continued . . .

Wild Inferno

Sandi Ault

BERKLEY PRIME CRIME, NEW YORK

THE BERKLEY PUBLISHING GROUP
Published by the Penguin Group
Penguin Group (USA) Inc.
375 Hudson Street, New York, New York 10014, USA
Penguin Group (Canada), 90 Eglinton Avenue East, Suite 700, Toronto, Ontario M4P 2Y3, Canada
(a division of Pearson Penguin Canada Inc.)
Penguin Books Ltd., 80 Strand, London WC2R 0RL, England
Penguin Group Ireland, 25 St. Stephen's Green, Dublin 2, Ireland (a division of Penguin Books Ltd.)
Penguin Group (Australia), 250 Camberwell Road, Camberwell, Victoria 3124, Australia
(a division of Pearson Australia Group Pty. Ltd.)
Penguin Books India Pvt. Ltd., 11 Community Centre, Panchsheel Park, New Delhi—110 017, India
Penguin Group (NZ), 67 Apollo Drive, Rosedale, North Shore 0632, New Zealand
(a division of Pearson New Zealand Ltd.)
Penguin Books (South Africa) (Pty.) Ltd., 24 Sturdee Avenue, Rosebank, Johannesburg 2196,
South Africa

Penguin Books Ltd., Registered Offices: 80 Strand, London WC2R 0RL, England

This is a work of fiction. Names, characters, places, and incidents either are the product of the author's imagination or are used fictitiously, and any resemblance to actual persons, living or dead, business establishments, events, or locales is entirely coincidental. The publisher does not have any control over and does not assume any responsibility for author or third-party websites or their content.

WILD INFERNO

A Berkley Prime Crime Book / published by arrangement with the author

PRINTING HISTORY
Berkley Prime Crime hardcover edition / February 2008
Berkley Prime Crime mass-market edition / March 2009

ISBN 978-0-425-22638-4

BERKLEY® PRIME CRIME
Berkley Prime Crime Books are published by The Berkley Publishing Group,
a division of Penguin Group (USA) Inc.,
375 Hudson Street, New York, New York 10014.
BERKLEY® PRIME CRIME and the PRIME CRIME logo are trademarks of Penguin Group (USA) Inc.

PRINTED IN THE UNITED STATES OF AMERICA

10 9 8 7 6 5 4 3 2 1

For Dimi

A fiery, spirited woman,
beautiful, strong, wise, and good.
Everything I always wanted to be.

Acknowledgments

A community that has been threatened by wildfire will forever mark time against that event. If there was victory, it will always be celebrated as their moment of triumph. If there was devastation, it will ever be their scar to bear. In the course of a few hours to a few weeks, the present and future of an area and its citizens can be completely altered.

Wildland firefighters have one thing in common: a zeal for the taste of danger, for pitting their skills and courage against a terrible and deadly foe. There are heroes. And sometimes there are martyrs. For the firefighters, the pace and the power to change lives and landscapes is a heady drug. Most firefighters come from government jobs where little changes from day to day through the course of an entire career. But a wildfire offers the opportunity to accomplish something life transforming—often in as little as two weeks.

I received an outpouring of help and support for this project from the men and women who work to preserve and protect our country's natural resources. I would especially like to thank Ed Guzman, USFS Fire Management Officer for the Boulder/Clear Creek Ranger District; Greg Toll, Wildland Division Chief for the Boulder Fire Department; Gary Fairchild, District Archaeologist for the Pagosa Ranger District, San Juan National Forest; Glenn Raby, Geologist for the Pagosa Ranger District, San Juan National Forest; Jimmye L. Turner, Fire Prevention Specialist for the Walla Walla Ranger District; Steve Hentschel, Fire Management Officer for San Juan Public Lands, Pagosa Ranger District; Chris Buckman, Durango

Interagency Dispatch Center Manager; Rich Gustafson, Fire Management Officer, Southern Ute Agency, Bureau of Indian Affairs; Marc Mullenix, Fire Management Officer, Mesa Verde National Park and the Four Corners Park Group, and Incident Commander for the Rocky Mountain Interagency Management Type 2 Team A; Lynn Barclay, Mitigation/Education Specialist, Bureau of Land Management, and Lead Information Officer for the Rocky Mountain Area Type 1 Incident Management Team; Jim Furlong, Fire Operations Specialist for the Pacific Northwest and Incident Manager for the Pacific Northwest Type 2 Incident Management Team; Roland Emetaz, retired USFS and Lead Information Officer for the Pacific Northwest Type 2 Incident Management Team; Jerome Martinez, Training Specialist for the New Mexico Type 2 Incident Management Team; Dr. J. McKim Malville, archaeoastronomer and father of the Lunar Standstill Theory at Chimney Rock; Stephen H. Lekson, Curator of Anthropology, University Museum, University of Colorado, Boulder; Justin Dombrowski, Director of Emergency Management for the City of Boulder and Boulder County, Colorado; John Wallace, Senior Resident Agent, Durango Resident Agency for the FBI; Marilyn Fagerstrom, Public Information Officer for the Left Hand Fire Protection District, who mentored me as an Information Officer; and the brave firefighters of the Pinewood Springs Fire Department, with whom I am proud to serve.

Author's Note

This is a work of fiction, and the characters and events herein are figments of my imagination. However, I have taken some license in placing this story over the backdrop of a real landscape and a very real phenomenon known as the Lunar Standstill. I have also alluded to some real myths, traditions, and rituals from several Native American cultures—however, out of respect for their right to keep and to define their own culture, I have mixed and changed these myths and rituals and created some fictitious ones.

Time before time, the chiefs in the Center of the World could talk with fire and receive its knowledge and power. They used what fire told them to hold the moon unmoving in the sky.

—From an old Pueblo story

◄ 1 ►

The Burning Man

Wednesday, 1100 Hours

In his last conscious moment, the burning man spoke three words. I got there just in time to hear them.

It was mid-July. High temperatures and months of drought had parched southern Colorado. For days, waves of dry storms had pounded the peaks and mesas with lightning, sparking dozens of wildfires. Local crews were unable to respond to all the smoke reports. One small fire smoldered in a remote part of the Southern Ute Reservation. As soon as the Three-Pueblos Hot Shots got there, they were sent in to quell the blaze.

But high winds had driven the flames of the fire up into a huge convection shaft, surging with sparks, embers, and smoke. Airborne incendiaries rocketed across the hotshots' burned-out buffer lines and colonized dozens of new spot fires in the adjacent patchwork of national forest, private property, and Indian lands. The head of the Chimney Rock Fire began to expand on two sides. The northern lip advanced rapidly, sending flaming emissaries across narrow washes. On the eastern front, embers caromed across rocky outcroppings and erupted into a maze of arroyos, each of these drainages a potential new head for the fire and a perfect chute to feed the flames up the steeply escalating, heavily forested slopes to the national historic site known as Chimney Rock.

When I arrived, my first order of business was to find an old man—a Ute known as Grampa Ned, who had reportedly snuck around barricades and entered an area to one side of the fire. My name is Jamaica Wild. I work for the Bureau of Land Management, and I was the liaison officer for the team that had been called in to take over the fire's management.

At the staging area, Bob Pinsler, the acting incident commander from the local agency, helped me pinpoint Grampa Ned's last known location on a map. "A woman from the Ute tribe saw him go down this dirt road toward that old mine. You flag the turns you take, and don't get off the road. If you don't see him, come on back out."

I pulled onto the highway, drove a mile to the east, and turned left onto a gravel track, skirting the barricades. Torn yellow caution tape fluttered in the wind. An orange cone lay smashed in the center of the path. I swerved around it and went on. A sign at the bridge crossing Stollsteimer Creek warned:

> SOUTHERN UTE INDIAN LAND
> NO TRESPASSING
> VIOLATORS WILL BE PROSECUTED
> UNDER TRIBAL OR FEDERAL LAW

"Not today," I muttered as I drove past it. "A fire doesn't care who owns the land." As I crossed the bridge, the twin spires of Chimney Rock loomed high above me, topping a narrow, rising ridge. To the west, a roiling cloud of thick gray smoke engulfed the sky.

At a fork in the road, I turned left, and the path played out at the entrance to the abandoned mine. No sign of anyone nearby. I turned and followed the road back, taking the other fork, and stopped to tie pink flagging to a tree. I followed this track for a quarter mile until it, too, gave out. But this time there was a white pickup parked on one side, its tailgate down. I plowed to the end of the gravel, hooked a U-turn, facing my Jeep out in case I needed to make a quick exit. I got out and crossed the road, checked out the white pickup. The truck was unlocked, the windows down, the seat and floor littered with empty cigarette packs and candy wrappers.

I cupped my hands around my mouth. "Hello?" I called. "Anybody here?" I climbed up on the running board, pressed the truck's horn, and gave three short blasts. "Hello?" I called again, louder.

Looking around, I noticed a footpath leading up through the pines. I yelled up the path, "Hello? Grampa Ned? Ned Spotted Cloud? Are you up there?"

No answer.

You're not going to make this easy for me, are you, Grampa? I opened the rear hatch of my Jeep, snatched my helmet and shoved it on my head, grabbed my fire line pack and strapped it on. Then I pulled on my gloves and tied a tail of pink flagging to a pine branch at the head of the path, went twenty yards into the forest, and flagged the trail again. I took my radio off scan, dialed to tactical channel 1, and opened the mic. "Liaison Wild to Command," I said.

"Pinsler. Go ahead."

"Update: there's a white pickup at the end of the east leg of the fork in the road. Unable to locate driver. Heading up a trail now a little way—I think he might be up here."

"You're breaking up. Request repeat."

I hiked upward, breathing harder with the exertion of the climb as I talked. "Update: I'm—"

"Liaison Wild, please repeat. Couldn't read you."

"I'm heading up a path at the end of the road."

I stopped again to tie flagging to a tree, then examined the radio. There was no response to my latest transmission. I flipped the switch to scan. It squawked with static and traffic. Terse voices demanded weather updates, GPS coordinates. Bits of bad news competed with attempts to exact order and discipline: *... winds picking up ... strong southwesterly gusts expected ... try to get air support from Durango ...* It squealed, clicked several times ... and then nothing.

I turned the set off then on again as I kept moving. A few spurts of static followed by silence. I heard a low, throbbing drone, like thunder rumbling in the distance. The smell of smoke was strong, the air was murky. I glanced up the trail ahead of me and hesitated. The radio crackled: "... ck ... ck ... Liaison ... ck ... ?"

I pressed the mic. "Wild. Go ahead."

The rumbling sound grew louder, and the air felt unbearably heavy, as if the sky were sinking, the cloud of smoke collapsing downward, pressing the oxygen out of the atmosphere. *Not good,* I told myself. *This is not good!*

I pressed the mic again. "Wild to Command," I said. "I haven't found the party yet, but I think I better get out of here."

"Ck ... ck ... ck," the radio sputtered.

Then to one side of me an explosion detonated, a tumult that hit me with a blast and made me feel as if my chest would cave. My ears rang, I was stunned. But in an instant, I could hear the fire roaring, ripping the earth open—a noise so great that my whole body trembled like a tuning fork. Adrenaline spurted into my bloodstream, and I broke into a fast run. I heard cracking limbs. A wall of heat and pressure pushed me down the trail. My legs burned from exertion, my ankles and knees rang with the impact as they jarred against rocks and roots. My fire shelter banged hard against my behind, smacking me with every stride. The weight of my pack bounced on the wide belt at my waist as I loped forward, wondering as I went whether I would have to deploy my shelter. Could I survive a burnover? My lungs ached from lack of oxygen. It seemed there was none in the air around me.

As I reached my second flag, hope gave me new speed and vigor—just twenty more yards and I could jump in my Jeep and drive!

But as I neared the end of the trail, a sound like a cannon shot made me start, and a huge limb thundered to the ground in front of me, knocking me down. I heard a thousand firecrackers going off at once as the canopy above lit up with red light. Flames devoured the treetops and the boughs began snapping and falling around me. A cloud of smoke and ash engulfed me.

I staggered to my feet and pulled the bandana at my neck over my nose and mouth. In the haze, I saw a flash of color at the head of the trail—a yellow shirt, someone moving. I willed my legs to run the rest of the way to the road.

At the trailhead, a tall firefighter stood, back to me, smoldering, a cloud of steam encircling his body like a halo, his pack and fire tool in a heap on the road beside him. He began wavering, obviously about to collapse. I ran to him and grabbed him from behind. Heat surged from his body, and I felt as if I'd just embraced an enormous burning log. "Get in the Jeep," I screamed, but he couldn't hear me—the din of the fire's consumption threatened to blow out my own eardrums.

I tried to walk him the few steps to the back of the car,

but he stumbled, off balance, and I tripped as he fell onto the rear deck, where I'd left the hatch open. A flaming branch dropped onto the back of my leg, and I kicked it to one side. I put a knee up on the deck and felt his neck for a pulse—weak, thready. His face above his bandana was blistered and red. His eyes were clouded over, the lashes burned off, and the skin was starting to pull away.

"We've got to get out of here," I yelled. "Can you hear me?" I tugged at the bandana that covered most of his face.

His gloved hand caught my wrist as I pulled the cloth away. Scorched, cracked lips parted, and he tried to swallow. His grip on my arm tightened with urgency. "Save the grandmother," he sputtered. And then he closed his eyes.

◄ 2 ►

The Inferno

Wednesday, 1230 Hours

I didn't have to worry about getting the firefighter down to Medical. Before I got to the fork in the road, a host of vehicles came toward me—first a brush truck, then a Forest Service engine, a crew truck filled with firefighters, and finally an ambulance. I pulled to the side of the road and got out just as Kerry Reed, my longtime boyfriend and a division sup on our team, scrambled from the driver's seat of the brush truck. "Jamaica, are you okay?" he yelled.

"Firefighter down!" I shouted. "Get the medics!"

A team of paramedics examined the man who—because of his powerful thermal imprint on my body—I knew only as "the burning man." Nearby, the newly arrived firefighters began to gear up, pulling on their line packs and gloves and grabbing their tools. The percussive *thwack* of a helicopter's rotors drowned out even the noise of the fire as a bucket suspended on a cable below the chopper lowered into Stollsteimer Creek with amazing accuracy, filled with water, and lifted straight up into the sky. In a matter of seconds, the ship vanished into the cloud of smoke.

Even as the fire raged to one side of them, the crew of helmeted, yellow-shirted men and women with their distinctive, low-riding line packs calmly gathered on the road in a semicircle around Kerry, who was pointing to a map spread across the hood of his truck. When they broke, the saw team left first in their heavy chaps, carrying gas and chain saws, going ahead to fell trees and cut down the snags. Smoke hovered above the ground like low-lying fog as they disappeared into the gray haze. The remaining squad members lined out in a row, each one holding a tool on their right. Every firefighter carried fuel for the saws in addition to a forty-pound line pack, except for the last four men on the crew. They carried medical kits and sleds for moving the injured.

I pushed the paramedic's hand away from me. He'd been examining my eyes, asking me what year it was and who was president. "Why so many sleds?" I asked. "Just one old man up there, right?"

"You may end up looking like you got a sunburn," he said. "Your face is a little red. Anything else hurt?"

"I'm fine," I said. "Is it the hotshot crew? Are they in trouble?"

"What about your arm? Your shirt's torn at the shoulder. Are you burned? Did you get hit by a snag?"

I looked at my right shoulder, reached to touch it with my left hand. It hurt. "It's nothing. It will be okay," I said.

He lifted the ripped cloth and peered under it, then straightened up. "You probably ought to have it looked at—and your face, too, just in case." He pointed a thumb at the ambulance, where the other medics were working on the burning man. "I think they're going to have Life Flight land on the main road. We better get him down there."

"Can you tell me what's going on?"

"With the hotshot crew?" he said as he packed up his kit. "I heard they had to deploy shelters. We haven't heard anything since."

"And the guy I found?"

"I don't know."

"Is he going to be all right?"

He shook his head.

"Please tell me."

"It doesn't look good." He tossed me a cold pack. "Put this on that shoulder," he said, "and use that burn gel I gave you on your face." He turned and jogged back to the ambulance.

Kerry Reed yelled into his radio: "Charlie, get an air tanker, get anything. We need more air support. I don't care if we've lost the initial attack—we've got firefighters in the burn, and we've got to get this fire flanked, or we'll never get to them! Break." He lowered the radio for a moment, reached under the rim of his helmet and rubbed his forehead, took a deep breath, then continued: "We're going to tie in here at the road, try to flank to the east. I'll get coordinates to you. Out." He glanced up and saw me. He reached out a hand and squeezed my arm. His hand was shaking, and his grip was painfully tight.

"I went up to get a man who snuck around the barricades," I said. "I never got to him. I knew there was a crew up above there, but . . . what's happened?"

"I don't know the whole story. The local team here was monitoring the Three-Pueblos Hot Shots' radio traffic. The Three-Pebs had started to hike out when their superintendent gave the order for them to deploy shelters, and that's the last anyone has heard from them."

"Well, there's some dead spots up there," I said.

He looked at the map. "Yeah, the terrain looks treacherous."

"No, I mean I couldn't get through on the radio. Maybe . . ."

He started nodding his head up and down, still searching the map for answers. "Yeah, maybe."

"And the firefighter I found?"

"One of the hotshots. Someone said he had a Three-Pueblos patch on his shirt."

"Oh. I guess I didn't have time to notice."

"My guess is he couldn't stand it in the shelter. Some guys can't take it, lying there baking in that foil envelope while the fire rages over them. Damn! I hope the rest of the crew fared better than he did."

Just then, the chopper returned for another dip in the creek, and the howl of its rotors, the pressure of air beating down on us in rhythmic pulses, made communication impossible. Kerry grabbed at his map as it started to take flight and—fighting it all the while as it flapped—headed around the truck to the driver's side. He pushed the map into the cab, climbed in behind it, and began shouting again into his radio.

In my peripheral vision, I saw red and blue lights flashing. I turned to see the ambulance driving away. I walked to the place where it had been parked and watched it disappear down the road. I closed my eyes, made a small circle in the air with my left palm, and sent a blessing to the burning man.

Then I turned and looked back at the conflagration behind me. This normally peaceful mountain valley with the two stone pinnacles of Chimney Rock in its center had become a war zone. On one side, an angry wind drove a hungry fire to desecrate and demolish the land, while on the other side, a helicopter's blades thundered through the sky, and an army of green-and-yellow Nomex–clad soldiers swarmed to the line to fight a life-and-death battle. Thick smoke rolled off the inclines above and filled the saddles, but a gust of wind suddenly lifted the gray curtain. Red-orange flames on the slopes stabbed at the sky and shot in long daggers as high as seventy feet in some places. A fire whorl rose up like a thin red tornado, then disappeared between the trees, which stood in dark relief against a low, crimson glow. The heat of the monster's breath parched my lips and made my face hurt. The forest cried out in a chorus of groans and piercing snaps and pops. Every few seconds, a large, flaming ember flew out of the sky like shrapnel and struck the road, leaving a litter of smoldering charcoal confetti sprinkled across the gravel. The high-decibel din of destruction assaulted my ears, my mind, my body. I suddenly felt as if I might faint, and then as if I were floating upward, drifting away from danger, away from the sound and the heat and the urgency. I heard my own thoughts like a voice from outside of me: *Why did the burning man leave his crew? What did he mean by "save the grandmother"?*

What would make him risk incineration in a wild inferno?

◄ 3 ►

Team Work

Wednesday, 1330 Hours
Command and General Staff (C&G) Meeting

Every wildfire comes down to a story. Like the dragon in tales of old, the fire makes a lair in an untamed and often inaccessible place, then proceeds to ravage the land and terrorize its citizens. The locals muster forces and fight, but when the beast proves too much for them, a call goes out for the dragon-slayers.

My pager had sounded when I was on my way to work at a little before six a.m. that day. I hit the road with my fire gear within an hour, driving from Taos. This scene repeated across the Southwest and beyond, as more than a hundred firefighters rushed from their regular jobs, from their homes and their families and all that was routine, to join in a battle for which they had trained and qualified to exacting standards.

Unlike most government workers, I didn't lack any excitement in my regular job. I was a resource protection agent for the Bureau of Land Management, where—until just over a year ago—I had patrolled remote wilderness areas as a range rider. But when a backcountry standoff turned deadly, my boss, Roy, had pulled me from that solitary assignment and appointed me to serve as liaison for the BLM to one of the local Indian pueblos near Taos. And there soon proved to be plenty of peril in my new post.

Since Roy was IC—incident commander—on the fire management team, he drafted me into the job of liaison officer on the team. He did this partly out of respect for the strong relationships I'd managed to forge with the Native Americans at Tanoah Pueblo, and partly, I suspected, to try to keep me out of as much trouble as he possibly could. I didn't go out with the team every time, but when the incident occurred on Indian lands, I deployed with the rest of the Command and General Staff.

For this fire, Incident Command Post—or ICP, as we called it—had been set up in the visitors' center at Navajo State Park, on the Colorado–New Mexico border. Around it, a city of fire tents had sprouted up in the campsites along the shores of Navajo Lake. Catering trucks, shower trucks, supply trucks, a field commissary, and a medical tent found their places near the center of camp, surrounded by the individual spike tents of line crew personnel. A helibase had been set up in a flat stretch of meadowland. Together, all this composed Incident Base, commonly referred to by its inhabitants as Fire Camp.

While I was waiting at the ICP for the Command and General Staff meeting to begin, I looked around for some water. My throat was raw from the smoke, and I felt dehydrated. I spied an ice chest in the hallway and made for it. As I was opening a bottle of water, I saw a woman through the doorway of an office. She was dressed in a T-shirt, khaki shorts, a hat, and dusty boots, and she stood with her back to me, studying a map on the wall. She turned around and seemed startled at my presence.

"Sorry," I said. "I didn't mean to sneak up on you like that."

She made a weak attempt at a smile. Now that I'd seen her face, she seemed older than her lean, muscular body had suggested from the rear.

"Do you work here in Navajo State Park?"

"No, I'm an anthropologist."

"Oh." I nodded my head as if this explained everything. "Are you working on the fire then?"

"No." She shook her head vigorously. "Well, technically, I'm working right now in the Columbine Ranger District. The border between the two ranger districts is right up on top of that ridge above the Piedra River, to the west of the fire. I have a grant to do some site surveys on the ruins up there on the Piedra Rim. But years ago, I helped excavate sites at Chimney Rock. The fire management officer for the Pagosa Ranger District asked me to come here. He thought maybe I could help out with site protection."

"I'm sure we can use all the help we can get. From what I see on the map, the whole Chimney Rock area is littered with archaeological sites."

Just then, a man came down the hallway toward me wearing the standard uniform: green Nomex pants, a clean yellow fire shirt, and wildland boots. He was young and handsome, with dark hair and eyes, and his lean body exuded energy and vitality. "Are you on the incident command team?" he said.

"Yes, I'm the liaison officer."

"Hello." He smiled. "I'm Steve Morella. I'm the archaeologist with the Pagosa Ranger District. I'm here to brief your IC and his command staff about the Lunar Standstill."

"Jamaica Wild," I said as I shook hands with him.

"Jamaica? That's a pretty name."

I forced a polite smile. "The Lunar Standstill? What's that?"

"We're going to talk about that in a minute, I hope. Where are you from?"

"I'm a resource protection agent with the BLM in Taos."

"Well"—he grinned—"even if a fire had to bring you, welcome to Chimney Rock. If I can help you in any way, if there's anything I can show you or . . ." He happened to glance to his left and see the woman in the office. "Oh, Elaine. I see you two have already met. Good! Well, come on then." He started down the hall.

"Hi, I'm Elaine Oldham," the woman said, half-apologetically, as she ducked through the office door in front of me. "I don't really know what I'm doing here," she muttered, hurrying to follow Steve Morella down the hall. "I'm an anthropologist, not a fire person."

※

"This isn't going to be your ordinary C&G meeting. I sent a few people here early to tie in but we haven't yet assumed command of this incident. We've just been briefed by the local agencies and the team here who's been managing this fire. We're expected to take over at the next operational period. I'm going to tell you a few things," Roy said, "then let our ops chief talk while I go take a ride in a chopper.

"This was a bad one when we got here, and things have gotten worse since then. We've got a shot crew somewhere in the burn area, and their superintendent called for them to deploy shelters. We haven't heard anything from them since, and that was almost three hours ago. We've got a hotshot from that team in the burn unit in Albuquerque in a deep coma. We've got a missing Ute man who is possibly somewhere in the burn as well, but we haven't found him yet. Folks, as you know, this is an 'incident within the incident,' and I'm having my division sup, Kerry Reed, break off from our team and act as IC for that—we'll call it Rescue Command. He'll pull some folks from the main group to work on his team, and he'll brief you after he's had a chance to do his own size-up. Now, I know that's not much, but we don't know a great deal right now, so let's move on. We've got a fire that is winning the fight. We lost the initial attack, and we have limited resources—I'm going to let Charlie talk to you about that."

Operations Section Chief Charlie Dorn stepped up to a map and took a pointer from the table. "Air support is what it's going to take to fight this fire, and air support is going to be hard to get. The single-engine air tanker in Durango has been assigned over in Grand Junction, so we can't use that. Colorado has fires all up and down the Front Range, and those teams are shouting 'structures threatened' and getting all the air resources." He turned and pointed to a red line on the map representing the known perimeter of the fire. "We have no roads and this terrain is tough—if we try to hike people and supplies in to fight it, they got nothing left by the time they get in there. We can't even use dozers in this country. We're going to have to use helicopters to paracargo in all our personnel and supplies, and I don't know when—or even if—we're going to get those birds. We have one chopper now doing bucket drops, and I think we can hang on to it. Beyond that, I don't have any more news about additional resources, air or otherwise. They have a helicopter at Mesa Verde they're going to loan us so we can do some surveillance for the shot crew and to check out the size of this fire—Roy's going up to do that in just a few minutes. But we can't keep that bird either, so we're going to have to make good use of her while she's here. The fire is within Southern Ute tribal lands, the San Juan National Forest, the Chimney Rock Archaeological

Area, and privately owned property. So it has potential to impact residences and prehistoric and spiritual sites. If we get another wind event like we had earlier and the northern flank expands, there's homes, businesses, and a major highway—on the other side of which is a one-hundred-twenty-five-kilovolt power line that feeds from Durango to Pagosa Springs—that are all in its path."

Roy put a hand up to signal Charlie to pause. "Folks, I'm going to have to go take a ride. But before I go, I got one more thing to add that we need to keep in mind: there's a Native American ceremony going on this week up top, at the ruins at Chimney Rock. It's a sacred event, some deal that only happens every eighteen point six years. We got representatives from thirteen tribes in attendance. And the eastern flank of this fire could easily run up to the top of Chimney Rock if we don't get it contained." Then he looked at me. "Jamaica, I want you to come with me."

"Okay, Boss," I said, and I followed him out.

"C'mon, walk with me," Roy said as he strode at a fast clip down the sidewalk in front of the Incident Command Post. Across the parking lot, a truck idled in the shade of a lone tree, the air around it shimmering in heat wrinkles from its exhaust. "I need to take a look at this fire and see what it might do next, and we're going to locate that hotshot crew. When we spot the Three-Pebs, we'll try to find a place near 'em to land a chopper and get them out. I want you there with the first rescue team."

"But why me?"

"This is a Pueblo hotshot crew. They're all Tiwa, some of 'em from Tanoah Pueblo. We may need your expertise."

"Wouldn't it be better to have a human resources specialist?"

Still walking fast, he pulled off the beat-up straw cowboy hat that was his trademark and exchanged it for a white helmet he'd had tucked under his arm. "I'll order an HR person, but this can't wait until the order gets filled and we get a warm body here. We need someone now." He opened the door of the ground support truck. "And Jamaica?"

"Yes?"

"I want you to do two things right away. First, get up on top of Chimney Rock and make contact with the tribal representatives. Let them know that we are doing all we can to protect their chances to continue with their ceremonies, but don't shine 'em on. Tell 'em we're trying to flank the fire but it blew up on us today, so we may have to evacuate if things don't improve. Then, go into Ignacio and see a woman named Clara White Deer. She's a member of the Southern Ute tribe, and the one who reported your missing guy—what's his name—Grampa something?"

"Grampa Ned."

"Yeah—anyway, go talk to White Deer. She works at the intermediate school there. Assure her that we did everything we could to try to find the guy, and see if you can get her calmed down. Evidently she was real upset when the sheriff talked to her. He asked me to send someone from the team."

"Okay, Boss."

"Another thing, Jamaica."

"Yes?"

"Go to the comm van and get a satellite phone and call me with the number. I don't want you on the slopes without a way to communicate. The minute we find the Three-Pebs, I'll call you."

"Okay."

He slid into the passenger seat. "You know you're going to have to do a critical stress debriefing as soon as we can get someone here to do it. There will be an investigation."

I bit my lip. Roy and I had both been through investigations before, including one that nearly lost me my job. He accused me of being able to find trouble wherever I went. And when I did, it wasn't small-time trouble. Lives hung in the balance. People died.

As he gestured for the driver to leave, I said: "This time I didn't do it!"

◄ **4** ►

Bearfat

The posted sentry, a volunteer from the Chimney Rock Interpretive Association, sat in a folding chair with an attached umbrella, reading a book. I pulled up to the iron pole gate that stretched across the entrance near the highway. By the organizers' request, the site was normally closed to non-Indians during the sacred ceremonies, but now—due to the fire—it was off-limits to anyone trying to enter except members of the team. Once I was through the gate, the volunteer closed it again behind me and returned to his reading.

I drove across a stretch of flat scrub, then trees began to form at the sides of the dirt track and the elevation started to rise. I passed through the parking lot beside the tiny log cabin that served as the visitors' center, where a group of Native American men and women sat at a picnic table under some trees. From there, I drove up a curving dirt and gravel road that climbed sharply as it wound up the side of the slope to the parking lot near the top. The two natural stone towers of Chimney Rock topped a cuesta—a slender, rising ridge with a nearly vertical, shaley escarpment on one side, and a steep, forested slope on the other, where the fire now burned. This stunning formation was centered in a bowl-like valley rimmed by mountain ranges, all higher than Chimney Rock with only three breaks—one to the south toward Huerfano Mesa in northern New Mexico, one to the north through Yellow Jacket Pass, and one to the east toward the Continental Divide.

Motorcycles, cars, vans, and several motor homes jammed the paved parking lot near the top. As I steered my way through, I noticed a group of about forty dark-haired people under some trees near the western rim, many of them sitting on benches and reinforced stacked-block walls that had been created in the style of Chacoan architecture. I passed the small building housing restrooms and a water tap and parked on the side of the road leading out, where low-hanging piñon branches scratched the top of the Jeep.

As soon as I was out of the car, a handsome, brown-skinned man wearing braids and a T-shirt bearing the slogan FREE THE REDSKIN came toward me. Behind him trailed a young woman in jean shorts and a tank top. I could tell by the way the man carried himself that he was about to try to evict me from the premises—he'd probably seen my blonde hair and concluded I had no business at the Native American ceremonies.

"Can I help you?" he asked.

I pulled on a brown BLM ball cap, walked to the rear of my Jeep, planted my boots in a wide stance, and straightened up tall, indicating that I intended to stay put. I smiled and stuck out my hand. "I'm the liaison officer with the fire management team. I'm here to see what we can do to make sure the tribal representatives have everything they need, and let them know we're here to help."

"Oh. Okay, then." He shook my hand and gave me a big smile. "I'm Bearfat, Southern Ute."

"Jamaica Wild."

He nodded his head up and down, still smiling. "Good name. I like that."

"Mr. Bearfat, are you one of the coordinators for these ceremonies?"

He examined me as if I were fresh meat, his dark eyes dancing over my BLM T-shirt and my Nomex-clad hips. "Just call me Bearfat," he said. "I'm not a coordinator, but I am a member of the Southern Ute tribe."

"I see." In spite of his ogling, I found myself wondering if he might know Grampa Ned. But with the old man's fate uncertain, I dared not ask.

"We Utes don't do the ceremonial stuff here—that's the Pueblo tribes' deal. We do our storytelling and our dances down in the parking lot below by the visitors' center. By the way, I have offered to arrange for a blessing ceremony for your fire crews."

"That's very kind of you, Mr. Bearfat. I'm sure we can use all the blessings we can get. Can I help in any way with that?"

"Call me Bearfat," he said again. "And, I don't know, Miss Wild. *Can* you help in any way with that?" His eyes continued to wander over my figure. Behind him, the young woman tired of watching the banter and started chewing on the end of one of her long braids.

"What will you need for the blessing ceremony?"

"Well, if I conduct it, I will need a clean space."

"You mean a room or something?"

"Not necessarily. It can be outdoors. Just a clean space."

"You mean cleared of debris? Smooth ground? What exactly should we do to prepare the space?"

"No women at their time of month."

"I beg your pardon?"

"No women within a half mile who are at their moon-time." He gave a leering smile. "You're not at your moon-time, are you, Miss Wild?"

I used my best diplomatic voice. "You know, Mr. Bear-fat, while we appreciate your offer of a blessing ceremony, I don't feel we could provide what you need. We have a lot of women firefighters on our crews as well as on the over-head team, and I will not be able to certify the standards you require."

He pretended to think about this a minute. "I guess some-one else will have to conduct the blessing then. I have my principles."

"I understand," I said, not meaning it. My job was to grease the wheels between the team and the local tribe, and that often meant biting my tongue.

"I don't think you're at your moon-time, Miss Wild; you're too sweet. May I call you Jamaica?"

I forced myself to stay calm. "I don't think we need to discuss this issue any further. I brought some coolers of bottled water for the folks up here. Maybe you could help me get them out of my Jeep and we'll put them over in the shade by the restrooms."

He grinned and nodded approvingly. "You got a good warrior spirit. I like that."

I turned around and opened the hatch of the Jeep and pulled two heavy foam coolers to the edge.

"Got any coffee in there?" Bearfat asked.

"I'm afraid there's not much call for coffee in the mid-dle of a scorcher like today."

"Oh, Jamaica Wild," he said as he reached into the Jeep and picked up one cooler and set it on the ground. He straightened up and looked me in the eyes. "Heat is good for you. Heat is power, it's energy. There's so little of it in the universe, we should be grateful we have Father Sun to give us life." At this, the young woman nodded her head in affirmation. Bearfat lifted the other cooler out and set it atop the first, then picked them both up and walked toward the comfort station.

I started to speak, then closed my mouth.

His companion looked at me and arched her eyebrows. Then she turned and followed him.

◂ 5 ▸

Mountain

I crossed the parking lot and headed down a path toward the circle of people I'd seen sitting in the shade of the piñon trees on the other side of the narrow mesa. A blur of movement emerged from the group—two figures wrestling? Then a flash of blond and black fur bowled toward me down the walk and shot toward my chest like a heat-seeking missile. The animal struck me with such force that I fell backward onto a patch of dry, dusty earth and my head banged the ground. I saw stars. The wolf stood with his feet on my shoulders and licked my face, whining and puffing. A small, dark woman bent over me, her head and shoulders wrapped in a tan blanket in spite of the scorching heat.

"Momma Anna?" I asked, looking up into her dark eyes. "What are you doing here?" As I spoke, the wolf whimpered and grunted at me, still furiously licking my neck, my ears, even my hair.

The old woman shook her head and frowned. "He tell me bring him you. I come, do ceremony here."

I pushed the wolf off of me and got to my hands and knees, but he continued to lick at my face, whining as he nipped gently at my ears. "But you said you'd watch him for me. I can't have a wolf on a fire!"

"He say you need him. I have ceremony do here."

I held up a finger to indicate to Momma Anna to hold that thought, then stood on my knees and put my arms around Mountain's neck. "Hey, buddy," I said, trying to calm him. He lunged into me, nearly knocking me over, huffing and vocalizing angrily.

I put one foot down to stabilize myself, keeping at eye level with the wolf. "Shhhhh," I said, "it's okay." His tail pounded against my arm, my shoulder, and he pressed his haunches against my chest. He cried and snorted, his fur flying with his anxiety. I placed a firm hand in the cleave between his hip and his abdomen and held it there while he wheezed and panted and whined. He turned in a circle, nipping at my chin as he passed, and again pressed his back end into my chest. I pushed my hand against his flank once more and tried to hold him in place, but Mountain weighed more than I did, and was twice as strong. He flipped around and again challenged me with a lunge toward my face.

"Okay, buddy," I said, as I managed to stand up. "You asked for it." I grabbed his hips and wrestled him to the ground, not an easy task. He yipped as we tussled and I forced myself on top of him, pinning him at the shoulders so that he lay on his side. His back legs clawed my pants and pushed against my thighs. Finally he submitted, laid his head down, and was still—except for his rapid panting. I could feel his heart pounding in his chest, see fear and anxiety in his eyes. "Shhhhh," I said again, still lying on him, as I loosed my hand from his shoulder and stroked the side of his face, the tufts of hair in his ear. "It's okay, Mountain. It's okay."

This four-legged companion of mine had come to me more than a year ago. A wildlife ranger had found him as a young cub, just a few weeks old when Mountain's mother had been shot outside of Yellowstone. He was the only one of his litter who had survived. Because I lived alone on a remote stretch of land outside Taos, and worked almost exclusively in the backcountry at the time, I had agreed to adopt him.

From the beginning, the wolf and I had struggled with his fear of abandonment, so characteristic of pack-oriented animals. He wanted me never to leave him—even for an hour or two—and he ripped my home apart on the few occasions when I did. But I couldn't take him everywhere I needed to go, so we had both adapted gradually to my short absences through a series of often costly trial-and-error experiences. Finally we had reached a point where Mountain was comfortable in my cabin and could be trusted to remain there for up to four or five hours every once in a while without shredding my clothes or chewing up furniture in an anxiety-driven frenzy. And I had adjusted to having a near-constant companion who went almost everywhere with me, including to work.

But we were still acclimating. Our latest struggle was over pack order. As the wolf matured, he often vied with me for the alpha position. I found myself wrestling and pinning him more often than before, contending for dominance, or at least equality.

I took my weight off Mountain and slowly got up, still standing over him. He lay on the ground, his ears back, panting, his eyes dilated. "Okay," I said, and he jumped to all fours and circled me again, his tail wagging. This time, he let me hold his flank—which was normally a means of comforting him when he was distressed. Otherwise I ignored him, playing down our reunion so he didn't sense any emotional electricity that could fuel his anxiety.

Finally, I nodded my head at Momma Anna. She had been patiently watching the encounter from one side. She made a little *tttch* sound with her tongue. "You and that wolf," she said, shaking her head, "in love. Maybe just go get marry."

Momma Anna handed me the leash and bridle for Mountain, and I slipped the loop over his nose. Similar to a horse's halter, this allowed me to pull his head to the side if he veered from the direction I chose. The wolf wouldn't go where he couldn't see, so this usually helped control him. But Momma Anna said, "He take off."

"What?"

"That. He see you, he take off, that."

"Maybe it wasn't on right," I said, disbelieving that the wolf could perform such a feat. I checked the bridle and tightened it a little to be sure.

"You see next other time," Momma Anna said, and she gave the wolf a friendly smack on the rump. Mountain wagged his tail at her.

Now that I had calmed the wolf, I wanted to speak to my Tiwa medicine teacher, the Tanoah Pueblo woman who had adopted me one Christmas season when we'd met at an art show. She'd invited me to Christmas dinner at the pueblo then, and over time had included me in numerous family events. Once I'd revealed to her that I loved to write and longed to produce books about the Southwest, Anna Santana had instructed me in many of the ways of her people, despite fierce restrictions set by the tribe prohibiting the sharing of their culture. Almost a year ago, I'd witnessed her son's death in a buffalo stampede at Tanoah Pueblo, and Momma Anna had charged me to find out the truth about how he had come to be there. My investigation led me deep into the clandestine rituals of the kiva societies, the peyote church, and beyond. Ultimately, I did learn the truth, but not before more lives were lost.

"Momma Anna, when I brought the wolf to you early this morning for safekeeping, you said nothing about needing to leave Tanoah Pueblo. I told you I might be gone as long as two weeks."

"You come next other time. This time, I come Fire Mountain."

"Fire Mountain?"

She made a 180-degree sweep with her arm. "Here."

"But you must have known you were coming to these ceremonies when I brought Mountain to you. You said nothing about them."

"Next other time, I am home. Now I am here."

Typical. Time had always been a challenge in dealing with the residents of Tanoah Pueblo, even in my work as liaison to the pueblo for the BLM. Their concept of time included only *now*. Everything outside of that could be classified—in Momma Anna's words—as *next other*. Often in the past when Momma Anna and I had arranged to meet, she would show up much later than the time we agreed on, if she showed up at all. But she always declared me late when I came to visit her at a prearranged time, no matter how prompt I was—because she was already there, in the *now,* the only time she knew.

"Well, how long will you be here?" I asked her, even though as soon as I spoke the words, I knew she wouldn't be able to tell me. "What am I going to do with Mountain? I have to work the fire."

"He say you need him."

I snorted. "Yes, well, Mountain would say that, no matter what. But I agreed to work this fire, and I can't take a wolf with me."

"Why not?" she asked. "Wolf and fire live same place, time before. He know how not get burn."

"It's too dangerous. You shouldn't even be up here, and neither should he."

"I am told be here. You do not tell me where go."

"But the fire . . ."

"You go. Do fire. I keep wolf."

"But it's not safe!"

"We got story now," she said, and she turned and started back toward the group on the west rim.

◄ 6 ►

The People

Following Momma Anna, I approached the group of Native Americans with Mountain on his lead. Clearly, he'd already met most of them, because many of them smiled and reached out to pat him or scratch behind his ears. He nuzzled them like old friends. The group was quiet, though, and no one spoke.

In the center of a large, flat floor of stone, one man held a tall staff in one hand. The tip rested in a shallow, pecked-out basin, perhaps two inches deep. The top of the staff was crowned with a pair of eagle talons, with the long joint of the legs—complete with downy feathers—extended outward from the top, resembling a pair of short antlers. The possessor of this wand was dressed in jeans, moccasins, and a bear hide. Sweat rained from his face and upper body, which was bare. His eyes were closed, and he was taking long, focused breaths. After what seemed like several minutes, he finally began to speak in a deep, thunderous voice.

"Time before time, the chiefs in the Center of the World could talk with fire and receive its knowledge and power. They used what fire told them to hold the moon unmoving in the sky.

"Far to the north, many priests lived and worked on Fire Mountain, learning the Way. From their round tower there, and from the ridge across the river, they made many studies, watching Grandmother Moon and Father Sun rise over the shoulders of the Earth Mother. They measured with sticks and a hole they made in the rock, and they counted days with lines of dots and brush marks, or with piles of pebbles. They built great night fires and used big, flat stones to shoot the light of the flames far, very far. They sent their wisdom on nights when Moon was hiding, so the fires could be seen in the sky. Three-days-walking to the south, on Red Mask Mesa, the fire tenders received the messages, then built blazes of their own, and—using the same kind of stones—sent the fire's light another three-days-walking to the south, to the Center of the World. The chiefs of what they now call Chaco Canyon would see the fires, read their messages, and the Way would be known.

"The People would gather at the temples, and the chiefs would say: *On this night, I will tell the moon where to stand, and it will come to that place because I say it must!* The People would watch and see.

"And when Moon obeyed, and came to the appointed place in the sky, the People knew that the chiefs were very powerful. The fires had bestowed their gifts."

When he finished, several of the women ululated in high-pitched calls, and a few of the men shrieked and whooped loudly. Nearly all the rest of the people watching the storyteller uttered a grunt and nodded their heads in agreement. Then those seated got up and began to mingle around, and those standing wandered here and there. Some walked away, up the path toward the parking lot.

"What a beautiful story," I said to Momma Anna, finding a place in the shade so Mountain could escape the blazing sun.

"He good, talking stick," she said.

"Was that the talking stick that he was holding?" I asked.

Momma Anna frowned at me and shook her head. The Tanoah considered questions rude, yet asking them was so ingrained in our culture that I often forgot. Momma Anna almost never answered me, but instead found ways to teach me through her daily activities: making pottery and jewelry, cooking, baking, gathering herbs, wild spinach, and piñon nuts, and gardening. Most of the time, I would come to visit Momma Anna or she would ask me to take her someplace, and I knew that the occasion would provide me with a lesson, and perhaps information for the book I hoped to write on the customs of Tanoah Pueblo.

"I need to find out who's in charge here," I said.

"Nobody in charge," she said.

"Well, then, I need to know who is organizing the ceremonies."

"Maybe you pray. Creator in charge." She got up and walked away from me.

For a time, I sat and watched the crowd, trying to determine from their behavior who might be acting as a coordinator for the group. A round, brown woman wearing Hopi ceremonial dress seemed to be preparing to do the next storytelling. Her companions were smoothing her hair and fussing over her apparel. I got up and led Mountain around the assemblage until I found Momma Anna again. She was standing next to a group of women, and they looked to be deciding who was going to take the seats on the benches and rock walls and who would be left standing.

"Momma Anna," I said, careful not to phrase it as a question, "I would like to give some information to these people from those of us managing the fire."

She smiled approvingly and removed the thin, tan blanket from her head. She stepped to the center of the flat stone area, near the recessed place where the last storyteller had staked his staff. She stood there for a moment as the group grew quiet and took places in a circle around her. Then she waved to me to enter the center of the gathering. I handed Mountain's lead to Momma Anna. "Hello, I'm Jamaica Wild. I'm the liaison officer with the fire team. I'm here to let you know that the incident command team is doing everything it can to contain this fire so that you can go on with your ceremonies uninterrupted."

The crowd rumbled, and one man spoke up. "We're not going nowhere. You can lock that gate down there so nobody else can come, but you can't make us leave. This is our sacred time." Those around him nodded and grunted in agreement.

I held up my hand. "I understand. I do. We're not there yet, so let's not get into a disagreement right now about that. I wonder if there is one person, or perhaps a small group of a few people, with whom I could speak, an individual or council who might want to carry the message or speak for the rest of you?"

They looked at me in silence.

I waited patiently for several minutes, a skill I'd learned in working with the Tanoah. This demonstration of a tolerance for quiet—for comfort without conversation—often earned me respect among the tribe. After some time had passed, I could see more acceptance in their faces. Finally I said, "Okay, well, I can talk with all of you now, and perhaps if you'd like to later, we will arrange another way to carry our messages. I have been chosen to speak to you on behalf of the incident management team. We want to do anything and everything we can to ensure your safety and your comfort. Now, I've brought some cold bottled water up for you, and I wonder if there is anything else I can do. Do you need meals?"

They remained mute. Dozens of sober faces looked at me with expressions I couldn't read. I puzzled for a moment, then realized how many customs I'd just violated with my last remark—not only had I asked a question, I'd suggested that they needed something from me instead of simply offering them hospitality. Most Native Americans are fiercely proud and do not like to be seen as needy in any way.

I hung my head and closed my eyes. I felt ashamed, frustrated with myself. When I opened my eyes again—my head still lowered in humility—I saw that my clothes were covered with dirt and wolf hair from my recent challenge with Mountain, and I realized how unkempt I must look to them. If the rest of those gathered here were anything like my Tiwa family at Tanoah Pueblo, then cleanliness was a prized virtue. I drew in a breath, faced the assembly, and—turning slowly to look at each one of them in turn—I spoke very softly. "Please forgive me. I am so sorry, so ashamed of that last thing I said. I know you do not need me or anything from me. It was a mistake for me to insinuate that you might. I ask your forgiveness."

Then I waited for what I knew would be a long time.

Ultimately, one of the women sitting on the block wall raised her hand and stepped into the circle. I had the good sense to step back next to Mountain. Momma Anna did not look at me. The woman in the center spoke, "This white girl seem like she is okay. I say we let her speak. She cannot be too bad if she has the love of a wolf." Everyone laughed at this last, and Mountain—sensing he was being talked about—gave a happy yip and wagged his tail. The woman opened her arm to invite me back into the circle.

I stepped to the center again, brushing my clothes with my hands. "Thank you. I will not make the same mistake again. I am sorry if I offended you. I would like to offer some meals to you tonight. I would like to know how many people so we can bring plenty of food. I want to send anything else you might use and enjoy, too: tents, sleeping bags, sunscreen. If any of you would like to have some first aid or medicine, I would like to have someone come. It would be good if there was one person or a couple people from among you who would agree to be the ones to carry messages to me so I don't have to interrupt your stories and rituals. And if I can ever do anything for you or get anything for you, please let me know. I will do my best to help."

Heads nodded approvingly, and a few women smiled at me. A small spattering of applause broke out. I returned to take Mountain's lead. Momma Anna gave me a little nod.

I walked away from the gathering to permit them to confer about what I had said. Mountain was panting heavily in the heat, so I went to the comfort station, took a bottle of cold water from one of the coolers, opened it, and squirted water from the pull-up nozzle top onto his tongue. He closed his mouth around the plastic tip and drank from it eagerly, just as he had when I'd bottle-fed him goat's milk as a tiny pup. It reminded me of when he was just a baby, and I smiled, my heart remembering the tenderness of that time. When he had drunk all the water in the bottle, I dipped my hands into some of the melted ice in the foam chest and scooped icy cold water onto his back. I wiped my cool hands across my own brow.

I knelt down to finally greet Mountain. I put my arms around his neck and hugged him. "Hey, buddy," I said. "Did you think I'd left you? I was going to come back. I just had to come work on this fire. And I have to leave you with Momma Anna again now, but I won't be gone for long, okay? I'm going to see you every chance I get—and then, when we get the fire out, we'll both go home. You can ride home with me, in the Jeep." The wolf smiled and wagged his tail wildly. He licked the side of my face, his tongue cold and rough.

Momma Anna approached, her blanket pulled over her head for sun protection. She gave a little smile when she saw me hugging the wolf. I stood up and smiled back. *Perfect!* I thought. *Momma Anna and I already know one another. She'll be the ideal person for me to liaise with.*

"That Ute guy," Momma Anna said as she reached us.

"What?"

"That Ute guy. You talk him."

"What Ute guy?"

Just as I said it, Bearfat strutted toward me like a peacock—this time without his young companion. "Guess we'll be working together, Jamaica Wild," he said, leering.

Clara White Deer

Wednesday, 1600 Hours

Before I left Chimney Rock, I radioed to Logistics to request meals, basic first aid, and some comfort supplies for the Native Americans. But the trucks full of ordered supplies were en route to Fire Camp, so Logistics was not prepared to provide provisions until the next morning at the earliest. They agreed to contact the Red Cross and local emergency services and get the list filled. With the first item on my agenda complete, I headed for Ignacio to perform the next assignment Roy had given me.

I drove south down Highway 151 past Navajo Lake, then west across high desert country into the next county and the small town of Ignacio, home of the Southern Ute Agency and the Sky Ute Casino. Heat shimmered on the asphalt and the temperature in my Jeep was sweltering.

At Ignacio Intermediate School, I asked the summer classes coordinator to help me find Clara White Deer. I was directed to the music room—past the empty gymnasium and down a quiet hall that rang with my footsteps. When I looked through the glass window in the door, a slender woman with long black braids was alone in the room, dusting off the music stands. She wore a turquoise tank top, jeans, and sandals. I knocked, then opened the door enough to stick my head in. "Ms. White Deer?" I asked.

A tawny, good-looking face with high cheekbones and large, dark eyes turned toward me. She was stunningly good-looking, perhaps in her midfifties, and I could just imagine how beautiful she must have been in her youth. The woman pushed her chin up in a gesture of pride and said, "I am Clara White Deer."

"May I come in?" I asked, opening the door a bit wider. "I'm the liaison officer with the incident command team on the fire. I wanted to talk with you a moment."

She returned to her dusting, rubbing the stand in front of her with sharp, quick strokes. "Did you guys find him?"

I stepped into the room and was quiet a moment. Then I said, "Could we sit down and talk?"

She stopped dusting and looked at me. "I don't want to sit down. I can't."

I moved forward, coming around so I was in front of her. "I believe someone from the sheriff's office talked to you."

"Yes. He didn't have any news. Do you have any news?"

"I wonder—is there someplace I could buy you a glass of iced tea?"

Clara White Deer tipped her head to one side. "Did you find him or not? Just tell me. I don't need a glass of iced tea, and even if I did, I can buy my own. In fact, I should probably buy yours—you work for the US government, so I bet you don't make too much money doing that. I probably make a lot more than you do just for being a member of the Southern Ute tribe." She started wiping her hands on her dust rag, then cut in front of me and walked to the desk at the front of the room.

"I just thought perhaps we could sit down someplace so we could visit," I said.

"We can visit right here," she said, locking eyes with me as she dropped the rag on the desk and brushed her hands together loudly to signify that she was done with the chore.

I stepped forward so I was standing in front of the desk. Clara White Deer never let her eyes leave mine. I spoke in a calm voice. "I just wanted to tell you that we did everything we could to try to find Grampa Ned where you last saw him. The fire blew up, and we had to suspend all activity in the area. We had firefighters in danger at the time, and we couldn't even go after them. We still don't know about any of them—Ned or the firefighters."

Finally, Clara White Deer looked away. She shook her head back and forth. "That old man," she said. "That stinking old man. I ask him for one thing, one thing. I never asked him for anything before. But I ask Ned Spotted Cloud for one little thing, and he goes and gets himself burned up in a fire."

I held up a hand. "Wait! We don't know that. He could be anyplace. We have no evidence."

She shook her head even faster. "I don't need evidence. I saw him going down that road toward the ruins back there by the mine. He drove right through the yellow tape and broke it. He ran over one of those orange cones that was set across the road. I honked at him, and he just waved his hand out the window. The sheriff said you found his truck back in there, right?"

"Yes, we did. But we didn't find him. He could have walked out."

She made a sardonic grin. "Not Grampa Ned. He drove everywhere—he's always been a smoker and he doesn't have such good wind anymore."

"Well, maybe someone met him, picked him up."

"Ned Spotted Cloud didn't have a friend in this world, Miss . . . what'd you say your name was?"

"Wild. Jamaica Wild."

She leaned forward, pursing her lips and studying me. "That's a funny name for a white girl."

I shrugged. My name was always the source of curious comments and strange reactions. I searched for something to say. "It's not nearly as nice as Clara White Deer," I finally managed. "That's a beautiful name."

She lifted her chin even higher, narrowing her eyes suspiciously. Eventually she nodded. "There's a little café a block from here. I'll buy you a lemonade. Their iced tea tastes awful." She picked up a handbag from beneath the desk and started for the door.

⊛

A half hour later, we were sitting across from one another in a booth, sipping lemonade. "Why do you call Ned 'Grampa'?" I asked. "Is he any relation to you?"

She laughed. "Now, that's real funny. No, he's no relation to me, none whatsoever. Everyone calls him Grampa. It started as a joke years ago, but it just kept on going. Ned was always a ladies' man. He had so many girlfriends that everyone used to say that four out of five kids on the Southern Ute Reservation were his children. Then, as he got older, they just started teasing him, calling him Grampa."

"Did he ever marry?" I was thinking of the burning man's words: *Save the grandmother.*

"Grampa Ned?" She snorted. "No. He never cared about anyone but himself."

I watched her as she rummaged in her purse and pulled out a tube of lip balm. She smeared some on, then said, "What? Why are you looking at me like that?"

"I'm sorry. It's just that . . . well, a little while ago when you were saying you were sure he was dead . . . I mean, I guess I thought you were upset because you cared about him and we couldn't find him."

"Oh, don't worry," she said, plopping the tube back into her purse. "I probably care as much as almost anyone does about Ned Spotted Cloud. He's a Southern Ute, a member of my tribe. I guess I care for that reason. But you won't find anyone around here who will say anything nice about him." She paused a moment and put her hand to her chin as if she had thought of something. Then the hand came away and she held it up in the air as if she had surrendered whatever had come to mind. "At least not anyone who really knows him. You think I'm making this up? You ought to speak to Mary Takes Horse. You know the trading post on the corner downtown? That's her place. She's one of the tribal storytellers—she'll give you an earful about Grampa Ned."

When the waitress brought the check, I grabbed for it, but Clara White Deer was faster.

"I'll get that," I said. "It was my idea."

"No, I'm buying," she said. "You did me a favor. I'm calmer now. It was good to just talk—you know, say it how it is? Besides, I told you, I probably got more money than you. The Southern Utes are well off—we're not some starving, illiterate tribe looking for government handouts to get by."

"I didn't mean . . ."

"We're the richest tribe in the country. Our people are very savvy. We have excellent health care and good education for our children. And we take care of our own: every member of the Southern Ute tribe gets a check every month whether she works or not—a big check. It's from the investments our tribe has made with the income from our gas and oil leases and our casino."

"So why do you still work at the school?"

"I've been teaching music here on the reservation since

I was a young girl. I needed the money back when I started, and for a long time after that, before we got our tribal growth fund going. But now I do it because I love it. I love the kids."

"Do you have any children?"

She smiled. "I have a beautiful daughter named Nuni. She went away to school, married a boy from another tribe, and after a long time away, she and her husband have moved back to the reservation."

"Any grandchildren?"

She lowered her head. "No. No grandbabies," she almost whispered. When she raised her head again, I thought I saw moisture gleam in her eyes.

I considered asking Clara about her husband, but I noticed that she was not wearing a ring.

We started to scoot out of the booth. "You said you asked Grampa Ned for one thing," I said. "What was it?"

Clara White Deer looked at me, then stood and gathered her purse from the seat of the booth. "It was something he stole from me," she said.

I got up and tugged at my Nomex pants to straighten them. "He stole something of yours?"

"Yes. A long time ago. And—wouldn't you know it?— after all these years, I finally asked him to give it back, but he wouldn't do it. And now he's gone and gotten himself burned up."

"We don't know that," I said again.

"I'm sure of it. I saw him drive in there when I was on my way into Pagosa Springs this morning. They found his truck. No one's seen him. The sheriff said the fire burned right down to the road where he parked. It's just like that old man to die and deny me the one thing I ever asked of him."

"Was it something of value?" I asked as we strode toward the cash register.

Clara White Deer plunked down a twenty-dollar bill for

the two lemonades and waved at the waitress, calling, "Keep the change." She started toward the door and I followed.

When we got out on the sidewalk, a gust of 106-degree air blasted us. She looked at me in my BLM T-shirt, my Nomex pants, and my smoke-jumper boots, and said, "You must be hot in that getup."

"I'm used to it," I said. "The winds are picking up. I better get back to the ICP. Thanks for the lemonade." I reached in my pocket and pulled out a card. I scribbled the number of the satellite phone on the back of it. "Here's a phone number where you can reach me while I'm on this fire. If you ever need anything, if there's anything I can do for you, just give me a shout." I held it out.

Clara White Deer was slow to open her hand and take the card. She was looking at me with a curious expression. "What Grampa Ned took," she said, "meant a lot to me. Maybe not to anyone else, but it was priceless to me."

I studied her face. "Do you have any idea what Grampa Ned might have been doing in that area where you last saw him?"

She shook her head, obviously finished with the conversation.

And then my sat phone rang.

◀ **8** ▶

Dead and Alive

Wednesday, 1745 Hours

The burn area was still smoldering as we walked in our heavy boots through smoking duff and charred embers. Specially trained wildland medical crews worked on a high rock outcropping well up the slope of the mountain at a flat place used for a helispot. The Three-Pueblos Hot Shots, the elite Type 1 hand crew whose members all came from the three Tiwa-speaking pueblos—Taos, Picuris, and Tanoah Pueblo in northern New Mexico—had been found alive but in varying stages of serious to critical condition. Area hospitals had dispatched two emergency medical helicopters to airlift the victims to the nearest burn unit in Albuquerque. The medics had just finished shuttling the last of them on sleds to the choppers.

A member of the newly formed rescue command team had been designated to take photographs and document everything he saw and heard. "Did you get to talk to any of them before they were taken away?" he asked.

The noise of the choppers battered at my consciousness. "No. They were all too . . . they needed medical care."

He pressed his lips together and shook his head, readying his camera to take another shot. "The winds are making it tough for the pilots," he said, as he hurried off to a better vantage point.

The winds had been creating problems for more than the pilots: on my radio, I heard chatter about flying embers and spot fires to the north and west of where I stood, in the burned-over area called the black. I followed the sight line downslope to the place where I'd parked my Jeep earlier that day when I was looking for Grampa Ned. It was a long way down to the road, which looked like a tiny vein of dust from here. Stony outcroppings sprang up along the descent and blocked the view of the exact place where I'd found the truck—and the burning man. I continued to study the terrain below me. I sipped water from the tube of my Camel-Bak and reached into the case on my belt for my field glasses. The heat was already unbearable, but the smoldering ground and glowing coals beneath me made me feel like a roast on a spit.

As I studied the southwestern aspect of the mountain, I tried to imagine what route the burning man would have taken when he left his crew—how he got all the way down to the road ahead of the blowup that entrapped his fellow crew members for hours. It seemed too far, the terrain too difficult for even the fittest firefighter to escape on foot. While scanning through my binoculars, a glint of silver gleamed in the corner of my left eye. I steadied the field glasses and panned slightly back to the left, then held solid. There it was again! A little more than halfway between the place where I was standing and the place at the bottom of the mountain where I'd parked my Jeep and started up the footpath, something glimmered against blackened ground.

❀

An hour later, Kerry pointed at the silvery metal edge of a tool. "It was the blade of this shovel reflecting the light. That must have been what you saw." The partly carbonized metal spade with only a stub of charcoal for a handle rested on the ground.

"You think the hotshot dropped his tool here and ran?"

Kerry nodded and pointed up the slope to where they had found the Three-Pueblos. "Well, this shovel is here, right along a fairly direct line from where his crew was to where you found him down there at the road." His extended hand began to shake, and he drew it back to his side self-consciously. He looked down, acted as if he were brushing something off his pants.

I felt shaken, too. I looked around, then down the slope toward the trailhead. "I don't get it. It's too far to the road for anyone to think they could have made it. He was a well-trained hotshot. They're the best of the best. Why would he panic and run? That doesn't make sense."

"I don't know, but that has to be what he did."

"Why would he be so far from his crew? He couldn't even have been a lookout—he was way below them."

"Yeah, that's strange. Maybe he was trying to hike out for some reason. It looks like he was headed toward the road."

I thought a moment, then remembered my first glimpse of the burning man, wavering on the road, his body smoldering. In my mind's eye, I saw the pack and Pulaski, a fire tool with two heads—an ax on one side and a short, sharp hoe on the other—sitting on the road beside where he stood. "This can't be his shovel," I said. "He had a Pulaski with him at the road."

"Well, then, whose shovel is it?"

I scanned the area. "What's that mound over there?" I asked, pointing to the northwest.

We walked to the blackened hump, an ash-covered mound of rocks and dirt that was next to a recess in front of a shallow rock cave, an alcove no higher than three feet, and not as deep. "Someone's been digging here," Kerry said. He pulled a multitool out of the case on his belt, crouched, and poked at a small pile of dirt and ash. "The soil is loose; this is recent. It needs to be documented. Let me get the photographer." He thumbed his radio. "Documentation, this is Rescue Command."

"Documentation. Go ahead," his radio crackled.

"Are you about finished up there?"

"A-firm. I'm already headed down to you."

"Bring your camera. We found something." Kerry put the radio back in his harness.

"That's funny," I said. "I experienced a dead zone with my radio right below this spot."

"Seems to work fine here."

"You think the hotshot was digging here for some reason?" I asked, gesturing toward the mound of ash-covered stones and earth.

Kerry shrugged, shook his head, and walked a few yards upslope, staring toward the place higher up where they had found the hotshots, watching for the photographer so he could signal him as to our location.

I stayed by our find and looked around. The land, the sky—everything was gray or black, covered with ash and soot. The only color was a faint orange glow in the haze to the north of us, where the fire still blazed unabated. On the ground all around me tiny stems of smoke danced from jumbles of charred and unrecognizable matter. Dark monoliths that were living trees just hours ago jutted skyward like broken fingers reaching for mercy, obviously denied. Red veins still glowed across the scorched back of the land, pulsing as they drank the last of its life, while the real fury of the fire—its raging heart—devoured everything in its path just over a quarter mile away. A strange clump of twisted matter a few yards below me caught my interest. I studied it for a moment, then realized what I was seeing. I moved toward it to confirm, desperately hoping I was wrong. But I was not.

A burned and blackened body was sprawled in a heap on the ground, its skull tipped at a strange angle.

"Oh, God," I whispered. I instinctively made a small circle in the air with my left palm, a blessing I'd been taught to give to any living thing who had passed beyond the ridge. I winced, then squatted on my heels to take a closer look. As I did so, I felt intense heat emanate from the ground into the backs of my thighs and buttocks, the core of my body. For a moment, I couldn't breathe. I wrestled with a wave of dizziness, forced myself to draw in some of the stifling, smoke-filled air, and then blew it out slowly. "Who are you?" I said to the corpse, noting a solitary fluttering tuft of gray hair clinging to a flap of singed flesh that had come loose on one side of the skull. "Are you Grampa Ned?" I tipped my head to the side to study the deceased. "Please don't be Grampa Ned. I was supposed to find you. Bring you out. Not like this."

I stood and dusted off my gloved hands, as if I'd touched something dirty, then noticed that the leather palms were black with soot, like everything else. I walked a few paces away from the cadaver, from the acrid smell. I swallowed, my throat raw from the smoke. I tasted grit on my tongue, and I cleared my throat. "Hey, Kerry," I called. "I think I found our digger."

◄ 9 ►

The FBI

Wednesday, 2000 Hours

Kerry came over and put his hand on my back. "Aw, babe," he said. "You think that's your guy?" He bent his head and peered under the rim of my helmet at me, then reached a gloved hand up and pulled my sunglasses away from my eyes.

"I don't know," I said. "Probably." I put my shades back on.

"You okay?"

"Yeah, I'm . . ." I shook my head. "I'm okay."

"There's no way we could have gotten him out." Kerry tapped buttons on a GPS device to determine the latitude and longitude of the body.

We? I thought. *It was me that was supposed to . . .*

Before I could finish my thought, he said, "It looks like this is part of the Southern Ute Reservation. I'll call the co-ordinates in to Dispatch. I bet the feds are going to want to see this one."

Kerry was right—the FBI had jurisdiction over any suspicious death on Indian lands. "I'll stay," I said, jutting my chin in the direction of the deceased. "I'll wait for them."

Three men arrived on foot after what seemed like an eternity. They were wearing new-looking fire-retardant clothing and fire shelters, probably issued from the supply cache at Fire Camp. Kerry had hiked down to the trailhead, flagging the way, and met them at the road where he had staged his rescue command team.

Two of the new arrivals went to examine the corpse while the other came up to me. "Ron Crane, FBI," he said, showing a badge. "You the one who found the body?"

"Yes."

"I brought an investigator with the Southern Ute police and the county coroner with me."

"I'm Jamaica Wild, liaison officer for the incident management team," I said. "I'm a resource protection agent for the BLM in Taos." I wanted him to know that I was a law enforcement officer as well.

"That's good," he said, giving an approving nod. "Okay, then, let's see what you got."

After the three men had walked around the body and taken pictures, Crane returned to speak with me on the sidelines. "Notice how his head is twisted?"

"Yeah, I saw that. I'd hoped you'd tell me he fell wrong or something."

"I don't think so," Crane said.

"I didn't really think so either." I'd spent a long time alone with the body while Kerry went down the slope to flag a path for the law. I had avoided walking around in case there were any clues left after the burnover. There was nothing to do but wait. And listen. And I knew somehow from that time spent in quiet with a spirit in transition that this had been a violent death. And not, probably, by fire.

"Looks like he—or somebody—had been digging just above here. Do you have any idea how long he'd been here before the fire burned through?"

"Not too long before the eastern flank blew out, I don't think. A member of the Southern Ute tribe told someone on the initial attack team that she'd seen a man named Grampa Ned drive in through the yellow tape. If this is him, it couldn't have been more than an hour."

"Well, I'm pretty sure this is Ned Spotted Cloud."

"Is it? I mean, it seemed likely, but I hate to draw any conclusions."

"Well, that's his truck down below. And that body looks about the right size. And the woman who reported him entering the mine area?"

"It was Clara White Deer."

"I don't think I know her. I know most of the Utes. I've been here for sixteen years."

"She works at the intermediate school in Ignacio. She's the music teacher."

"Probably never gets in trouble. The kind I know are the ones who do."

"Did you know Grampa Ned?"

"Oh, yeah. I knew Grampa Ned all right."

"So he was the kind who got in trouble?"

Ron Crane looked at me and smiled. "He made trouble like the Southern Ute Growth Fund makes money. All the time. Hand over fist."

Crane returned to the body and talked softly with the coroner and the other investigator. I saw them examining the back of the dead man's head. The coroner pointed at the skull with the end of a slender silver pen. Crane stood up and took several measurements, then used a digital camera to snap some pictures of the deceased and the surrounding ground, including a large, blackened stone near the body.

He walked back upslope to the disturbed earth before the little cave and unfurled a large plastic pouch. He was wearing gloves, but he was careful to use only his thumb and forefinger to pick up the part of the shovel that once connected to the handle and put the spade into the pouch. Then he returned to speak with me.

"He's had a blow to the head," the agent said.

I nodded.

"Whatever it was," Crane said, "it made a pretty good gash in his noggin. Even though the body's burned, it's easy to see that he was struck with something, right at the base of the skull. Probably the blade of this shovel." He held up his plastic pouch. "But we'll have to have the medical examiner look more closely at the wound, and we'll check this thing out, too, and see what we can find."

"So you think Grampa Ned came up here a little while before the fire blew out to the east. And he or someone else was digging. And then Ned came down here by this tree—or what used to be a tree—and someone hit him in the head before his body burned?"

Ron Crane screwed his lips to one side, looking back at the body from where we stood. "Looks like it to me," he said.

"But who?"

"It's usually the spouse," he said, "except Ned didn't have one." He grinned.

I winced. It seemed an odd time to be making jokes. "It just seems that no one else could have been here without getting seen or burned, too," I said. "I was coming up that trail when the fire started crowning on this side." Then I widened my eyes. "Oh, no!"

"No, what?" Crane asked.

"The burning man," I said. "He was the only one who . . ."

"Yeah, I heard one of the hotshots tried to outrun the fire and got burned. Tell me about that."

"I was coming up the trail looking for Grampa Ned. I saw his truck parked down there, and I was just going to see if he was close by. The fire started to crown, and I raced back down the path. I saw the hotshot on the road. He was standing a few yards away from my Jeep. His body was steaming, right through his Nomex."

"Did he say anything?"

I had a terrible feeling of sadness as I spoke. "He said, 'Save the grandmother.'"

"The grand*mother*?"

"I know. It seemed odd to me, too. I wondered later if he'd meant to say *grandfather,* meaning Grampa Ned, but was just too disoriented from his burns."

"The grand*mother*!" Agent Crane shook his head as he walked back to talk with the medical examiner.

I shook my head, too. It didn't make sense to me—why would a highly trained hotshot from New Mexico leave his crew in the middle of a blowup and go hit an old Ute man with a shovel?

Agent Crane returned. "It's starting to get dark," he said. "I don't think there's much more to see here anyway—the fire's pretty much burned everything up. But we're going to tape this area off just in case, and then we'll carry the body down. Here's my card." He pointed to the phone number. "Just call me if you think of anything else. Have you got a contact number here?"

I took out my card and a pen. On the back, I wrote the number of my satellite phone.

"I'll be in touch," Crane said.

◄ **10** ►

Coyote Tactics

Wednesday, 2100 Hours

I rode back to the ICP with Kerry. He was never much of a conversationalist, but now he was as silent as a stone. I noticed his hand trembling on the steering wheel.

"You all right?" I said, giving a little smile. I reached out and touched his arm.

He flinched, then forced a little laugh. "You startled me."

"Talk to me," I said.

He shook his head and pretended to be fascinated by the pavement ahead of us.

"Hey, come on. Talk to me."

"What?"

"Your hands are shaking. You jumped when I touched you."

"It's just the adrenaline," he said. "I wanted to go get those guys, to save them. There was nothing I could do."

"I know."

"I keep going over it in my mind, trying to think of anything we could have done. All we could do was tie in at the road and try to flank the fire farther down. I couldn't go in there, I couldn't send anyone in there. There was nothing I could do. And then to find them like that, all in such bad shape . . ."

I reached across the cab of the truck and held my hand above the steering wheel for an instant so he could see I was about to touch him. I drew it back across his arm and gently stroked his shoulder. "It's all right. I feel the same way about Grampa Ned. I was sent to go get him, to bring him out. It doesn't even seem real, it hasn't quite sunk in for me."

"And I could hardly think, it was so damned loud . . ."

"You mean . . ."

"I can still hear those frigging choppers in my ears—they won't stop. It's like I'm hearing that throbbing *thwack* all the time, and it feels like everything's in slow motion."

"It's all that—the noise, the heat, the smoke. On top of everything else."

"I haven't worked that close to a chopper since I was in Somalia. I forgot how loud they can be."

"You were in S—"

"There is nothing worse," Kerry cut in, "than having your guys in trouble and not being able to go get them. Nothing."

I waited to see if he would go on, realizing he'd just begun to open up and talk, but he'd said all he was going to say. I leaned out the open window and let the air blow against my face. We rode in quiet for the rest of the way.

🌀

When we got to the ICP, the mood was grim in the war room. Roy and a few of his staff were hunkered over a large map spread out on a table. The men's T-shirts were sweat-stained and a few of them had smoke-smeared faces. They all looked up when Kerry and I walked in.

"You two need to do a critical stress debriefing," Roy said. "There's supposed to be someone coming tonight. Make sure you hook up with her, then take some time off, whatever you need."

"No, I'm okay, I'm staying," I said.

"I'm staying, too," Kerry added. "Have you heard any news about the Three-Pebs?"

The Boss reached with one hand and took off his cowboy hat while he pushed his other hand through his hair. He jammed his hat back onto his head. "They all made it so far. That's all we got."

"My guy died," I said without thinking. I was surprised as soon as I'd said it. "I mean, they think the body I found was Grampa Ned."

Roy narrowed his eyes at me. "You sure you're okay?"

"Oh, yeah." I nodded. "It was just so hot in the burn area, I'm . . ."

"Get yourself some water, sit down, take a breather," the Boss said. "Go to Medical and get an IV to hydrate you if you need to."

"What's the fire doing?" Kerry asked.

Roy looked down at the map and waved him in closer. "We're having a helluva fight with this one."

Kerry went to the table and joined in the huddle with the other men.

I grabbed a bottle of water out of a cooler, sat down in a chair, and leaned back against the wall. My mind felt numb. My feet and legs hurt from going up and down the blackened slopes. I closed my eyes and must have dozed off for a few moments. I woke when I heard Steve Morella's voice.

"We couldn't get here in time for evening briefing," Morella said. The archaeologist's yellow shirt was no longer clean and his nose and cheeks were sunburned. Elaine Oldham, the anthropologist I'd met with him earlier, stood behind him.

"Well, come on over and we'll bring you up to speed," Roy said. "We got a real vicious one here. We've had to change our strategy, and this blowup we had today has thwarted any hopes we might have had for direct control. We're going to have to go the whole fire with coyote tactics."

"Coyote tactics?" Morella asked.

Kerry spoke up. "Self-sufficient crews that go in, work their shift to construct their line, then stay there, sleep right near the fire line with a lookout posted, get up after a few hours' rest, and go after it again."

"What about food? And water?" Elaine said.

"MREs—meals ready to eat. Freeze-dried stuff," Kerry answered. "The firefighters carry them in their line packs. Water, too. The only way we can get anything into this terrain is to airlift it. Once we drop the crews in, we'll have to leave them there and try to air-drop supplies to them later."

Roy cut in. "But that's the problem right there: we can't get any air support. This whole zone is dry as a twig and there's fires everywhere. To really do this right, we need to get an air tanker and order the mud and keep it coming."

"Mud?" Morella asked.

"Fire retardant. Slurry. We can't get in on the flanks of this fire because there's no roads and the terrain is steep and treacherous, and there's spotting on both sides. The only good way to fight it is to bomb it with mud, use it to create buffer zones so the crews can get in. Or let it burn— better than putting firefighters in harm's way."

"And you have no air resources at all?" Morella said.

Roy shook his head. "We've got one chopper dedicated to this fire. We can either use it to drop buckets of water or to carry people and supplies."

Steve Morella studied the map, the red line showing the perimeter of the fire, now exploded in size from earlier in the day when I saw it during my brief attendance at the Command and General Staff meeting.

Roy took a pen out of his pocket and used it as a pointer. "We got a ranch, about twenty homes, and a quarry up on the east edge of the river, out ahead of the northern head of the fire," he said. "There's some open meadowland on that ranch, but the river area is thick with trees and dense undergrowth. And we've had so much curing—"

"Would you explain curing?" Morella interrupted. "Dr. Oldham has never been on a fire."

The Boss nodded. "Drying and browning of the vegetation ahead of the fire's front. The hot winds, the heat, it acts like a convection oven and bakes everything ahead of it. When the fire gets in the trees, it crowns—gets up in the tops of them and runs from branch to branch. That's what we had down here today." Roy pointed to the area where we'd found the hotshots—and the body. "We got ponderosa pine already bone dry from the drought, some piñon and juniper, both of which are highly flammable, and plenty of oak brush—which is downright incendiary—all in through there." He swirled his pen in the air over the map. "If the winds don't die down, this fire will run up every one of these drainages and right through your Lunar Standstill ceremony at Chimney Rock, and there's not a damn thing we can do. The flames could easily run through these trees all along Devil's Creek, where we got a Ute tribal youth camp. And if it continues to push northward and gets into that dry meadow grass on that little ranch, it will run. And maybe even blow across the highway and into the national forest on the other side, where we got a hundred and twenty-five–kilovolt power line that feeds Pagosa; if that goes down, Pagosa will be dark."

Morella sighed heavily. "You said something about letting this fire burn. You're not going to do that, are you?"

Roy looked him right in the eye. "I'm gonna try like hell not to, but we're talking about a force of nature over which I truly have no control, Dr. Morella."

"But the Lunar Standstill—it only happens every eighteen point six years. In a little over two days, the new moon will rise between the spires. We have about forty people up there—elders, spiritual leaders, indigenous people of the Southwest—preparing for the event. They've come from all over just to be here for it. I didn't get to brief you and your staff at the afternoon meeting because there were more urgent—"

Roy held up his index finger to interrupt. "I know about the Native Americans up at Chimney Rock. The Bureau of Indian Affairs talked to me about it. I'm going to try my best, but if we can't get this fire under control, the Archuleta County Sheriff's Office is going to go up there and evacuate them. That's for their own safety, Lunar Standstill or not."

Steve Morella raised his hands, palms upward in resignation. "Is there any good news at all?"

Roy gave a wry grin. "Two things. One, we found all the Three-Pebs, and they're in the burn unit in Albuquerque. Even the one Jamaica found earlier today is still hanging in there. And two, we got plenty of water around here for the chopper to dip from. Sometimes that's a real problem, but there's the Piedra River, two creeks, a couple little ponds, and Capote Lake on the other side of Chimney Rock. But it ain't gonna be enough with just one chopper doing all the work."

Morella said, "That is good news about the hotshots."

"The bad news, though, is that the northern head of this fire is still running hot and strong, and it's after nine o'clock. Most of the time, a fire will make a good run in the afternoon, and then she'll lay down at night. We'll just have to see what she does as the night goes on. If we can get crews in to flank this baby, we'll want to take one of your field people with every crew, have them advise the firefighters so we don't disrupt any archaeological sites."

"That's what I'm here for. I have a group of summer research assistants that will be ready first thing tomorrow. But we also came to take your staff up to the top of Chimney Rock and explain to you about the Lunar Standstill," the archaeologist said. "I think if you understood the importance—"

"Jamaica," the Boss interrupted, looking at me, "you can do that in the morning after briefing. Go, and then come back and give us the high points."

"Where am I going?" I asked.

"Up on top of the ridge at Chimney Rock, right next to the two stone pillars," Morella answered. "There's a historic fire tower up there."

◄ 11 ►

The Story of
Two Brothers

Wednesday, 2200 Hours

I had a little time to wait before the debriefing, so I decided to check on the native Puebloans before I left off my duties for the night. I drove up the steep, curving road to the parking lot on top in the dark, and parked in the same place on the side of the road. As soon as I got out of the Jeep, Mountain came bounding toward me. I planted my feet and got ready. He slammed right into me, almost knocking me over, and started his usual anxiety-driven circling and vocalizing, his tail thwacking me and thumping into the side of the car. I knelt down to put myself at eye level and I held and stroked him. I put my arm around his neck and pressed my face into the side of his. He huffed a few times, as if he couldn't get enough air, whimpered a little, and then finally began to settle down. I reached between his front legs and rubbed his chest, one of his favorite things. I could feel his great heart beating, and suddenly—for no particular reason—I thought I might cry. It had been a rough day. And it wasn't over yet. I took a deep breath and pulled my face away and looked at my best friend, my only family. I gave him a little smile, and he sat down and wagged his tail. "How are you, baby wolf?" I asked.

He tossed his head back and gave a quick yip.

I mimicked his head movement. "Oh, you're mad at me, huh?"

He nipped at the air, making a *pop* when his jaws snapped shut.

"Okay, I can see I've got a lot of making up to do."

He leaned forward and nuzzled his snout into my breast, poked his nose under my arm, and then stood there, tucked into me. After a few moments, he pulled away, stood up, and circled in front of me, then pressed his haunches into my chest, inviting me to scratch his bottom.

I saw Momma Anna coming toward me holding up the bridle and lead. "He take off," she said, shaking her head. "He know you come."

I stood and nodded to my medicine teacher. "I think he knows the sound of my Jeep."

Momma Anna studied my face. "You got sadness."

I raised my eyebrows. "It shows, huh?"

She nodded.

"It was a rough day on the fire."

She waved her finger at me. "Sadness like that fire. You must put out."

I remembered a time when Momma Anna had performed a ritual with a corn pollen mixture to cure sadness in a family member before a wedding. She had told me then that the sadness could make everyone sick and the wedding could go bad. And I remembered in the days after her son's death and the death of her brother, Momma Anna had not indulged in grief, but rather had done the tasks that were before her and even found occasion to laugh and to enjoy good food. The Tanoah believe that each of us comes to this life for a purpose, and that purpose is all that matters. Even in the face of loss.

"I don't have any corn pollen with me," I said. "I have a medicine pouch in my Jeep—"

She interrupted with a scolding sound: *"Tttch!"* She stepped to the side of the road and pulled some piñon needles from a tree. "Take this," she said, reaching for my hand and placing the prickly greenery in my palm. She nodded at me expectantly.

I hesitated, not sure what I should do.

"Ask," Momma Anna said, softly.

"What should I—"

But she cut in. "Not ask me! Ask put sadness out."

I drew in a breath, the air still hot from the stifling day, the smell of smoke heavy in my nostrils. I closed my eyes and raised my palm in offering, but the smell of the fire only reminded me of the charred body of Grampa Ned. After a minute, I opened my eyes again and saw Momma Anna staring at me with pursed lips. I sprinkled the pine needles in a circle above my head, felt them falling into my hair and around my shoulders.

"Now, do," Momma Anna said.

"I will do," I answered, knowing that meant for me to get on with my purpose.

"They do story down there." She pointed down the road heading back to the bottom. "You take me down," she said.

"To the visitors' center?"

She didn't answer, but instead started around the car to the passenger door, stooping to avoid the branches of the piñon.

The woman Clara White Deer had told me about was the storyteller for the occasion. She introduced herself and told her clan lineage in the Southern Ute tribe. Then she began the storytelling ceremony. She lifted a rawhide and willow stick rattle from a basket near her feet. The rattle bore a painted bear design on one side of its round hide globe, and strands of thong and feathers where the hide was tied to the handle. Mary Takes Horse closed her eyes and shook the rattle in an arc over her head, then held it high and made three percussive stabs in the air. She opened her eyes and looked out at the silent gathering. "They say there were two brothers who loved the same woman. It was a long time ago, when the People were moving all the time from camp to camp, and they had stopped one time for a long while to pick serviceberries. This woman was very beautiful and both the brothers wanted to have her for a wife, so they all the time tried to help her make up her mind. While she was out picking berries all day, they would hunt up a rabbit or a deer and leave it in front of her lodge. Each brother had a way of painting his arrows so that she would know which one of them had brought her meat, because they would leave the arrow in there.

"It took the woman a long time to make up her mind, and she had a lot of good meals for her and her parents while she was trying to decide. Finally, her dad told her that she had to choose or the brothers would get tired and neither one of them would want her for a wife. Well, both the men were handsome, but one of them was a lot bigger than the other. He had a big, strong chest, and he stood taller than his brother by a head. She thought the big one would make a better husband in certain ways . . ."

At this, all the women giggled, and Mary Takes Horse smiled and waited until the laughter subsided.

"So anyway, she told the big man she would marry him, and off they went to the wedding lodge. Now, this was in the summer, okay? And when they were together that night, big man told her she could sleep next to him, but that he was not going to make her his wife until spring."

The women in the audience all groaned and hissed. Again, Mary Takes Horse waited, smiling.

"So the next day, this woman talks to her mother and tells her what big man is doing. Or what he is *not* doing."

A round of laughter ensued from men and women alike.

"And her mother told her all kind of things to try to make big man change his mind. 'Put bear grease in your hair, make it shine like a river,' her mother would say. Or 'Cook the rabbit with this herb so the whole camp will smell it and be hungry for what you made.' But nothing the beautiful new bride did would make big man change his mind. One night, she was combing her hair when big man got ready for sleep. He opened his buffalo robe, inviting her to come lie beside him. 'Why won't you make me your wife?' she asked him. He told her that she must wait until spring. That next day, she put his things outside the lodge and this told the world they were no longer married."

The audience applauded. The man to my right put two fingers between his teeth and whistled loudly. Mary Takes Horse held up her hand.

"But that's not the end. This beautiful woman decides she will take the other brother, the little guy."

The women hissed and booed.

"So the first night they are together, little man gets right down to business. He takes his pleasure from the woman, smacks her on her bottom, and turns his back and goes right to sleep."

More hissing and booing from the women, but a few of the men nodded and winked at one another.

"And the next day, you know the woman is back talking to her mother again, saying how unhappy she is with this one. But the mother tells her she has made the stew and the meal is already cooked, so she can only eat it now, there is nothing else to do.

"Well, things go on and little man is happy to take pleasure from his beautiful young wife any night he wants, but he does not make sure she is happy in return. And the summer goes on.

"Pretty soon, the frost is there every morning and the People are leaving for a winter camp. They choose a place out by Red Hill, along the river, and they settle in for the winter. Meantime, that little man starts gambling with the men, and he rides off for long times saying he is hunting elk, but he does not bring the young woman back any meat, and she has to go to her family's lodge for dinner many nights through the winter. And one day in early spring, while the beautiful woman is outside helping her mother stretch a hide, she sees the big man bringing a deer he has killed to the lodge of another woman in camp. And that woman is a little bit older and not so pretty, but big man continues to bring her gifts and this not so pretty woman decides to accept the big man. And so big man and his not so pretty bride go into the wedding lodge, and it is spring."

The audience laughed and clapped.

"Then the summer comes, and the People stop to pick serviceberries again. And pretty soon all the women in camp have made the last of the serviceberries into pemmican and the leaves of that tree are turning into the colors of sunset and fire. Frost paints the lodges again, and the People choose a winter camp, this time in Sagebrush Valley. They settle in and the snows come. The young woman notices that big man and his new bride don't hardly come out of their lodge much at all."

Whoops and more clapping.

"Every once in a while, big man's bride would come out and gather some firewood and then she went right back in the lodge. And every time she did come out for wood, the People noticed that her skin looked softer and smoother, that her hair was shiny and strong, and her body was nice and round, that she was growing more pretty every day somehow, spending her days and nights all the time in that lodge with big man. Finally, the spring comes, and big man and his new bride come out of their lodge with two little bear cubs. Over the winter, big man has grown hair all over his body, and he has become a bear. At first, the People are afraid, but then they watch and see the tenderness and devotion he shows to his little ones and to his bride, and they see that he is a wise being. Big man has become a bear, and his bear spirit just needed the right wife to help him find his path.

"And the bear gave the People a lesson. There is a time for all things, even for things we love, things that bring us joy. Everything that happens is someplace on the medicine wheel, and the wheel is always turning. The bear knows that the spring is the best time to make love. Because on the medicine wheel, love is on one side, and children come around after that. So the wheel turns, and a spring marriage makes winter children, so the babies can sleep with their mother in the den as they grow fat and healthy, without hunters coming. And the bear also tells us that spring and summer are the time for hunting and gathering, because winter comes around on the wheel after that."

"But what about little guy?" one man yelled.

"Aw, he was a coyote," Mary Takes Horse said. "He ran off and went his own way. You know how they are."

◀ 12 ▶

Debriefing

Wednesday, 2300 Hours

When I got back to Fire Camp, I headed for the chow tent. I knew they wouldn't have supper this late, but there were usually a few goodies one could grab—they often left them out for crews who arrived in camp late. It was still over one hundred degrees, so the first place I went was to the beverage area. I took my plastic bottle out of my belt holder and filled it first with crushed ice. Then I poured in a couple packets of sweetener and a pouch of the fake lemon juice they had for tea. I filled the jug to the top with water and shook it to mix up my improvised lemonade. I poked around the coolers set up along the chow line and found some ice cream bars in one of them. I sat down at one of the tables and began unfolding the wrapper from a frozen fudge bar. A small gust of wind blew through the tent and a strip of the paper I had pulled from the ice cream flitted back and forth and then stuck again in the frozen fudge. I remembered the flap of flesh on the singed face of the corpse, the tuft of hair fluttering in the breeze as I examined

the body that was almost certainly the remains of Grampa
Ned. I set the fudge bar, still in its wrapper, on the table.
For a moment I felt queasy, and I forced myself to breathe
slowly. *Calm down,* I told myself. But my mind was not
calm. *What was Grampa Ned doing there? Who hit him on
the head?*

Kerry wandered in and looked around. He got himself a
cup of coffee and came to sit across from me.

I leaned back in my chair, welcoming this distraction.
"Coffee?" I asked. "This late?"

"I won't sleep anyway." He pulled a small round container from his Nomex pants. I watched as he opened it,
pulled out a pinch of chewing tobacco between two fingers,
and stuffed it between his lip and his lower jaw.

I knew that Kerry had struggled with this vice for years
before giving it up. He called it "dipping," and he had tried
several times to quit before he met me. Finally, he'd used a
course of nicotine patches, and that had worked, or seemed
to have—he had not had a dip in the year and four months
that I'd known him. Until now.

I leaned forward and reached across the table to stroke
his hand.

He seemed nervous about being touched. "I had to have
a dip," he said. "I got a can at the gas station in Arboles."

"I know. I'm stressed, too."

He pointed at the table. "Your ice cream bar is melting."

"I'm not hungry." I got up and threw the fudge bar into
a trash container, then returned to sit down.

"Yeah, me either."

"I almost cried when I saw Mountain a little while ago."

"You saw Mountain? Here?"

"Oh, I forgot, we haven't had time. He's with Momma
Anna up at the Native American ceremonies on top of
Chimney Rock."

"Oh, that's not good. We don't have good containment

on that side. Just because the fire's moving north now doesn't mean it won't blow out on the east again if we don't get a good fire break in there somehow."

"I know. I guess they've established some trigger points—factors that will determine if and when the Indians have to evacuate."

"Let's hope they're right, and it's enough time to get everybody down."

"God, what a day. The woman who's coming to debrief us should be here any time now."

He gave a snort. "Yeah, there's a real waste of time. As if I didn't have enough to do with this fire going like it is. Man, I've never seen a wildfire like this one. It's been totally unpredictable. This thing has run as fast downhill as it does uphill, which a fire never does. It's spotted way out beyond the lines, embers flying like tracer bullets."

I tipped my head to one side and looked at the man with whom I often shared my spare time, my bed, and my most intimate thoughts. "You okay?"

He pulled up. "Why do you keep asking me that?"

"A lot has happened today. You seem really amped up."

"I'm amped up? You're the one who said you almost cried. Listen, there were firefighters in the burn and I couldn't get to them. Don't I have a right to be concerned when there's an enemy out there I'm supposed to fight, and I can't figure out a way to fight it?" He'd raised his voice enough that crew members walking past were staring into the chow tent.

I was quiet a moment. "Of course you have a right to feel concerned. I'm just—"

"I'm fine, okay?" He gave a false grin. "Stop worrying about me."

"You mentioned Somalia earlier."

"What?"

"You mentioned being close to a helicopter in Somalia."

"When?"

"When we were driving back to Fire Camp, in the truck."

He looked confused. "Well, I was probably talking about working around the choppers."

"You never talked to me about Somalia before."

"Nothing to talk about. Army ranger stuff."

"Well, you just called the fire an enemy. And a minute ago, you mentioned tracer bullets."

He got up from the table, pushed his chair back under it, spit tobacco juice on the dirt to the side, and said, "It was just a way of describing things." He started to walk away. "We've both had a long day, babe. Let's leave it at that."

"But what about the critical stress debriefing?" I said, getting up from my chair.

"I wouldn't miss it for the world." He winked and gave a corny smile.

๑

Kerry was right. The critical stress debriefing was pretty much a waste of time. Most of the CSD team had gone to Albuquerque, since the hotshots were there and families were being transported in. So it was just me, Kerry, and the facilitator, a young woman named Barb who barely looked old enough to drive. Kerry did very little talking, and only answered the questions in terse replies. Neither of us had truly had time to take in the events of the day. When I told Barb what had happened, it felt like I was describing a movie I'd seen. "I'm not in real time," I told her.

"Not in real time?" she said.

"A lot has happened today. It feels like it's been a week, and it's been less than twenty-four hours."

Kerry and I answered a few questions about how we felt. We watched as Barb scribbled on a paper clamped to a clipboard. "Watch yourself and your teammates for signs of stress," she warned. "Talk about it with one another if that feels right, or call us and we'll come back and talk with you. Let us know if there's anything we can do. Seeing someone in death—even just the injuries you saw today alone—can cause extreme trauma for the observer."

When she left, Kerry walked out, too, but I remained and fixed myself another jug of iced lemon water. I shook my head, thinking about our facilitator. *Sweet,* I thought. *She's so sweet. She's just trying to help.* But she didn't know that I'd watched three men die less than a year ago—one of them Momma Anna's son. And there were more deaths before that, but that was another story. *Lately,* I thought, *I see death more often than I see my neighbors.* Of course, I don't really have any neighbors. Unless you count coyotes and mountain lions. Deer and elk. And bears.

◀ 13 ▶

Fire Camp

Wednesday, 2330 Hours

After the debriefing, I walked to the newly emerging supply cache, which consisted of three long tables and some yellow caution tape defining a perimeter around pyramids of boxes, mounds of sleeping bags rolled tightly into sacks like fat sausages, crates of bottled water, sunscreen, and other items. I grabbed a form and made a list requesting the things I needed to do my job: pens, paper, a clipboard; a whiteboard, tripod, and markers so I could leave notices by the restrooms up in the parking lot at the top of Chimney Rock. "Where do I order meals?" I asked the supply clerk.

He pointed to the logistics chief, who was strolling toward the ICP.

I made out a requisition for forty-five breakfasts and bag lunches, and got the paperwork into the right hands.

Then I went to my Jeep and drove to one of the three furnished cabins there at Navajo State Park. Two had been assigned to the men on the Command and General Staff, and the third was for the high-ranking women—there were twelve of us on the team. I hauled my red firefighter travel bag, complete with small spike tent and sleeping bag, in the door of the women's cabin and found that the six bunks were already taken and women on sleeping bags occupied most of the floor. I noticed Elaine Oldham lying on her side, still awake, in one of the upper bunks. We exchanged smiles. There was no place on the floor except for the middle of the room, where the others would need to walk to get to and from the bathroom. I plugged my sat phone into one of the wall outlets, then took my kit back outside and set up my spike tent on the lawn. But it was too hot to get inside. Instead, I sat on the grass before the opening, a hot wind occasionally gusting over me.

I reached to untie the laces on my leather smoke-jumper boots. These lifesavers were made with a raised heel and a lug sole designed specifically for fighting wildfire. They were sturdy, the pair weighing eight pounds, and they had a dozen sets of lace hooks and eyelets. I started unwinding the leather laces and felt pain in my right shoulder where the burning branch had struck me.

I pulled on the buckle of my belt and drew it through the belt loops, rolled it up and put it in one of my boots, along with the pair of heavy wool socks and the thin pair of silk ones I wore as a liner next to my skin. My feet felt like throbbing red knobs—hot and swollen. I must have walked fifteen miles that day. There was no one around and it was dark, so I stood up and dropped my Nomex trousers. My shirt had tails that reached the middle of my thighs, so I climbed out of my cotton panties without exposing anything of consequence. I rummaged in my kit and found what I wanted: the stretch bike shorts and oversized T-shirt I wore for pajamas on incidents. Once clad for sleeping, I pulled out my ditty bag and squeezed paste onto my toothbrush, then stood and walked around in my bare feet on the dry, crunchy lawn while I brushed my teeth. I spit onto the ground and rinsed my mouth using water from the Camel-Bak in my pack. I drank more of the water after I'd finished, then used some of the lip balm attached to a clip on the pack to try to soothe my parched lips. My face felt as dry as a sheet of parchment, but I was too tired to go inside and wash. I took my hair out of its ponytail holder and ran the brush through it, then set the alarm on my watch for 4:30 a.m.

Still unwilling to climb into the hot tent, I used it to shelter my belongings and stood and probed the darkness with my senses, searching for a good spot to sleep.

I knew from looking at a map that here, on a wide peninsula, the cabins and a small campground were surrounded by the waters of Navajo Lake, which stretched like a long, twisted root into New Mexico, down to Navajo Dam, and then back up a slender branch called the Pine Arm toward Colorado again. I could hear waves washing against a beach, and I followed the sound, walking about fifty yards to the edge of the lawn nearest the water. I spread my sleeping bag out on the grass, stretched out on top of it, and prayed there weren't any snakes, spiders, ants, or other biting beasts that intended to join me for the night.

I listened to the water lapping gently at the shore of the lake. I wondered if Kerry would stay up all night in the war room. He'd always had trouble sleeping, as long as I'd known him. When he spent the night at my place, I would often wake and find him sitting at my kitchen table alone in the dark, or even propped up on one arm watching me slumber.

I turned on my side, the way I liked to sleep. I missed Mountain. I thought of all the times we'd sat on the stone outcropping near my cabin at night under the stars—me wrapped in a blanket, him snuggling into my side or at my feet. We often dozed off like that and slept the whole night, waking only when the sun's rays pierced my eyelids. I knew that if he were here right now, I would welcome him onto my sleeping bag and put my arms around him, no matter the heat. Mountain and I knew how to share thoughts. And silence. I longed to have him beside me, to connect with his simple understanding of life. I remembered Momma Anna's words about the wolf and fire: *Wolf and fire live same place, time before. He know how not get burn.*

That's more than I can say for some of the rest of us, I thought, remembering the singed corpse I had seen just hours before, and also the tremendous heat that I felt when I embraced the burning man. I squeezed my eyes tight and tried to block out the memories. I had to turn on my other side because my right shoulder was throbbing where the tree limb had struck it.

⚚

I dreamed of Grampa Ned as I tried to sleep in the heat on the hard ground. His black, fire-shrunken body was lying opposite me, and when I opened my eyes, I saw him looking at me with glazed pupils. A scorched hand reached for my bottle of icy lemon water. I offered it to him, and he took it and drank eagerly. Then I became aware of my own thirst, and I demanded that he return the bottle, but he would not. I tried to take it from him, but he crumbled into a heap of ash. I was startled by a tap on my shoulder. I turned over to see the burning man lying beside me on the sleeping bag, his body emanating heat. His cracked lips opened and mouthed the same words he'd said to me before: *Save the grandmother.* But instead of making the sound of those words, his voice made a noise like fabric ripping.

◄ 14 ►

Morning Briefing

Thursday, 0430 Hours

By the time my watch started to sing its soft, high-pitched *tink-tink, tink-tink* alarm, there were already lights on in the cabins and I could see shadows moving around in the windows. I got up, rolled up my sleeping bag, and scuttled back across the dry grass to throw it in the tent. But the tent was collapsed, the fabric drooping in toward the center, hanging in pieces from the supports. I walked around the ruined shelter and saw that the back side of it had been punched through with something sharp at the top, and the fabric had been split down the middle to the ground. Someone had shredded my tent in the night!

I searched around under the dangling folds of nylon. My red bag, which held my firefighter gear and personal effects, must have been missed by the assailant. I looked through it, checking my items from memory. I always packed my red bag the same way so it was ready to grab at a moment's notice. The extra pair of Nomex pants was always rolled along the left side, the two extra yellow shirts along the right, with the shoes on the bottom, their soles to-ward the outside of the bag. Many times, on a fire, I got to bed long after the rest of the crews and had to find my things in the dark. Or, rising early, I might need my ditty bag and a change of clothes before the sun came up. A flashlight or my headlamp would work if I wasn't sleeping in a space where others were still snoozing. But if I was, I knew how to find what I needed by feel and memory of my standard packing order. It didn't appear to have been dis-turbed.

I grabbed my clothes and went inside to pee. Most of the women were still asleep, so I moved quietly to the bath-room. The team's lead information officer stood in front of the sink, brushing her hair. She gave me a silent smile, picked up her ditty bag, and vacated the bathroom so I could use it.

When I came out, my face washed, my hair pulled back in a ponytail, and my skin slathered with sunscreen, I grabbed my sat phone from where it was charging and took it outside. I punched in the security officer's number and re-ported that my tent had been ripped into.

"We'd better get a line around Fire Camp, and get those campers out of here," she said. "Obviously someone was looking for money or valuables. They didn't take anything, did they?"

"No. My red bag was untouched. Not that there was anything of much value in there."

"Yeah, wrong target if a thief wanted to make a big find. Firefighters are not the richest folks I can think of."

"Not in economic terms, anyway," I said.

"Well, I'll report it to the park ranger here. We're setting a camp perimeter today. It was just chaos yesterday. There wasn't much time to—"

"No, I know. I know. I just wanted to inform you about the tent."

"I don't think we'll have any problems once we get the campers out of the park."

"Yeah, I'm going to leave my red bag in there if you're setting a perimeter. It will probably be just fine. Whoever it was—if they saw something they wanted, it would already be gone by now."

When I went back into the cabin to get the phone charger, a couple of the women who'd slept on the floor were stirring, pulling on their pants and lacing their boots. Seeing them preparing for another hard day on the fire lines was awe-inspiring to me. If a fire is worth fighting, then every fire-fighter is bone tired at the end of the first day. And every day after that, it gets worse. The fatigue escalates along with the demand on the body's physical and mental reserves, the smoke, the heat, the stress, the danger. Firefighters will sel-dom get more than a few hours of sleep a night on an incident—and often not in such decent conditions as this cabin. And yet, they rise faithfully to the sound of a portable alarm or the squad boss's gentle shove. Up they get, doing what they have to without complaint.

Most wildland firefighters are innately physical people—they stay in shape. But more than that, they are people in love with the land. When a firefighter is out in the wild and sees a beautiful piece of the earth she might never have seen, it makes her fiercely determined to preserve and protect it.

None of the women in the cabin would rather spend their summer days lying on a beach slathered with suntan oil when they could be carrying fifty-pound packs, digging fire line by the chain and cat-holes for their toilets, and wearing hot clothes and a helmet eighteen hours a day. Some had probably quit their jobs to be here. Jobs are easy enough to find—fires are literally the call of the wild. No self-respecting wildland firefighter hesitates when she hears that call. I put my head down for a moment and thought of Momma Anna's instruction: *Now, do.*

This is what we do on a fire, I thought. *No matter how hard it is or how tired we are, we get up and we go out and we do the job we're here to do.*

I headed for the chow tent and saw the Navajo Hot Shots marching in tool order to breakfast—all in a straight line, as they would form up in the field according to the tool each man carried. Pulaskis first, then shovels. They were dressed in their yellows and greens, every shirt tucked in neatly, the hotshot patch identifying each as a member of this crew sewn exactly the same distance above the left shirt pocket, every pair of gloves hung from the belt on a carabineer on the right-hand side, every bandana the same color. When they went through the line, they stayed in formation, and they sat in that same arrangement at the tables at the back of the chow hall.

I found Kerry and Roy drinking coffee across a table from one another, both looking haggard. I took my plate of grub and sat with them. Roy said, "So you guys got de-stressed last night?"

I looked at Kerry. "I guess you could say that," I said.

"Yeah, we debriefed," Kerry said, and he got up with his plate still full of scrambled eggs and bacon and headed for the trash.

Roy looked at me and winked. "Don't worry. I got my eye on him."

☸

Most of the team was at the morning briefing, and additional crews had come in overnight. A meteorologist who had joined us from Durango gave a detailed spot weather forecast. The safety officer warned of the dangers of having crews working out ahead of the fire and of altitude sickness, dehydration, and sunburn. The information officer quelled rumors that one of the Three-Pueblos Hot Shots had died. She promised to get more information as soon as possible, and to have a camp newsletter and bulletin board up within the day. But she did not mention Grampa Ned's death because we'd been requested to suppress the story if possible until there were more details from the FBI, and until positive identification and notification of the next of kin could be made.

Ops Chief Charlie Dorn said the fire had made a run during the night, and was now threatening Camp Honor, the Ute tribal youth camp. "Structure protection crews are working in there now, but like Safety said, they're ahead of the fire, and that's not good. We've given them some trigger points to use to determine if and when they need to pull out and get back to the road. The Navajo Hotshots have arrived this morning, and we may have another Type 1 hand crew here by noon. The San Juan Hotshots are normally stationed in this area, but they're working a fire in California, so they aren't available. Durango Helitack has called back its chopper and crew of nine from Grand Junction, so we expect to get them busy here by early this afternoon. We did have a wind shift last night, so the northern head is the one that's most active now."

"We're sending an archaeological resource advisor out with every crew," Roy added. "There are literally hundreds of sites in the fire area and surrounding. For that reason, even on the flatter ground up north, we can't use dozers, and we'll need to be careful about digging line as well. The smoke is now making travel on Highway 160 between Durango and Pagosa Springs very dangerous. To top it all off, folks, we had a report of a good-sized black bear during the night, so your lookouts are going to have to watch for that, too.

"Now, before we disperse for the day, we want to make you aware that we will receive a blessing ceremony from the elders of the Southern Ute tribe. For those of you who wish to participate, we'll meet directly after the briefing at the park's amphitheater."

As the crews dispersed, the Boss waved me over. "Can you take the meals you ordered up to the Native Americans when you go up to the high mesa with the scientists this morning?"

"Sure, but that means I'll probably have to drive by myself. All that food is going to take up a lot of space in a rig."

"Well, do that, then try to get back down here quick as you can. The Navajo Hotshots want a designated space for spiritual ceremony. I want you to talk with them about that, get them what they need. Then, here's a number." He handed me a slip of paper with a phone number and the name *Nuni Garza* written on it. "It's another Ute woman looking for that Grampa Ned guy. Have you heard anything back from the FBI?"

"No. But it was late in the evening when they recovered the body. I expect I'll hear something this morning once they do the autopsy."

"Listen," Roy said, putting his sunglasses on, "when you're at the ruins on the mesa up there this morning, talk to them about preparing for an evacuation. Just in case."

"They already told me that they weren't going to leave."

"Well, we don't have any authority to make them, that's for sure. And the governor of Colorado, the agency rep for the Bureau of Indian Affairs, and about six different tribal nations have pressured me to hold off on recommending an evac. But I'd hate like hell for this fire to march up that hill like it started to do yesterday, and take a life, maybe a lot of lives."

"I know. But, Boss, some things are even more important to the Pueblo people than their lives. They believe they're part of something greater—sort of like points on a continuum."

He shook his head. "I just want to keep them *live* points on that continuum."

"Me, too. By the way, who's doing the blessing ceremony for the Southern Utes?"

"There he is now." Roy pushed his chin in the direction behind me.

I turned around, and Bearfat approached with his scantily clad young companion. "Good morning, Jamaica Wild," he said, grinning.

"Hello, Mr. Bearfat. I understand you've arranged to give a blessing ceremony here. I thought you needed what you called 'a clean space' to do this," I said.

He shook his head. "That would be the case if I were doing it. But I'm not doing it. I just arranged it for the elders. Here they come now."

◄ **15** ►

The Blessing

Thursday, 0545 Hours

A delegation of six men and women from the Southern Ute tribe stood in the performance area of the amphitheater. I recognized one of them. It was Mary Takes Horse, the woman who had told the story at the storytelling ceremony the previous night. The first speaker was a man who called the assembled to prayer for the hotshot crew in the hospital. The firefighters removed hats and helmets and stood in silence as the elder offered a Christian prayer. The gathered forces were completely silent. Next to me, a woman firefighter dabbed at her eyes with the corner of her bandana. Another man in his greens and yellows kept pinching his nose, swallowing hard. Sensing the stillness, a small bird near the lake began to chatter, adding voice to the prayer.

After that, Mary Takes Horse began to speak. "They say a long time ago, Creator put the four-leggeds and the wingeds, the crawling things, the swimming things, and the slithering things on the earth before the two-legged human beings. Back then, the world was always dark, and it was very cold because they had no fire here. When the two-legged human beings came, all the animals wanted to welcome their new brothers and sisters and make them happy. So the animals talked to Creator. They asked for a way to make the human beings warm, a way for them to cook their food, a way for them to light their way at night. And Creator told Father Sky to give fire to the earth. And so Father Sky gathered great clouds and wind, and cold and heat, in the same place, all fighting with each other to have power over the other. And soon, all that angry energy broke one of the clouds open and a ribbon of fire leaped from the sky and shot down to the earth like a beautiful shining arrow. The place where it landed burst into flames, and there was warmth and light. And all who lived here on this earth knew that fire was good."

Then one of the men stepped forward. "For many generations, Native Americans have lived peacefully with fire. We used fire as a tool, both as individuals and as nations. We have managed the land and the things growing on it using fire. We have used fire to keep the forests in good health and the grasslands renewed.

"But since the United States federal government started taking over the land and trying to control both the land and fire, the forests have grown too thick and heavy, the grasslands have not been renewed and refreshed, and fire has become an enemy and no longer a friend. When this energy comes from the sky now, it is not as a beautiful shining arrow, but rather as an enemy comes—destroying our villages, eating our forests and grasslands until there is nothing left, robbing us of the beauty and peace in our world.

"We do not want to be like the warriors in the Sky World when they fight—the clouds and the wind and the heat and the cold fighting one another for power. We hope to work together to find a way to bring the warmth and light back to the world of people.

"And so we bless the warrior firefighters, Indian and non-Indian, who have come here today to fight this fire. And we bless the animals and the land. And we bless the fire, too, that it will find its right place of power and no longer be an enemy, but rather come to renew the land and not destroy it. We are all brothers and sisters here. Fire knows no boundaries, and it strikes all communities—native and nonnative. Today, we must be as when the first beings lived on this earth: welcoming to our brothers and sisters who have come to fight this fire. Welcoming and offering to help in any way we can."

◀ 16 ▶

Lunar Standstill

Thursday, 0630 Hours

Steve Morella, Elaine Oldham, and I met in the parking lot at the top of Chimney Rock. The day was already promising to be a scorcher. The smell of smoke from the fire below us permeated the air. I gestured to a pair of men walking by and let them know the meals for the Native Americans were in my Jeep, and they promised to take care of moving and distributing the food. Elaine, who had not uttered a word yet, excused herself to use the ladies' room.

I turned to Steve Morella and said, "How long do you think the Native Americans will stay up here with the fire on the other side of that ridge?"

"They are afraid that if they leave, they won't be allowed to come back in for the completion of their ceremonies. So they will remain here, camping or whatever, until the Lunar Standstill."

"Have you seen their ceremonies before?" I asked.

"Every July, over a dozen tribes send representatives to

our social dances. It's really wonderful—they tell stories, perform dances, hold ceremonies. This year, because of the Lunar Standstill, they are performing special rituals to mark the rise of the moon between the spires. We have always welcomed them here. We believe this is their place, not ours."

"But they *are* right in the path of the fire," I said. "It might become necessary to evacuate them. The IC wants me to get them ready, but I hope it doesn't come to that."

Steve Morella smiled. "I imagine if you try to evacuate, these people will refuse to leave. They feel pretty strongly about the sacred nature of the Lunar Standstill, and it only happens once every couple decades. Most of these folks are from southwestern pueblos. They can be pretty stubborn when it comes to their sacred rituals."

"Amen to that," I said.

"You have some familiarity with the Pueblo peoples?"

"Yes. I work as a liaison for the BLM to Tanoah Pueblo. And I have some personal experience with Tiwa people as well."

"Tanoah Pueblo? Oh my, that's probably the most guarded of the pueblos. Even more so than Santo Domingo. Many of the Tanoah would rather die than give up anything about their culture."

"Don't I know it," I muttered.

We left the pavement, passed by the barely discernible rubble outline of a ruin known as the Parking Lot site, and hiked upward across a thin rim of rising ridge no wider than a few yards. Each side of the narrow causeway fell away sharply. I looked to the south and west of us and saw a swath of boiling smoke laced with red welts as Vulcan's child ravaged the earth. Directly to the west and northwest, a thick curtain of gray haze obscured the view. "Wow! You can see quite a bit of the fire from up here," I said.

"Oh, yes. I guess our geologist brought the IC up here to

the fire tower late last night. But what he wanted to see was right below, and that's one place you can't see well from there. They decided the view of the fire was better from over on Peterson Ridge, so they posted a lookout over there." Morella stopped at a place where the path narrowed slightly. By then, Elaine was back, offering only a sheepish smile.

"There was once a round structure here," Steve continued, waving his hand in a circle. "It's called the Guard House site, because originally the scientists who excavated the ruin looked at this slender ridge and thought that something straddling it across the narrowest point was built to protect those living above from intruders. It completely blocked the path from below to the upper mesa. But the evidence showed that there were no weapons or defense items inside. Instead, there were ceremonial objects."

"You mentioned it was a round structure," I said. "Was it a tower?"

"No," Morella answered. "But there was a tower here. It was on the highest part of the east-facing cliffs. It's often referred to as the Sun Tower site."

"I'm fascinated by the ancient towers. I've camped near some ruins above Tanoah Pueblo, next to what is almost certainly a guard tower. It almost has to be, by design and placement."

"Well, we thought so about the Guard House for a long time. But since the Lunar Standstill was discovered, we have some different ideas about that. So you like towers? Have you been to Hovenweep out on the Colorado–Utah border?"

"Yes," I said. "What a mysterious place—all those rock-block towers along an arroyo in the middle of the desert."

"Elaine has worked there for many years."

"Oh, you have?" I said, politely.

Dr. Oldham merely nodded.

Just then a young Native American man approached. "Hi, there," Steve Morella said.

The man carefully skirted the area where we were standing. He didn't speak, but hurried around us and down to the parking lot.

"He's probably Navajo, or possibly even Ute," Morella said. "Most of them won't go in the ruins. Probably wouldn't speak to us because we're standing in one."

I thought of Grampa Ned's body lying near a mound of disturbed earth, the charred shovel. If what Morella had said was true, it seemed unlikely that Grampa Ned had been digging in a ruin.

We headed upward, climbing a series of rock shelves until we reached the Great House Pueblo, bordered on the side where we approached by a massive wall that looked like the same architecture as the majestic ruins I'd seen in Chaco Canyon. I could hear drumming and chanting somewhere above us. Steve Morella led, I followed, and Elaine Oldham brought up the rear as we traveled an upward-sloping path alongside the wall of the Great House. We came to the top, where a circle of people were seated atop a circular stone wall inside the Great House Pueblo, their legs dangling into the restored ruins of a great kiva. The music was coming from down in the center. Morella gestured with a finger to his lips for us to be silent, and we walked quietly past on the path.

Just above the kiva stood the fire lookout tower, only yards away. The mesa was so narrow here that rock walls extending six feet from either side of its base spanned the width of the ground, which dropped off abruptly on either side down steep cliffs. Beyond the lookout, a knife edge of sharply sloping shale led to the two stone columns, Chimney Rock and Companion Rock. Morella stood before an iron gate that blocked the single flight of steps leading up to the observation area of the tower. He turned to face me and Elaine. "This fire lookout was originally built in the 1930s," he said. "It was closed in 1959. By that time, we were starting to use airplanes to get our eyes on fires. The Forest Service took the deck and cabin down, and only the original stone base was left. Later, they decided to rebuild it, as it had historic significance to the agency. They drove the last nail in the rebuild in 1987, and in 1988 the Lunar Standstill was discovered—or I should say rediscovered—by modern scientists. What we know now that we didn't know when it was being built is that this fire lookout stands exactly between the Great House and the two rock pillars, and the Lunar Standstill can't be seen except from the fire tower as a result. We also discovered during some of our observation nights up here that the Guard House site was probably the original observation site for the rise between the two rocks."

"But what exactly *is* the Lunar Standstill?" I asked.

"You know how the sun seems to rise on the eastern horizon farther to the north in the winter and farther to the south in the summer?"

"Yes," I said, watching Morella take out a ring of keys and search for the one to the large black lock on the gate across the stairway leading up to the fire lookout.

"Well, the moon makes the same journey across the horizon in only a month, not a year, like the sun. It rises from the most northerly point of its cycle to the most southerly point in the period between full moonrises. We call this interval between the two full moons a month. But, just like the sun, the moon begins its monthly cycle by rising at different places on the horizon throughout the year. The most northerly monthly moonrise occurs every eighteen point six one years when the moon completes a long journey across the horizon. There, it appears to rise at the same point, or 'stand still' on the horizon, for approximately three and one-half years. Hence, the name 'Lunar

Standstill.'" He unlocked the gate and swung it open. "Ladies first," he said, and Dr. Oldham and I went up the long flight of steps to the deck surrounding the glassed-in fire lookout.

"And this"—Steve Morella swept his hand across the sublime view of the two spires—"is the only known natural observatory which documents this celestial event. The moon rises exactly between Chimney Rock and Companion Rock during the Lunar Standstill. And we are smack in the middle of the Lunar Standstill now. For the first six months of the year, the moon rises during the day. But in July—in fact, this Saturday morning—the moon will rise between the rocks as a barely visible new moon. We will witness just the tiniest glimpse of her right before dawn. And each month from now until the winter solstice, the waxing moon will rise as it grows from a crescent to nearly full. Finally, the full moon will rise between the rocks on or near the winter solstice in December."

"And this is important to the Pueblo people," I said. "This is a sacred time."

At last, Dr. Elaine Oldham spoke up. "This is a sacred time, and this is a sacred place. We believe that the ancient Puebloans traveled from miles away to come here to witness this very event. We also believe that the discovery of this phenomenon by the ancient ones permitted them to make long-term calendars. Before they saw the Lunar Standstill, they could only use things like the solstices and equinoxes, the monthly cycles of the moon. It made planning ahead very limited. And considering that we now think that Chaco Canyon was a place of great ritual pilgrimage, we have to think that the Chacoans had a means to determine when things would happen there so they could plan ahead. Some people might have had to walk for days to attend a festival there, or a ritual or a trade fair. Think about it: if you started even one day late, you could miss the whole thing. The people had to know how to plan for long journeys and great gatherings." As she spoke, she seemed the perfect picture of a student of the ancients. Her skin, moisture-starved for years and roasted in sun-seared digs, was like tanned leather. Her long blonde hair—which she wore pulled back at the neck and dangling in whitened wisps from under her khaki hat—was nearly stripped of its color by the same punishing solar rays.

"Well! The anthropologist has a voice!" I grinned. "That's the most I've ever heard you say."

She smiled, embarrassed. "Don't get me started. I could talk your ear off about this stuff."

"So if the calendrical calculations were done here, how did they get them to Chaco Canyon?"

Elaine Oldham's face grew animated. "That's the most exciting part of all. Right on this spot where they built this lookout, the archaeologists who first studied Chimney Rock found evidence of a massive fire pit. If you look right below here on this side nearest the pinnacles"—she pointed to the ground below us—"you can still see one of the large pieces of stone that was part of what they thought was a fire reflection box. And they also found great slabs of pyrite and obsidian, which they believed were used as mirrors."

"Mirrors?"

"Yes. Walk around here on the other side of the deck and look straight to the south. The atmosphere is smoky, but you can still make out Huerfano Mesa. See it?"

I looked at the pale blue mountain with the slender, flat top. "Yes, I see it. That has to be a long way from here."

"About seventy miles." Morella joined in. "And guess what they found atop Huerfano Mesa?"

But Elaine didn't wait for me to answer. "A fire reflection box with an obsidian reflector, aimed directly at Pueblo Alto in Chaco Canyon, another eighty or so miles to the south-southwest, but in direct line of sight."

"That's mind-boggling!" I said. "They were transmitting the data by signal fires?"

"We're fairly certain of it," Morella replied. Elaine nodded in agreement. "Chimney Rock was the Greenwich of its time."

As I looked back at the two stone pinnacles, I remembered the storyteller with the eagle talon staff at the stone basin who had told the tale about the ancient ones telling the moon where to stand. "I'm guessing the person who figured out how to predict when the moon would rise between the pillars was probably pretty powerful in his day."

"Exactly," Morella agreed. "This knowledge must have provided tremendous power. There were probably priests or scribes who worked for the high chief at Chaco living here, watching the heavens and calculating the astronomical events. But the Great House up here was used mainly for ceremonies and pilgrimages, not to continuously house a lot of people." Morella walked to the west side of the deck and pointed across the river. "Elaine is working on that ridge across the Piedra River to survey sites there that have never been excavated. From what we can tell, those are also aligned with events on the horizon. Look over to the east there, at the Continental Divide. Do you see how jagged the horizon is because of those peaks?"

I nodded my head.

"Well, that had to be very useful in marking the position of the sun and the moon at various times of the year. It offered a tremendous advantage to the timekeepers of this area. In contrast, when you go to Chaco Canyon, the priests or timekeepers there had to build a structure—the sun dagger on Fajada Butte—to mark the solstices and lunar cycles. Or the windows at Mesa Verde, painstakingly built to align with the solstices and equinoxes. But this"—he pointed at the two rock pillars—"was not built by the ancient Puebloans. It was created by the same force that made the sun and the moon."

"How amazing!" I said, filled with wonder.

"It gets more intriguing the more you find out," Morella continued. "We happen to know that a Lunar Standstill occurred the year that work first began on that Great House down below us. And another occurred the year a second phase of building occurred. The building's walls are aligned with astronomical events. I don't know if you happened to see the stone basin down below the narrow causeway leading up here to the high mesa area." Morella held up a sheet of paper with a simply drawn map of the ruins atop the Chimney Rock cuesta. He pointed to the spot denoting the Stone Basin site.

"I did, in fact," I said. "They were doing storytelling at that spot yesterday." I studied the map, then looked at the ridge below us. From this vantage point, I could see down the back of the cuesta past the Great House Pueblo just yards from the fire tower, down the causeway to the Guard House site, then the Parking Lot site and the lot itself, and beyond it, at the far end of the meager mesa, the area known as the Great Kiva Loop Trail, where the path to the Stone Basin site led to another set of ruins, including one known as the Great Kiva.

"We now think that basin—which is carved right out of the bedrock there, and is just like similar basins found throughout the Chacoan empire—was used as a means to observe and survey the perfect alignment of the building's north wall with the sunrise at summer solstice, possibly using a stake or a lance with a branch or a fork to use as a sight. We also know—thanks to papers produced quite recently by astroarchaeologists—that the Taurus Supernova appeared in the night sky above these mountains in the year AD 1054. It would have been the third brightest object in the sky, after the sun and the moon, and was visible—

even in daylight—for about three weeks. It rose right before the sun rose each day during that period. We have evidence that ancient cultures around the world observed it, and there is a pictograph at Chaco Canyon that seems to illustrate it. It's likely that one or more of the ancient watchers of the heavens was using the Stone Basin site to observe and mark this event, because the south wall of the Great House Pueblo is aligned with the point where the supernova would have appeared in the sky when observed from the stone basin. Since we know the Chacoans were masterful architects, and well capable of creating near-perfect square angles and other complex aspects in their buildings, this seems to be the only reasonable explanation for a building that is several degrees off square in a culture so architecturally advanced."

I walked the entire perimeter of the deck, looking out across the landscapes this small fire lookout surveyed. Looking again back toward the way we came, I could see that the cuesta was shaped like a spear, with a long shaft that was the causeway. The wide base of the spear tip, directly below, was the Great House Pueblo with its two kivas, where the native Puebloans were doing ceremony. The fire lookout stood on the point of the spear, pointing at the two stone columns.

Elaine Oldham came up to me. "That pueblo below us is a machine, an astrological computer, a record of events. Their record is in their architecture."

Just then, there was a clamor on the wooden steps. I walked around the deck to the top of them and saw Mountain bounding up the stairs toward me, missing steps, trying to leap up them. Momma Anna stood at the bottom, again wrapped in her tan blanket. She turned her palms up and shrugged, pressing her lips tightly together. "He want you," she said.

"Mountain!" I said, as he rubbed his haunches against

me on the deck of the fire lookout. I squatted down to place myself at his eye level. "Mountain, you have got to stay with Momma Anna. I have work to do."

Elaine Oldham stood on the deck just past the glass doors. "Oh, how beautiful!" she exclaimed when she saw Mountain.

But Steve Morella looked wide-eyed through the opening of the sliding glass doors from the interior of the lookout. Mountain glanced in his direction and his ears went down, the hair on the ridge of his back raised.

"Mountain!" I commanded. "Down!" The wolf dropped to the floor, but his ears remained lowered, and he gave a little whimper. I looked back at the door to the one-room fire tower, trying to determine if Mountain had seen his own reflection in the glass doors or if he was startled to find someone in there. "I'm sorry," I told the two scientists. "He's usually quite friendly, but strange surfaces, unusual shapes, anything unknown to him will often put him on the defensive."

"Is that a wolf?" Morella asked, almost cringing.

"Yes, he's a wolf. His name's Mountain."

Neither of them moved.

"He's actually quite gentle," I said. "It's just that wolves are naturally shy of people. He's afraid right now, and that makes him defensive. Wolves aren't like dogs. They take a little extra effort to befriend."

"I don't want to befriend him," Morella said. "I want you to take him away." His voice was getting louder. "I want you to take him away from the door so I can get out!"

Mountain alerted on this and the ridge on his back spiked again. I had hold of his collar, but he wrestled to get free. "No, Mountain, down!" I said, and the wolf dropped again, but this time his ears were up and his eyes were fixed on the doorway. "Just calm down, Dr. Morella," I said to Steve. "Be quiet and be calm. If you show fear, he'll just pick up on it and become more anxious. Just breathe deep and let's all get calm, and I'll take Mountain back down."

"You do that," he said under his breath.

"I think he's beautiful," Elaine Oldham said. "Can I touch him?"

Morella spoke up before I could answer. "You're not supposed to have animals here at Chimney Rock Archaeological Area."

"He's here with the elders from Tanoah Pueblo," I said, working to turn Mountain around on the narrow deck walkway, still clutching his collar and keeping my body between him and the door of the lookout.

"Oh," Morella said, watching cautiously. "Well, I don't suppose we can tell them not to have him here. After all, we consider this their place. But I hope they're cleaning up after him. This is a very delicate ecosystem up here, you know."

I fought Mountain all the way back down the steps. There were no stairs at my place, and he wasn't used to them. It was one thing to bound uphill on them, like climbing a mountain, but quite another to navigate his way down. He struggled to leap, and it took all my strength to control him and go slowly so neither of us would be hurt. Momma Anna was waiting below. She held up his bridle and lead, and I put them on him. "They not like wolf?" she asked, jutting her chin toward the top of the stairs.

"Well, one of them didn't. And Mountain didn't seem to like him either."

"Smart wolf," she said as she led Mountain away.

◀ 17 ▶

Unclean

Thursday, 0730 Hours

After I made sure Steve Morella was going to be all right, I took my leave of the two scientists and ran after Momma Anna. "Wait!" I said, but she didn't heed me. Mountain balked and struggled, turning to look back at me, but she hurried down the narrow causeway, tugging at the wolf on his lead and bridle, until I finally caught up with them at the Parking Lot site.

"What did you mean when you said 'smart wolf'?" I asked.

She spun and frowned at me.

"I'm wondering if there is something I should know about that man—the scientist," I said.

She gave a wry smile. "There thing you not know, all men."

She resumed walking, and I joined in beside her, my hand on Mountain's back. I remained silent to see if she would go on with what she was saying, but she didn't. Finally, I said, "Speaking of men . . ."

She kept walking.

"That Bearfat guy. He's not a good choice to negotiate for the People. He was saying when I first talked to him that women on their per . . . women in their moon-time are unclean."

My medicine teacher stopped, turned, and looked at me. She handed me the wolf's lead. "You are unclean. That maybe why he say that."

My mouth fell open and I instinctively raised my hand to my breast. "I am unclean?"

"Yes," she said, and she resumed walking in the direction of a large piñon tree on the rim of the cuesta.

"But . . ."

As she walked ahead of me, she reached her right hand up and waved it in the air as if to wag me away.

I felt as though I'd been struck. I was too stunned to know what to do next, so I took Mountain for a brief romp to let him do his business. After a few minutes, I returned to where I'd seen Anna Santana heading. She had made a little camp under a tree, where all her things were neatly laid out. She sat cross-legged in the middle of her blanket on the ground. She looked as if she were expecting me. She patted the blanket for me to sit beside her, but Mountain accepted the invitation instantly and beat me to the spot. He lay down beside Momma Anna and panted in the heat, his face happy and eager.

I squatted in the dirt opposite my teacher. I picked up a twig and began fingering it between my two hands.

"You look good," she said. "Those boots. Look strong. It good, be strong."

I snapped the twig. "I am not unclean. And I'm not even in my moon-time, even if that were unclean, which it's not."

She shook her head. She made a little ticking sound with her tongue against her teeth, and the wolf perked up his ears at this. "Why you think we make story all time?"

"I don't know. To carry your culture and your memories to the next generation?"

At this she nodded. "Story do that." She kept nodding. "And summon ancestor. Like drum. Sound of voice like drum, each one different." She picked up the little round drum she always took with her to any important event. "This drum, my father make. I am little girl, he makes this drum, me. This drum, my father voice. Voice of love for daughter."

I sensed I was about to receive a lesson from my medicine teacher, and so I brushed off a corner of the blanket and sat down, facing her.

"Each life a story. Your life a story." She struck the drum once with the beater and pressed her lips into a thin smile. She blinked her eyes at me, and I saw compassion in her face. Or pity. I wasn't sure. She raised a finger and pointed it at me. "What make drum good?"

I thought of Momma Anna's father, Grandpa Nazario, who was once the head drummer at Tanoah Pueblo. Last winter, as I came and went from the pueblo in my duties, I watched as the ninety-seven-year-old elder taught his great-grandson the art of drum making. Nazario observed and coached as the boy hollowed out aspen logs, patiently chipping and rasping until the thick outer ring of wood was smooth inside and the center was empty. Then Grandpa demonstrated how to stretch a scraped and soaked piece of elk hide over the top of the drum, and another over the bottom. Using a wet leather thong cut from the same skin, he showed the boy how to lace the two pieces of hide together over the log, tightening it slowly as the skins dried, pulling them taut, letting them dry, and then tightening them again until the drum was ready to play.

I looked at Momma Anna, who was waiting expectantly. "Patience?" I guessed.

"No!" she snapped. She pointed her finger at me once

more, indicating I should try again. She struck the drum once more with the beater.

I closed my eyes and thought. In my mind's eye, I saw the boy scraping away at the logs—often working for days on the same piece of wood. One large log resisted all his efforts, and so, after the boy had carved and pared for days with little effect, Grandpa Nazario taught him how to burn the center of the log, then to use a little ax to chip away at the charred pulp inside it until it was clean and hollow. "The emptiness in the center?" I tried.

She raised her head up and pursed her lips. "Drum maker take away what keep drum from singing." She set the instrument carefully down on the blanket beside her and laid the beater across the top.

I still didn't see what this had to do with me being unclean.

She pointed a finger at me again. "Your story not come through that . . ." She wiggled her hand up and down in front of me.

"That what?"

"You not clean tree."

This was the frustrating part of having a medicine teacher from another culture. I usually had no idea what Momma Anna was trying to teach me. She spoke in riddles, gave strange instructions, and generally set me off on missions I didn't understand. As was often the case, I had absolutely no idea what she was talking about, yet I sensed she expected me to act on the information she had just imparted. "I don't understand," I admitted.

"You. Not clean."

I took in a deep breath and then blew it out in a frustrated blast. "Okay, then. I'm still not getting it." I moved to get up.

"You got it. Now."

My irritation was mounting. "Got what?"

She snapped her fingers in front of my face. "What you feel?"

"What do I feel? You call me unclean? You defend a guy who says women are unclean when they're—"

She clapped her hands this time, loudly, right in front of my nose.

I drew back. Suddenly I realized what she was asking me. I closed my eyes. I felt my pulse racing. "Angry. I feel angry."

"All time," she said softly.

"Not all the time." I argued, opening my eyes and engaging hers.

"All time," she said. "You good hide anger. Even you not see it. Deep inside."

"But that's . . ."

She held up a finger to stop me. She placed her hand on her chest. "Drum," she said.

I wanted to argue, to ask more questions, to find a way to process what she had just told me, but she brushed at the air with her hand a few times, as if to sweep me away. "We talk more maybe next other time."

I got up and dusted off my pants. Mountain got up to go with me. I leaned down and hugged his neck, and I felt a great, dull pain tugging at my chest—as if a stone were chained to my heart, pulling it down. It was a feeling of sadness and longing I had carried all my life but had worked hard to mask. As I rubbed the wolf's mane and felt him nuzzle my neck, I knew that Momma Anna had struck something deep in me, something old—as old and confounding as the sorrow I had been born into. Whatever I had used to keep the pain at bay was now useless and I felt naked. "Not now," I told Mountain, wincing, choking back tears. "You stay here. I'll be back. I promise."

As I struggled to compose myself, I approached my Jeep to find Bearfat sitting on the rear deck, shaded by the open hatch. He smiled at me.

I pushed my sunglasses on as I covered the last few yards. "Excuse me, but I've got to get back to Fire Camp." I hoped he hadn't noticed the quaver in my voice.

"You missed the dawn up here. It was beautiful."

"Yes, I imagine it was. The smoke from a wildfire usually intensifies it."

"Not just the smoke. The cradle."

"The cradle?"

He stood up. "Don't you know about the cradle that carries the emerging day like a newborn child?"

I could hardly wait to get in my Jeep and drive. I felt raw, every nerve tingling. Momma Anna had peeled back my protective covering and filleted me.

But Bearfat would not be deterred. "See, the moon is like a cradle, a deerskin sling like Indian mothers use to hold their babies." He clasped his arms and swung them gently as if he were holding a baby. "The moon carries the dawn tenderly away from the night and up to the Sun Father so it can grow into a good day. But when there is no moon, the morning stars have to form a cradle and carry the newborn day into the light."

"That's really lovely," I said, nodding my head, trying not to appear too eager as I reached up to close the hatch.

"But when the dawn is not carried tenderly," Bearfat said, stepping in front of me and taking hold of the hatch, "the new day, like a young child who has suffered, does not grow straight and tall. Those are not good days." He gently lowered the hatch until it snapped shut, then turned and smiled at me.

"Really?" I said, anxious for him to get out of my way. "And was the dawn carried tenderly today?"

"What do you think?" he said.

"I think I have to get back to work. Thanks for the story." I stepped around him and got in my Jeep and drove away before he could see the tear that had escaped and was rolling down my cheek.

On the way down the steep, curving road, I felt as if I were a small child again, watching my mother through the crack between the nearly closed bedroom door and the jamb.

> *"I see you there, Jamaica. It's all right. Mommy's not going anywhere. Take your thumb out of your mouth now, you're too big to suck your thumb, you're four years old."*
>
> *I pull my thumb from my mouth and reach to twirl my hair. I push the big, dark door and it swings open with a loud creaking sound that hurts my ears. Now I see the whole room with the big, high bed. It feels cold in there. I don't like it.*
>
> *"Come on in, honey. I'm just playing a game. But it's a secret, so you can't tell anyone, okay? Want to help me play?"*
>
> *I take two steps. I count them—one, two. That is enough. I eye the door to make sure it stays open.*
>
> *"I'm just playing a game here, pretending I'm going on a big adventure. I'm trying to see how many things I can fit in my suitcase. Want to help me? You can bring me my scarf from the dresser."*
>
> *I don't want to play this game. I don't move.*
>
> *She comes to me and squats down in front of me. She has tears in her eyes, but she is trying to be a big girl and not cry. "Now when he comes in for lunch, don't tell Daddy about our game, okay?"*

As I rounded the last curve near the bottom of the road, I realized my mind had stopped and was idling, empty. I drove through the parking lot at the visitors' center, feeling blessed numbness. I felt suspended in time, somewhere between the small child I had just been and the woman I now was. I tried to bring myself into the present, to focus. *You have a job to do,* I told myself. *You're on a fire, and there are people depending on you. Now, pull yourself together!* I forced my hands to loosen their fierce grip on the steering wheel.

But another memory overcame me. I was suddenly fourteen, lying in bed in my attic room in our lonely Kansas farmhouse, listening to my father swear and stagger downstairs, looking for another bottle, knocking things over, drunk and angry. I heard him cursing my mother's name even though it had been a decade since she'd left, cursing the piece of farm machinery that had taken one of his arms in an accident, and cursing me because I wouldn't come down and help him find more booze.

And because the older I got, the more I looked like my mother.

◄ 18 ►

Nuni

I'd missed the Navajo Hotshots before they left camp, but I figured I would catch up with them before the day was done to talk about setting aside a ceremonial area for them to use. I headed for Ignacio and called the number Roy had given me.

Nuni Garza gave me directions and an address, and a few minutes later, I pulled up before a large ranch-style house on a few acres on the outskirts of town. A woman was standing on the porch watching for me. She waved to me from amid a bevy of chairs, a metal table piled with auto parts, a gas can, two small chain saws, and assorted junk. The path to the porch was lined with two riding mowers, two push mowers, a wheelbarrow, and what looked like a collection of starter motors.

"Thanks for coming here," Nuni Garza said. She was a beautiful woman, perhaps in her late thirties, maybe early forties.

"You're Clara White Deer's daughter, aren't you?" She was almost as attractive as her mother.

"Yes. Come on in." She led me into a small entry hall. There, a coatrack was heaped with jackets. Countless pairs of boots and shoes lay tangled in a pile beside the door. A plaid wool muffler hung from the chandelier, and cobwebs tied it to every curve on the light fixture. I could see a large living room to one side, with a big stone fireplace at the end. Every available space in the room besides the seats of the well-worn leather sofa was full of bags, stacks of papers, or boxes and baskets with myriad items peeking out the tops. In the other direction was a dining room, where the chairs had been pushed against the wall and mounds of folders and papers obscured almost all of the long wooden table. "Let's go through to the kitchen," she said, "and I'll fix you a glass of iced tea. It's going to be another broiler today."

The kitchen was just like the rest of the house. Towers of red plastic cups, hills of disposable plates and bowls, unopened cans of soup, cereal boxes, and bags of tortilla chips littered the countertops. The table was stacked with more papers and files—some in cartons—and about twenty phone books, half of them with aged, brown edges. A small square of space in front of one chair was clear, just enough room to set a plate and cup. At the back of this tidy frontier was a line of amber plastic medicine bottles, perhaps a dozen of them.

Nuni Garza handed me a red cup with iced tea inside. "Don't worry," she said, "the place is full of clutter and it's dusty, but it's not dirty. That's a new cup, and I made the tea myself yesterday, in a clean jar."

I took a sip. "It's good, thank you."

"Dad likes iced tea, so I try to keep some made up in the fridge."

"Your dad lives here with you?"

She smiled. "I don't live here. This is my dad's house."

"Oh," I said. "My mistake."

"He's a pack rat. He saves everything. He's a collector and a saver and a never-throw-awayer. Is that a word?"

"Close enough."

"Let's go out back to the covered patio," she said. "It's got a couple of nice chairs where we can sit, and it's shaded. Dad had that room built on last year."

Just then, the doorbell rang. Nuni wound her way among the accumulations of things into the front entry. As she did so, my sat phone rang.

"Fire Liaison, Jamaica Wild speaking," I said.

"Crane, FBI. We've finished the autopsy . . ."

"Nooo!" Nuni screamed from the doorway. "No, it can't be him! It can't be him!"

I looked through the entry hall and saw a uniformed tribal police officer standing, cap in hand, in front of the wailing woman. His face was as sober as a stone. He looked at me and gave a slight nod.

"Agent Crane?" I said into the phone. "Let me call you right back."

◄ 19 ►

Lefthand

Thursday, 0840 Hours

I offered to wait with Nuni until her mother or husband could get there, but she told me she wanted to be alone. I quickly expressed my condolences to the sobbing woman, scribbled my sat phone number on the back of my regular BLM card for her, and left.

When I got to my Jeep, I could see that the rear passenger tire was flat. I went around to the back to get out the spare. The tail end of the car was sitting suspiciously low. I looked at the other rear tire. It was flat, too. I threw up my hands and blew air through my puckered lips. It was already so hot outside that my own breath felt cool as it tickled my nose.

A blue pickup pulled up behind me alongside the road. A magnetic sign on the door read, LEFTHAND CONSTRUCTION. An Indian man wearing overalls, a ball cap, and braids got out and came up to the car. "Somebody got a grudge against you?" he asked, looking at the two flat tires.

I shook my head. "I don't know."

He smiled and tipped his green John Deere ball cap. "I'm Alto Lefthand. I betcha I can help you out. I got a compressor in my truck. We can try giving them some air and see if the tires will hold long enough to get you back into town to the gas station."

※

Later, at the service station, while the mechanic took both tires off to patch them, I returned Agent Ron Crane's phone call.

"It's a homicide, just like I thought. No smoke in his lungs, no carbon particles in his throat like the ones you would see from breathing smoke from a forest fire, which means he was dead before the fire got to him. Struck on the back of the head with a sharp-edged object, probably that shovel, since the blade has a slight bend in it on one side. No evidence on the blade; of course no handle to get prints from. Since the body was so badly burned," Crane said, "we used dental records for identification. Fortunately, the Southern Utes have good medical and dental care. Anyway, it's Ned Spotted Cloud all right."

"I know. I was with Nuni Garza when you called, and a tribal policeman knocked at the door and told her. I guess Ned was her father."

"Yeah, one of the tribal investigators called on Clara White Deer to question her, and she told us that he had a daughter."

"*They* had a daughter. Clara White Deer is Nuni's mother."

"Oh, really?" Ron Crane said. "Let me make a note of that. I didn't get that from what the officer said."

"Yes, she told me she had a daughter named Nuni yesterday. Then today, Nuni told me she was at her dad's house, but I hadn't yet found out whose house it was until the tribal policeman came. And you called."

"Does Nuni Garza have any children?" Crane asked.

"No, I don't think so. Why?"

"Just wondered," Crane said.

☸

Alto Lefthand had been hanging around the gas station talking with the mechanics and watching them patch my tires. He came over as I was getting off the line. "Like I said, somebody must have a grudge against you, or they were playing a real bad practical joke."

"Yeah, not my lucky day, for sure."

"No," he said. "I mean, for real. Look at these." He held up several short, thick bead-headed tacks. "About eight of them were driven into the tires between the treads, right in the center. Somebody knew they'd cause a slow leak, I betcha. Could have left you stranded somewhere. You got lucky. I'll bet driving up that gravel road on the way to Ned's house, you busted the heads off a few of them, and that's why the tires went flat so quickly. Otherwise, you might have driven all day and then found yourself somewhere after dark, stranded."

"Well, I'm sure glad you happened along, Mr. Lefthand. Thanks so much. Can I pay you something for your trouble?"

"Nah, it wasn't no trouble, don't worry about it. They're just putting the tires back on now. Shouldn't be more than a couple minutes." He paused to look back at the Jeep in the service station's bay. "You working on that fire up by Chimney Rock?"

"Yes, I am. I'm the liaison officer with the incident management team."

"So, do you know Grampa Ned?"

"Not really," I said.

"Weren't you at his house when I pulled up?"

"Yes. I was talking with his daughter."

"Oh, yeah, her. She just came back to the rez. Grampa Ned never owned having any children before that. We all knew he had 'em, but he wouldn't own up to it. Then suddenly, here she comes, and she's taking care of him and coming over to his house and making him food and doing his dishes and stuff, telling everyone she's his daughter."

"Well, that must have been nice for both of them."

"It's more than that old coot deserves."

"I beg your pardon?"

"Ned Spotted Cloud is a rat bastard, and everyone here will tell you so. His daughter doesn't know how he is because she's been living someplace else. Old Ned's screwed everybody on this reservation one way or another."

"Including you?" I asked.

"Yes, ma'am. Including me."

"I'm sorry to hear that."

"I haven't figured out a way to get even yet, but I will."

I hesitated a moment. I might have mentioned that there was no need to worry about that anymore, but we had strict guidelines regarding the dissemination of information on our management team, and we were never to inform the public of a death until all of the next of kin had been notified, and only then through our information officer or a qualified public official.

Alto Lefthand didn't need any prodding to continue, however. "Yeah, Grampa Ned had me build that big covered porch on the back of his house last year. Had to get a Cat in there and level out the ground, then do a concrete pour to make that patio. Hired my nephew to help. It took the two of us over a week. When I got done, Ned refused to pay me."

"He did? Why?"

"I don't know. He said the sliding door on the back of his house wouldn't ever lock after I did the work, but I didn't touch his sliding glass door. You know, he's got plenty of money. He's an elder, so he gets seventy-five thousand a year from the tribal growth fund, plus more for holidays, birthdays, and special occasions. And he owns a rental property, plus he's got that big house. He has it pretty good. It's not about the money. Ned Spotted Cloud just screws everyone he meets, that's all. And I'm not the only guy trying to figure out a way to get even."

"Oh, really? Who else is mad at Ned?"

"Well, you'd be hard-pressed to find someone who ain't. But I heard that Ned's renter, Gary Nagual, is costing Ned money, which has to be getting Grampa's goat. That guy ain't paid rent in six months, I betcha. He likes to gamble. And drink. Even though he gets good money from the growth fund, too, he's always broke. I think Ned's getting ready to evict him. That's just one example. I could give you more."

Thinking of Agent Crane's question, and my own mandate from the burning man, I asked, "Well, since you mentioned you knew Mr. Spotted Cloud had kids, do you know if he has any grandkids?"

He laughed. "Why do you think everyone calls him Grampa Ned?"

"I mean that he admits having, like he admits Nuni is his daughter."

"I don't think he would've admitted she was his daughter if she hadn't marched in there and started doing so much for him. He never admitted it before, and everyone knows he ditched Clara White Deer when she was pregnant and just out of high school. So if he wouldn't admit it then, he probably never would have. It was all Nuni's doing. Somehow she made her way into that cold heart of Ned's."

Before I could reply, my sat phone rang again.

The moment I punched the talk button, I heard, "Jamaica, this is Roy. Meet me at the entrance road that goes up to Chimney Rock. The fire's jumped Highway 160 and is headed for those power lines."

"I've got to go," I said, snapping the phone off.

◄ 20 ►

Power Lines

Thursday, 1000 Hours

When I arrived at the entrance to Chimney Rock, Roy was pacing around in the wide turnout area, his satellite phone jammed into the side of his jaw, talking with the power company. I parked and got out of my Jeep and waited for him to get off the line. A hot wind started to lift my hat off. I caught it as a woman came toward me. I recognized her from earlier that morning when she had opened the blessing ceremony and from the storytelling the night before. She had been standing with a tall, lean man wearing a cowboy hat and Western boots and jeans.

"Are you the one who talks with the Utes?" the woman asked.

"Yes," I said, offering my hand. "I'm the liaison officer. My name's Jamaica Wild."

She took my hand and shook it. "I am Mary Takes Horse. I'm on the Southern Ute Tribal Council. That guy I was talking to over there is Oscar Good. He's the owner of the Laughing Dog Ranch."

"Hello," I called, and waved at Oscar Good. He gave me a nod and then went toward a pickup parked to one side.

"We are very worried. Camp Honor is our Ute tribal youth camp. We have some cabins and a gathering hall in the woods there. Everyone has been evacuated from the area, and we want to know what is happening."

"Let me find out the latest information," I said. "I'm about to talk with the incident commander. He called for me." I looked at Roy, but he was still on the phone. "In the meantime," I said, "I'd like to know if there is anything I can do for you, if you have places for everyone to stay, or if there are any specific things I might help you with."

"We just want to know what is happening to our land," she said.

"I'll find out as soon as the IC gets off the phone. While we're waiting, I want to say what a beautiful story that was that you told at the blessing ceremony this morning."

"My grandkids all like that one," Mary Takes Horse said. "We have many stories about fire. You know, Indians used fire in many ways. We used it to manage the land for hunting, and to keep the brush down around our camps and our medicine plants and sacred sites. We used it to send signals, and to keep the enemy from hiding nearby. A lot of times, we even used fire to keep our trails clear to and from our different camps and hunting places. And the fires we set always allowed for new things to grow to feed the animals we hunted. We believe that fire is a good tool."

I smiled. "We're beginning to understand that in the natural resources field. We could learn a lot from your stories and traditions."

She studied me. "Why don't you come to the storytelling tonight? It's the Utes' turn to tell the story again."

"I'd love to, so long as I'm not needed otherwise on the fire."

"Isn't your job to talk with the Utes?"

"And the other tribes here, yes. I'm the liaison between the fire team and the native peoples."

"Well, you need to come to the storytelling then. It's tonight at nine o'clock, at the visitors' center on the road up there before you climb the ridge." She pointed across the flats to the forested section inside the Chimney Rock Archaeological Area.

"Let me go talk to my boss," I said, "and find out the latest on the fire."

I walked across the dirt turnout to where Roy was talking to the information officer. The Boss waved a hand at me to follow him. When we got to the side of his truck, he turned and looked to the west. The two stone towers of Chimney Rock stood in sharp relief against a sky filled with surging brown smoke. "We're getting ready to do a press conference here," he said, "and there's a lot of ground to cover. The highway's closed, the fire's approaching those power lines, we had to evacuate all the homes there along the Piedra River, the youth camp, and that little ranch and the quarry. We've set up an evacuation center at Pagosa Springs Elementary School, and you'll need to check and see if there are any Utes there.

"The meteorologist is forecasting even hotter weather today than yesterday, with gusting winds, which is going to give this fire everything it needs to keep growing. But the worst news of all is that we still don't have any intelligence on our hotshots—they're still all in the burn unit in Albuquerque, and the doctors haven't released their updated condition. And we've had a homicide. Your Ute guy."

"I know. The FBI agent called me just a little while ago."

"Yeah, they're supposed to have someone here for the press conference to talk about that. Have you spoken with the local guy from the Bureau of Indian Affairs?"

"No, I—"

"You haven't even talked with the BIA rep yet?" he snapped.

"No, I—"

"Damn it, Jamaica, we're doing a unified command here—the BIA, the Southern Utes, the local agency, and this team. We're supposed to be working together, and you don't even know the key players? The BIA is your guy; you get with him right away and get him on your side. Do it first. Then I want you to talk with the governor's office in Denver. Here's a name and a number." He handed me a slip of paper. "See if you can get someone down here to help us talk to the Native Americans doing ceremony here. We're going to have to evacuate them, too."

"But Boss—"

"No buts." He held his hand up. "We've had enough losses on this fire. We're not going to risk any more."

He paused a moment. I nodded and then started to walk away. But Roy called after me. "Hey, Jamaica?"

I turned back.

"I wasn't done."

"Sorry, I thought you were."

"Well, when I'm done, I'll let you know." His voice had an edge. "Did you get with the Navajo Hotshots this morning like I told you to?"

"No, Boss. They'd already left camp by the time I got back from the top of the ridge."

"I told you to get with them before they left camp."

"But you told me to go up to Chimney Rock first, and they'd already gone by the time—"

"Well, you're going to have to kiss and make up with them now. I hope to hell they're not all stirred up. You're not taking care of your end of things, Jamaica."

My mouth hung open. I couldn't even think of a defense, I was so taken aback. Finally, I said, "Look, I got here early yesterday before anyone else, I tied in, I went after a guy—"

Roy interrupted again. "Take one of those archaeologists with you—you know those two that were in the war room last night? Don't take one of the summer field assistants. I don't want to leave anything to chance in this case. The Navajos don't want to be near any grave sites, and I want someone who knows what they're doing to work with that crew. We sent them up to Division Charlie; they're doing structure protection. Get in and put your resource advisor with them as soon as you get someone headed here from Denver. Don't wait, and don't do anything else but the things I told you in that exact order. You got that?"

I bristled. "Get with the BIA, get him on my side, call the governor's office and get someone down here to evac the Native Americans, get one of the lead resource advisors with the Navajo Hotshots at Division Charlie, check to see if any Utes are at the evac center, and get ready to have a big fight with the indigenous people up on top. Anything else?"

"No, that'll be it," he said as a gust of wind tried to take his hat. He grabbed the crown and pushed it down and got into the cab of his truck.

◀ 21 ▶

The Sad Story

Thursday, 1100 Hours

Fire Camp was taking on the look of a fully functioning tent city. The supply cache now sported a tent cover and a line roped off for overflow items too large to fit in the store. The information team had moved into an office trailer, and they had erected a big camp bulletin board, which was already covered with notes, ribbons, and good wishes for the Three-Pueblos Hot Shots. Plans had installed a satellite dish on the lawn of the ICP for the latest GIS—geographic information system—mapping data. This was the division where maps were made charting the fire's progress and the plan of attack. Plans was also where our bible—the Incident Action Plan containing the day's objectives, maps, weather reports and forecasts, safety messages, contact information, and an organization chart showing the chain of command—was created and printed twice daily, updated for each operational period. The chow tent had been upgraded with some climate control: it was lined on one side with a trailer holding a tank of water topped by a row of thundering fans that received timed squirts from misters to keep the dust down and provide a reasonably comfortable place for crews to get in out of the blazing sun and eat. And washbasins with running water offered the firefighters a chance to clean their hands as they entered the mess tent. Rows of porta-johns lined the public areas of camp. The shower trucks were now operational, complete with a big blue vinyl overflow pond-pouch to re-cycle the used water. The medical unit had posted signs everywhere illustrating the importance of good hygiene, hoping to fend off some of the inevitable cases of camp crud.

And now there were three refrigerated sleeper trucks with generators droning, each box lined floor-to-ceiling with compact individual sleeping units—or "cold coffins," as we firefighters called them, since they were only big enough to lie down in. These permitted the crews to sleep and recuperate in a cool environment free of biting in-sects or other critters. Since the fire management team was now running both night and day operations, the night crews who could get back in from the field currently oc-cupied the cold coffins. But the coyote crews continued to suffer the elements as they spiked out in harsh terrain on the eastern flank of the fire, without any of these modern benefits.

I caught up with Dr. Elaine Oldham in the chow tent, where she was sitting next to a fellow in green fire pants and a Forest Service T-shirt. Neither was talking; they were both hurriedly eating lunch. "I've been looking for you," I told her, as I sat down with a plate of salad and my bottle full of iced tea.

She looked up in surprise. "You have?" she said. "Oh! Where are my manners? Jamaica, this is Frank McDaniel.

He's the fire management officer for the Columbine District." She gestured to the man seated next to her. He had a tan face with salt-and-pepper hair. His lip sported a lush, full mustache to match his locks.

I offered my hand. "So you're the FMO over there? Jamaica Wild. Liaison officer for the team." I turned to Dr. Oldham. "I'm sorry to be so abrupt, but there's a lot happening. Elaine, the IC wants you to work with the Navajo hotshot crew. They're in Division Charlie today, and I'm supposed to take you up there to be their resource advisor. They refuse to work near any grave sites so you'll be there to make sure they're clear of any."

"But I'm working for Rescue Command," she said.

"I'll talk to the IC for Rescue. Roy wants you to work with the Navajo crew. And he's the boss. If you have any questions, you can talk with him. I'm just following his orders, and he said to take you up and get us both acquainted with the Navajo Hotshots."

Frank got up and picked up his empty plate and his soda can. "Well, if anyone knows the grave sites around here, it's Elaine. I'm sorry to be abrupt myself, but I've got to go. Nice to meet you, Miss Wild," he said.

Elaine Oldham got up, too, and began picking up her things. She spoke in a strained voice. "I have to go get my gear. Are you driving us, or do I need to see about transport? They told me I wasn't supposed to drive myself on business for the fire until some paperwork was processed."

"Well, that's the federal government for you. I can drive. Why don't we meet at the ICP in fifteen? Will that be enough time for you?"

"Well, I have a headache, and I'm going to go to Medical and ask them for something."

"It's probably from the smoke. That's you becoming a firefighter: dry eyes, headaches, and sore throats from so much smoke. I can meet you at Medical after I finish my salad."

"No need for you to come there," Dr. Oldham said. "I'll meet you at the ICP. I'll just hurry."

※

Kerry was alone in the war room, listening intently to his satellite phone when I got there. The light was off. I tapped softly on the door.

He started, then held out a hand indicating I should wait. "Nobody can do that better than me, Roy," he said. He jumped off the stool he'd been sitting on. He looked at me, then turned away, wiped his hand across his brow and through his hair, and said, "I'm fine, Roy. Hell, I've been through worse than this, you know that. I can't sit here and not do anything. Put me on Bravo. You want this fire flanked on the east side? Then let me do it. I got pulled off to do Rescue Command, but now that it's done, let me finish what I started. Okay, then. Yeah, we'll set up a spike camp down there. I'm on it." He switched off the talk button and looked in my direction.

I turned on the light, then flipped it off again. "How much sleep have you had?"

He shrugged, then headed across the room to the coffeepot. "About as much as anyone else," he said. "Roy wants Division Alpha to hold the heel of the fire and work along the river on the western flank to preserve habitat. He told me to take Division Bravo now that Rescue Command is pretty much over."

"Sounded like you had to push for it."

"A little bit. He knows I can do it, though, and the team needs me on tactical. I can't sit around and manage something that's already a done deal. We've got to get that east side contained or it's going to get in another one of those drainages like it did yesterday and shoot right up the slopes. Hey, did you hear that body you found was a homicide?"

"Yeah, I heard. Do we have an update on the Three-Pebs?"

"Not yet." He filled a coffee cup. His hand shook as he returned the pot to the coffeemaker.

I moved carefully toward him and touched his arm. "Hey."

He gave the slightest smile. "Hey, yourself."

"I'm worried about you."

I saw his eyes narrow. "Don't."

"Let's do another stress debriefing, what do you say?"

"We already did one."

"No, we just talked with the woman a few minutes. You barely said a word. It was all too fresh. I didn't get anything out of it. Let's schedule another one for later today. Want to?"

"I can't. I'm setting up a spike camp down east of the heel of the fire, and we'll be running night crews from there, too. I've got to get over there and get things going. Besides, I don't want to talk. If I want to talk about it, I'll let you know, okay?" His voice was as cold as the coffin-boxes in the sleeper trucks.

I pulled my hand back to my side. "Okay. I'm going to borrow your resource advisor."

"What resource advisor?"

"Dr. Elaine Oldham. She told me she's been working for you."

"Oh, that gal. I don't really need her right now anyway. She doesn't say much, does she?"

"Not unless she's really passionate about something."

"Well, I'm not using her at the moment. They have resource advisors assigned to Bravo already, and we'll get more if we need them. Go ahead and put her wherever you want."

I checked my watch. "I'm supposed to meet her here in about ten seconds."

He set his coffee cup down on the counter and gave me a halfhearted hug. "Did you hear? The fire jumped the highway," he said, breaking away. "They closed 160 down. Roy may need a separate team to manage the other side of the highway."

"Yeah, I know. Roy's up the wall. He really raked me over the coals just a little while ago. I'm still sore from it." But I thought about that and decided to forgive Roy instantly. Ultimately, the buck stopped at his door, and this incident had complexified geometrically since he took it over. And now there were even more risks, because working around high-voltage power lines requires a completely different set of techniques than just fighting a wildland fire.

Elaine stepped into the room. "Ready to go?" she asked.

I gave Kerry a smile. "Yup. My Jeep's out back."

✵

Elaine chatted easily on the way to Division Charlie. "Your wolf is beautiful. What's his name again?"

"Mountain." I smiled, thinking of my beloved four-legged companion.

"I could help you take care of him while we're on this fire. I'd love to spend some time with him."

"Thanks, but it wouldn't be as easy as you think. Wolves are not like dogs. They have no interest in pleasing you, so they're not obedient. You have to earn their respect and establish pack order, and even that is always up for challenge. They are escape artists, very willful, and often unpredictable. I had to go through some training, and then there was still a huge adjustment period while Mountain and I learned how to live together. It would just be too hard."

"How did you come to have a wolf?"

"His mother had been shot. He was just a tiny pup. One

of our wildlife rangers found him. They tried to integrate him into another pack, but the pack wouldn't accept him."

"So you raised him from just a baby."

"Yes, I bottle-fed him and everything. It helped establish our bond."

"You don't seem the motherly type," Dr. Oldham said.

I frowned, then reminded myself what Momma Anna had said about me being angry all the time. I looked across the cab of my Jeep at her. "Well, how about you? Are you the motherly type?"

She gave a big sigh. "Not especially."

"No children, then?"

"I didn't say that," she said. "I have a daughter."

"That's nice."

"Not really. She was born with Down syndrome. She's been institutionalized since birth."

"Oh, I'm so sorry. I didn't know . . ."

"Twenty-two years," she continued, "twenty-two years she hasn't been able to see at all or hear very well. She can barely dress herself. She doesn't speak well—it's hard to understand her, but you should hear her laugh. In spite of everything, she has this big, loud, incredibly contagious laugh. Her heart is not very strong . . ." Elaine bit her lip and took off her sunglasses. As she wiped them on her T-shirt, I saw moisture glisten in her eyes.

"That must be so hard," I said. "I can't even imagine."

She shook her head. "It's just that"—she paused a moment—"there's nothing I can do for her, nothing at all." Her voice quavered. "I'm sorry," she sniffed. "I didn't mean . . ."

"No." I reached out my hand and touched her arm. "It's all right. I understand."

"I don't see how you can," she said, and then she withdrew into silence.

◄ 22 ►

Red Hot Shots

Thursday, 1200 Hours

Since Highway 160 was closed, we had to work our way through heavy traffic on State Highway 151, which was no doubt the way the locals were getting around the fire. For them, it meant traveling down south, through the Southern Ute Reservation to Ignacio, and then turning back north toward Bayfield. All in all, it probably doubled the time, yet that was considerably less than the tourists had to travel. In order for them to get from Pagosa Springs to Durango, it meant a trip south to New Mexico and a long drive across some badlands from Chama to Farmington, then back north to Colorado. Half a day's drive at least, instead of an hour. The temperature had escalated steadily throughout the day and was now at 113 degrees. The asphalt road shimmered like a river with heat waves, and the stop-and-go traffic made the time in the Jeep feel like we were locked in a sauna.

I noticed Elaine licking her lips and offered her some lip balm. "That's a sign that you're getting dehydrated," I

said. "That could also be the reason you have a headache.
Better reach back and get one of those bottles of water out
of the back and drink it down. While you're at it, get a couple extra, would you?"

I pulled the front of my yellow Nomex shirt away from
my chest. The smell of smoke mixed with sweat rose to my
nostrils. Elaine started to roll up the cuffs of the new-
looking yellow shirt she was wearing. "No, don't," I said.
"They won't let you come on the fire lines if you're not
wearing full PPE."

"Not wearing what?"

"Personal protective equipment. It's your entire uniform, from top to bottom. You need to have your sleeves
down. When we get there, you'll have to put on your helmet and fire shelter and gloves."

She nodded but didn't speak. She rolled her sleeves
back to her wrists and fastened the cuffs.

"Hey, can I ask you something?" I said as I cracked
open the cap on a bottle of water. "You said you helped excavate sites around Chimney Rock some years ago?"

"Yes. Why?"

"Well, I just wondered if you were familiar with the
sites in Division Bravo. There are literally dozens of them
on the map."

"Yes, I'm familiar with them. Why?"

"What kind of sites are those where we had the burnover
yesterday?"

She blew out a breath and shook her head back and forth
rapidly. "They're just ancient settlements, nothing big, really. Little pueblos, or family group residences, mostly
Pueblo I and II. Nothing special. Not like on top of Chimney Rock, where you have the huge Great House and those
large kivas, the perfectly aligned walls."

"And the sites in the black—the burned-over area.

They've mostly all been excavated, right? I mean, most of them have site numbers, so . . ."

"Yes, they were excavated a long time ago."

"So, I would imagine . . ." I had to be careful not to reveal any details about the crime scene. "Well, no one like a pothunter or something like that would expect to . . ."

She turned to me and wrinkled her brow. "What?"

"Find artifacts to steal?"

She snorted. "I can't imagine anyone would think that would be the best place around here for that. In the first place, those were poor farmers in that area, not the rich priests and VIPs who lived up on top in the big, fancy Great House. And besides, everyone loves the more refined Chacoan artifacts, and those folks along the river and on the slopes above it weren't Chacoan."

"Really?"

"No. We believe that they were here before the Chacoans arrived. They lived in pit houses, which don't last for centuries the way Chacoan architecture does. Those ruins are heaps of rubble that can hardly be put back together. And besides, those sites have been sifted with fine sieves.

"But there are ruins up in Cabezón Canyon that have never been excavated. They're out of the public eye and completely unsupervised. *That* would be the place to find artifacts."

At Highway 160, we reached a checkpoint. The Forest Service employee warned us of heavy smoke and accepted the bottle of water I offered. Engines lined the shoulders of the highway, and flames licked up the trees on both sides of the road. Crews doused the grasses along the edges of the asphalt with water while others worked in the low flames pulling away limbs and hacking at brush. I veered down a dirt and gravel road that bordered Devil's Creek, then turned into the tribal youth camp. Before crossing the creek, in a dense fog of smoke, I saw a notice advising that it was Southern Ute land—like the sign I'd seen the day before when I went to look for Grampa Ned.

We drove across the bridge and back into some heavy stands of timber. Several cabins nestled in the woods beyond the creek, back against the clifflike slope leading up to Chimney Rock. Near these, I spotted the distinctive, box-shaped green buggies used to transport the elite Type 1 crews known as hotshots to their assignments. A few of the Navajo Hotshots were burning out brush and using saws to remove low branches and cut through the ladder fuels—growths of oak brush that caught flames from the grass and torched, launching the fire's height up several feet so it could easily climb up to the bottom limbs of the trees and from there into the crowns.

The rest of the firefighters were working in two squads putting in fire lines, one on either side of Camp Honor. Elaine and I watched the group nearest us for a few minutes. They worked in a row, spaced several feet apart with their low-slung packs on their rumps in the air and their heads and shoulders down. The six-man squad moved like a precision machine. Three hotshots with Pulaskis worked at the fore, using the sharp ax on the tool to cut through roots, and the short blade of the hoe on the other side of the head to scrape through thick duff as they walked steadily forward in rhythm with their tool strokes. Behind these three came a trio of shovels, the men cutting and scraping what was left down to mineral soil. One of the shovel-men yelled, "Bump up!" and all the firefighters ahead of him moved ahead a space to new ground, leaving the work they had left for the men behind them in the line. Together, they dispatched a tangled, overgrown swath of scrub into a wide, bare path sufficient to serve as a sidewalk in only minutes. It was so efficient, so clean, and so quick that I wanted to applaud.

"What did that guy say?" Elaine asked.

"Bump up. It means move ahead. He's running out of work where he is, or he's about to overtake the guy in front of him. Everyone ahead of him moves up a stretch and leaves the work for those guys behind, so nobody's standing around."

"But why *bump?*"

"That may be a firefighter's favorite word. We use it all the time. We bumped you over here from Rescue Command. People bump out to take a leak. When you finish marking the sites here, you'll probably bump back to Fire Camp. It can even be used to encompass the entire crew. They might bump over to Division Zulu after they get these lines in. Or they can even bump out to go to another fire when this one is contained."

I spied the crew's superintendent, and while Elaine unloaded her gear from the back of the Jeep, I strapped on my own pack and gloves, pulled my bandana up around my nose, slipped the goggles down off my helmet and over my eyes, and walked through low flaming grass—tongues of yellow fire licking at my boots—to go talk with him.

When I got there, I lowered my bandana. "I'm sorry I didn't get a chance to talk with you this morning. I understand that you will require some space to do ceremony?"

"Yes, we'd like to have—"

Before he could finish, my sat phone rang. "I'm sorry," I said. "Just a moment."

The BIA representative was on the line. He wanted to meet me at the Pagosa Ranger District in a half hour.

I turned back to the Navajo sup. "All right, let's give this another try, and I do apologize. A lot is going on. You were saying?"

"We want—"

Again, the sat phone rang. "I don't believe this," I said. "Just a second, I'm so sorry."

This time it was the governor's office advising me that they had someone on the way to the area, and not to speak of evacuation to the Native Americans up top.

Once more, I turned to the hotshot team leader. "I apologize again. So you need some space—"

And for a third time, the sat phone rang, interrupting us. "Fire liaison, Jamaica Wild," I said, holding up a finger and smiling at the hotshot.

"Jamaica," Roy snapped, "get back to the ICP quick as you can. We need you to accompany the FBI back out to the crime scene. And I got an update on the Three-Pueblos Hot Shots."

Bump!

‹ 23 ›

Scene of the Crime

Thursday, 1300 Hours

When I got back to the ICP, Roy was sitting at a desk doing some paperwork. He showed me a faxed list of the names of the Three-Pueblos Hot Shots and their medical conditions. I scanned down the list. One firefighter, Delgado Gonzales, age twenty-three, was in good condition and was expected to be released within the next day or two. Most of the hotshots were in fair condition. Two were in serious condition due to smoke and heat damage to their respiratory systems, and some burns. At the bottom of the list was the name of one man in critical condition: Louie Gonzales. He was unconscious, unstable, and had burns over 80 percent of his body. A note beneath his name said *Indicators are unfavorable.* His age was listed as twenty-one years. I ran my finger back and forth over the print on the page, as if I could feel his body, his temperature, his pulse through the paper. I dropped my head.

"We got one firefighter about to get out," Roy said. "And

most of 'em are doing pretty good, all things considered. But we got a few boys that are touch-and-go."

"Louie Gonzales," I said.

"What's that?"

"Louie Gonzales. That's his name. The burning man."

Roy stopped what he was doing and raised his head up. He looked over the tops of his little cheater glasses at me.

"Twenty-one years old," I said.

"Yeah, I know. He's the brother of Delgado, the one about to get out."

"Twenty-one years old."

"All this is getting to you," he said. He pulled off his glasses and set them on the desk, leaned back in his chair.

I bit my lip. "It doesn't get to you, Roy?"

He rubbed his forehead. "You know it does. I owe you an apology for the way I tore you up earlier. That was me being in a pressure cooker and not knowing what to do about it. I guess I just feel better somehow now that I have a list of names, knowing most of 'em are going to make it. It was not knowing anything that was driving me nuts."

"Well, I'm going nuts anyway. I'm supposed to be in three places in the next half hour. I need to meet the BIA rep in Pagosa . . ."

"I'll get Information to take care of that," Roy said. "They got about five trainees that just arrived. They won't like it, but I'll snag one and put them on that."

"And the governor's office . . ."

"You need to field that one, but if we have to babysit someone till you get back, let me know. The FBI wants you on scene because you're the one who found the body. I can't send anyone else for that."

My sat phone rang. "Fire Liaison, Wild speaking," I said.

There was no answer.

"Hello?"

The line was dead.

"Might be the FBI agent," Roy said. "He told me he'd call you when he was getting close and you could meet him down at the trailhead. Maybe he was getting out of range and got cut off."

"I'll head over there."

As I was walking through the door, Roy called after me, "Jamaica?"

I turned and looked at him.

"You'll be all right. You been through worse. You're tough."

※

Ron Crane and I were quiet as we hiked up to the crime scene—mostly because it was such an arduous climb and we were working hard just trying to get enough air into our lungs. For me, the time spent simply moving my legs and working my body gave my mind freedom to ruminate. I thought about Louie Gonzales, twenty-one years old and running for his life through a blazing inferno. But Louie Gonzales wasn't running when I found him. He was merely standing in the road, possibly too overcome with his injuries to move any farther. And what about his cryptic message: *Save the grandmother?* He could have told me to call his wife or sweetheart, to tell his brother he was sorry he didn't stay and deploy his fire shelter, to tell the hotshot crew they were his brothers, to pray for his soul, anything. Why *Save the grandmother?*

When we arrived at the top of the drainage where I'd found the body, Agent Crane bent over and placed a hand on each knee, puffing and panting. Around us, what was formerly forested slope now looked like a moonscape. A wide brown plume boiled to the north and west of us, and small pillars of smoke rose from stump holes and still-smoldering pockets of ground around us.

"It was starting to get dark when we were up here yesterday," Crane said. "I don't think there will be much of a crime scene since the fire burned pretty hot through here, but I thought we ought to take a look in the daylight anyway."

"Okay to walk around, then?" I asked.

"Let's try to be careful, but—yes, we've got to move around."

I moved as carefully as I could in my heavy wildland boots. I checked the ground before each step, walked in fairly straight lines from the trailhead around the perimeter, and approached the mound of dirt and loose stones piled up beside a depression. I reached into the cargo pocket of my fire pants and pulled out a map and studied it. "It looks like this is either right on or next to Site 8AA.104. Do you still have the lat and long that we radioed in?"

Crane leafed through a small notebook that he'd pulled from his shirt pocket and read me the coordinates. I checked them against the map. "I think this spot where Grampa Ned was digging is actually a few yards west of that site. That is, if he was the one digging."

"Oh, he was digging, all right, and not just with the shovel," Crane said. "We found lots of dirt packed under his fingernails, or what was left of them. One hand had been tucked under his body, and it was in better shape than most of the rest of him."

"But why? Everyone keeps telling me what a rich tribe the Southern Utes are, and I've heard that Grampa Ned owned property as well. I wouldn't think he'd be digging for artifacts. He certainly didn't need the money. Besides, the Forest Service archaeologist told me that most Utes won't go in the ruins around here."

Crane squatted down and started looking across the soil. "Well, if he was digging for artifacts, too bad for him."

"And who would come up here and hit him with a

shovel? I can't believe it's the hotshot. I found out today he's only twenty-one. He probably didn't even know Ned. He's from one of the Rio Grande pueblos."

Crane got down on hands and knees and lowered his head almost to the level of the ground. He scanned across the place where someone had removed the earth. "I'll be honest with you," he said as he studied the area. "Usually within a couple hours of something like this, I know who did it. I've been here long enough, I know these guys, and I have excellent cooperation from the Southern Ute Tribal Police. I usually talk to the family, find out what the victim had been doing, and come up with a short list of possible bad guys. Murder is all I do, and this is where I've been doing it for sixteen years. But this one is different."

I used his technique, squatting and scanning the ground. "You can't think of anyone who might have done it?"

Agent Crane stood up and brushed off his hands. "I can't think of anyone who wouldn't have wanted to. From what I can tell, Ned Spotted Cloud did not have a friend in this world, other than his daughter Nuni, who just recently found out she had a father and didn't really know him. But there's a list of folks as long as my leg with motives. Some of them better than others, but not enough to narrow the field much."

A tiny glimmer of reflected light caught my eye. I turned my head to the side and tried to lower myself even farther. "I think there might be something here," I said, "under the soil."

Ron Crane stepped carefully to the side of me and gingerly got to his hands and knees. He turned his head parallel to the ground as I pointed to the sparkle amid the ashes and charred soil. He knelt and took a pocketknife and carefully scraped the soil back. A minuscule bit of micaceous pottery emerged from the blackened earth, no larger than the tip of my pinky. "Well, what do we have here?" Crane said, as he used the point of his knife to gently pry up the tiny carbonized lump.

I recognized the figure immediately, having watched Momma Anna make countless numbers of them. "It's a bear!" I said. "A little pottery bear! A few of the women at Tanoah Pueblo still make them—they're like fetishes—medicine objects, power animals."

Crane managed to turn the diminutive bear over with the blade of his knife. He moved to one side to allow more light on the object. "There's a hole on either side of his neck," he said.

"It's for stringing it onto something—like a leather thong or yucca fiber—and wearing it around your neck. I know these bears. I know someone who makes them."

Crane took a small digital camera out of his pocket, squatted down again, and snapped a few shots. "This one looks pretty old. We're going to have to have one of your resource advisors come up and take a look at this before I remove it. Can you call on your satellite phone?"

✺

Steve Morella was astonished at our find. "What do you know?" he kept saying as he looked at the fetish, smiling. He took photos as well and made some notes. "There was a bear effigy like that, only larger, up at the Guard House site. They found it when they first excavated up there. That bear was almost four inches in length, though, not minia-ture like this one. Looks like the same kind of fine black-ened pottery—though the other one was not as sparkly as this guy is. We'll have to document the find."

"I'm taking it for evidence," Agent Crane said. "It could have fingerprints on it. After we check it out, we can arrange to return it to your possession."

"This is quite amazing!" Morella said. "Quite amazing! The site near here was a small family pueblo—Elaine would know all about it. She worked on the excavation of this very dig in the eighties. I believe it was a five-room block pueblo with only a few items found intact, nothing major."

"Well, this could be major," Crane said, "if it has fingerprints on it."

"There's just one thing that's kind of strange," Morella said.

"What's that?"

"The site was excavated twenty-some years ago. It was sorted, sifted, things were collected, labeled, and then covered over again. This bear effigy is lying nearly on top of the ground. Even where it looks like someone has been digging, they didn't get down very deep. I'm not saying it never happens that something washes up when we have heavy rains or something, but . . ." He stood and looked around him. "I just don't see signs of that kind of erosion here. It seems odd that whoever was digging here would find something so near the surface, an isolated find, not a group of pot shards or something like that. And that bear doesn't even seem to be clotted with soil, as it would be if it had been buried here for a century or more."

Agent Crane removed a small plastic pouch, then managed to scoop the tiny figure up onto the blade of his knife. He gestured for me to hold the evidence pouch open, then carefully inserted the knife and lowered the fetish into the sack. It fell in with a small *plumpf* sound and then appeared to look up at me from the bottom of the bag. Crane stood and held the container up to the light, admiring its contents. "Well, we'll just send this little guy down to the lab and see what he has to tell us."

After Morella left, Crane walked around and took more photos and some measurements. The blackened ground

still radiated heat, and the sun baked down on us from
above. I took a long look back up the slopes to the place
where they had found the hotshots who'd been burned
over. I remembered that I had seen a glimmer of silver
from above, that there was almost a direct line of sight between the two spots. Ron Crane saw me looking up the
slope and followed my gaze. He said, "Your burned guy, he
was a Pueblo man, right?"

I nodded. "Three-Pueblos Hot Shots."

"And this is a Puebloan ruin, right?"

I looked at him, but didn't speak.

"Maybe he spied old Ned digging here and came down
and stopped him."

I remained quiet.

"A Pueblo guy would probably take great offense if he
saw some old man digging in one of their sacred sites."

I shook my head. "I think the sacred sites are all up on
top by Chimney Rock. Morella said this was just a simple
little family pueblo. Besides, how would a hotshot from
New Mexico know there was even a site here?"

He wiped his forehead and blew air through his lips,
making a sputtering sound as if he were blasting a few
notes out of a trumpet. He looked up the slope again to
where the hotshots had been found. Then he looked back
down at the place where Grampa Ned spent his last moments. Suddenly, Crane started walking back downhill.
"I'm going to tell you what I think. I think he either saw
Ned here and risked his life to save him, or he saw Ned
here and risked his life to kill him. It's one or the other, because nothing else makes any sense."

Evening Briefing

Thursday, 1800 Hours

Kerry's Division Bravo had set up a self-contained camp near the front—known as a spike camp—to the east side of the heel of the fire, near the area where I'd found the burning man. Since I got down off the slope from the crime scene at a few minutes before six p.m., I headed to the spike camp for evening briefing. Agent Crane decided to tag along and listen. A crew of Hopi hotshots was about to airlift in to start the night shift, while the Blackfeet #3 Hotshot crew remained near the fire line, but stood down after a long day.

Smoke rolled off the slopes behind us as we gathered in a circle. The heat of the day was still so severe that I noticed the firefighters were reluctant to stand too close to one another.

Kerry's lower lip bulged with a wad of tobacco. "Listen up, people. This is a very hot division. The slopes and fuels are maintaining a lot of heat. We have the potential to maintain high to extreme fire activity tonight. Our spot weather

forecast says there may be some dry thunderstorms
overnight, and the wind effect from these could really kick
this up. The terrain here is very difficult, and we're trying
to burn out ahead of the fire. You all know how risky that is.
Strike team leaders, make sure every person on your crew
is thoroughly briefed, that you've got good communications, and that those communications are maintained during the firing operations. There's some radio dead spots up
there; we're right in the shadow of the repeater. You'll have
to make sure you use whatever means you can to keep
comms—use human repeaters if you need to. Even though
this is a night operational period, temperatures will stay
hot, and humidity is low. They've had a couple of heat
stress–related incidents on Division Alpha along the western flank, so maintain your fluids, watch one another, pace
your workload, take breaks. We've got two coyote crews
already in there, so tie in with them once you drop into
your zone, make sure you get a briefing from them." Kerry
looked at me. "Do we have any news on the Three-Pueblos
Hot Shots?"

I cleared my throat. "Yes." I addressed the group. "We
heard today. They're all alive . . ."

A clamor of whooping and cheering went up from the
camp.

"We have one member of the crew who is expected to
be released tomorrow . . ."

Another round of cheering. There was a perceptible lift
in the mood of everyone gathered there.

"And . . . I'll make sure you get any further updates as
they come through." I chose not to say any more, knowing
the good news would sustain the firefighters. That was
enough.

Ron Crane walked with me as I headed toward my Jeep.
"I heard what was said about firing operations. I guess that
old adage about fighting fire with fire is true."

"Yes, it is. Setting a backburn can often rob the fire of fuel and oxygen. And burning out ahead of it deprives it of fuel as well. Hotshots, in particular, do a lot of stringing fire. They're the best-trained firefighters we have, and they know how to manage it."

"It looks like a lot of work—those heavy packs, the long hours, the terrain."

"It's hard work all right. But there's nothing like it."

"Why do you do it?" he asked.

"I don't know. Partly it's that I love the West. But mostly it's the chance to work with all these brave people. And maybe also to sit at the end of the day on top of a mountain somewhere and see a beautiful view that maybe no white girl has seen before, and may not again soon."

"No *white* girl?"

I smiled. "I hang out with a bunch of Indians. Most of the women just call me White Girl. They never even use my name."

He laughed. "I'd call you Red Girl today."

"Yeah, I got a little burn. But almost everyone in camp is sunburned, so I fit in here."

"So, have you got someplace you have to go right now?" He stopped walking.

I stopped, too, wrinkled my brow, thinking. "I have to get some chow, then head to a storytelling this evening. Oh, God, I almost forgot. I have to meet with the governor's representative for Native Cultural Affairs."

"Well, I can take care of your chow if you'll let me buy you a sandwich or something."

The knot of firefighters was breaking up, the hotshots headed for the helispot to catch a ride to their new assignment. From across the road, I saw Kerry looking at me, his head tipped to one side in curiosity. He looked at Ron Crane, then spit tobacco juice on the ground and turned away.

"I can't," I told Crane, and started walking again. I looked at my watch. "I've got to meet with the governor's rep. I got all excited when we found that little bear effigy and I forgot all about that. I'm already really late. She's going to be pissed."

"I might need your help with the investigation." He hurried to keep up.

"Me?"

"Yes. You just said you hang out with a bunch of Indians. And I need to know what was going on with the hotshot that you found. He's Indian, right?"

"Yes, Puebloan."

"Okay, there's that. And you're on the inside as a member of the fire team. You'll hear things, maybe see things I won't be able to hear and see."

I furrowed my brow, trying to think of a polite way to refuse.

Crane continued, "And Clara White Deer evidently agreed to talk with you, right?"

"Only a little bit. We had a glass of lemonade."

"Well, she will hardly say a word to me, and the tribal police said the same thing. Said she doesn't like men. I was wondering if you could find out a couple things from her for me."

I made a grimace. "Listen, I'd like to help but I have stuff to do. I work long days on a fire. I don't have a deputy and I don't have a crew. If the IC thinks it has something to do with my job description, then I have to do it myself. And on this fire, that's been a lot."

Crane smiled. "Well, then, I guess I better talk to your IC."

◄ 25 ►

Walkingtree

Thursday, 1845 Hours

The representative for Native American Cultural Affairs from the governor's office had already arrived at the ICP when I got there, and she had not been idle. Shirley Walkingtree was a member of the Arapaho Nation, and she had let Roy know, in no uncertain terms, that the governor wanted the Native Americans at Chimney Rock to be protected and left undisturbed at any cost, unless and until flames were licking right at the walls of the Great House Pueblo up on top.

"Is a representative of your fire management team on-site?" she asked.

"No," Roy said. "Initially, we tried posting a lookout in the fire tower up there, but we ended up having a better view from the Piedra Rim across the river, and out of respect for the Native Americans, we didn't want to intrude on their ceremonies. Jamaica's been up there several times, and so have the resource advisors, but we don't have anyone up on top all the time. Besides, that's directly above an uncontrolled area of the fire, and I've tried to explain that nobody should be up there until we get that flank contained."

"What about at night?" Ms. Walkingtree asked.

"They haven't requested anyone stay up there at night," Roy said.

"What if they needed something? Had a medical emergency? Saw flames approaching?" Her voice was gaining volume.

"Now, Ms. Walkingtree, we've tried to show respect and attend to any needs or wishes of those folks, but they haven't especially wanted any of us to be there. They have cars, they're free to drive down to the visitors' center or even out of the gate."

"But I understand that if they leave the area, your fire crews won't let them back in."

"That's correct. But in an emergency—"

"So they're not going to leave unless it's a life-and-death situation," she said.

Roy tipped his hat back a bit on his head. "We'd be more than happy to put someone up there with a satellite phone or a radio, if that would be something they'd want."

Shirley Walkingtree leaned down and picked up her leather briefcase, set it on the chair, opened it, and took out a notepad. "I had a call from their liaison. He said that they would like to have Jamaica Wild—is that you?" She turned to me.

My mouth came open at the request. I quickly recovered. "That's me, and I'm sorry I'm late getting here. I was working with the FBI. A liaison for the tribes called you?"

Ms. Walkingtree raised her chin high and looked down her nose at me, making it clear she was suspicious of me and was making a mental file of my face for future target practice. "You're the liaison to those tribes for this team, are you not?"

"Yes, ma'am, I am."

"And *their* liaison has to call me, all the way in Denver, to get something?"

"Well, I asked for them to let me know if there was . . ."

She shook her head rapidly back and forth. "They appointed a liaison specifically to work with this team." She consulted her notebook again. "His name is Bearfat, he's Southern—"

"I know Bearfat. But he hasn't asked me for anything I was able to provide, and I didn't know—"

"Well, perhaps you haven't been willing to listen. You're late and you just interrupted me—that's considered rude in almost any culture." Done with me, she turned to Roy. "You have been given the authority to manage this fire, to control or contain it, and to make sure that it does not threaten or destroy valuable resources. This sacred Native American ritual ceremony is as valuable as someone's home or a section of forest. Great sums of money have been authorized to make sure that you have everything that you need so that you can do your job. The governor of the State of Colorado requests you to provide any support you can to make sure the Native Americans are allowed to complete their ceremonies. If this is not possible, I'm sure he will expect your personal phone call with a summary of the reasons."

Roy reddened. "Well, I'd just be delighted to do that, Ms. Walkingtree, if it comes to a question of putting my firefighters in danger to protect someone who refuses to evacuate when a fire is coming right at 'em, which is what we'll be talking about if the eastern flank of this fire erupts again. And the governor can just come figure out how to manage this fire hisself if he doesn't like how I'm doing it."

She gave a terse smile, picked up her briefcase, and walked toward the door. "In a few minutes, I believe you will be hearing from Senator Iris Littlebasket Carlos, a member of Nambe Pueblo. Her office indicated that she would be calling you personally to add her support for allowing the Native Americans to continue with their sacred rituals, as she has two family members participating in the ceremonies. I'll be in touch," she called behind her.

Roy turned to me, shaking his head. "Damn! Somebody who looked like me must have stolen her land."

I snorted. "Somebody who looked like me must have stolen her *man*."

Roy grinned, but quickly sobered again. "So, get your gear, take your satellite phone, and spike out on top with the Indians tonight. I don't have time to hold their hands, so you're going to have to do it. I gotta go up to the highway. They're having a helluva fight trying to keep the fire from getting in under those power lines."

My sat phone rang, and Roy hurried away as I was answering it. I heard a click, then silence.

◄ 26 ►

The Long Way Around

Thursday, 1900 Hours

I got in my Jeep and drove to the cabin where my torn tent was still pitched. I knelt on the grass, leaned in the small opening, and started to gather my things when I realized that my red bag was open. I examined the contents. It was clear to me that someone had gone to great pains to repack my things after looking through them. The pants were still rolled, but they were positioned down the middle. The yellow shirts were split on either side of the bag. And the shoes were turned upside down.

I sat back on my heels and looked around. As the security officer had promised, the civilian campers had been moved to another campground and there was no one but fire personnel in this part of the park. And I couldn't believe that a firefighter would have done this. I saw no one nearby. Most of the day crews were at chow, and with the fire still raging out of control, the overhead staff would work long into the night.

I gathered my gear and put it in the Jeep, then headed for the chow tent. On the way there, I saw Steve Morella and Elaine Oldham walking slowly along the road toward the cabins. I pulled over and leaned out the window. "How'd you do with the Navajo Hotshots?" I asked Elaine.

She spoke so softly, I could barely hear her. "Fine. There are only three known sites in that division, so I was able to locate and flag them within a couple hours." Her face was drawn and sooty, and she slouched and leaned against the side of the car.

"You must be tired," I said. "It's hot and smoky, and it's hard work out there on the line."

"I'm exhausted," she said, her voice rising. "I'm too old for this. My head is throbbing and my back hurts. And my feet! The Ground Support driver took my gear over to the cabin for me while I had some dinner. I don't think I could have carried it another minute. I'm going to take a shower and fall into my bunk."

Steve Morella spoke up. "I was just telling Elaine about the little bear. What an incredible find!"

"Yes, it was." I looked at Elaine. "Steve said you were there when the site was excavated some years ago. Did you find anything similar then?"

Elaine shook her head. "No." She rubbed her eyes. "I wish I had."

I felt sorry for her and tried to perk her up. "I'm sure you did find some interesting things when you excavated."

She shook her head again. "Besides the pueblo itself, and an even older pit house, all we found were some very basic things—a metate, some flaked stone, pot shards, that kind of thing. No effigies."

"A discovery like that could launch a career," Steve said, rubbing the palms of his hands together. "I can't wait to get it back from the FBI so we can analyze it."

I remembered his puzzlement about the piece being so

close to the surface. "So you believe the bear was missed during the original excavation?"

"We'll never know for certain, but we can do a clay analysis and carbon dating and see if it is likely that it belonged to that site."

I wanted to ask more: *How would Grampa Ned have known where to dig?* But I hadn't been here at Incident Base for the main evening briefing, so I wasn't sure if any information about the death had been released.

"Well, I'm tired, too," Morella said. "I'm going to hit the hay as soon as I wash up."

"Okay," I said, putting the Jeep in gear. "See you, guys. Have a good night's rest."

"Are you going up to the ICP?" Elaine asked.

"No, I have to run in to Pagosa Springs, and then I'm going to spike out on Chimney Rock," I said.

Morella looked surprised. "Really? Is it safe up there? I thought they were still fighting to get a line around the east side of the fire."

I shrugged. "Someone has to be up there from the team. I guess it's me."

☯

On my way to Pagosa Springs, I drove up the highway from Navajo Lake toward Chimney Rock. The sky was dominated by a titanic tower of billowing smoke, churning gray and brown and white, illuminated red in places by flames and sunset. Like an immense, evil giant looming over the land, the plume from the Chimney Rock Fire had sucked up all the space in the sky until what was not smoke was merely a small frame that served to focus the eye ever more on the herculean wrath of Nature toward those of us who might have forgotten Her power and our place in the scheme of things.

I would have passed right by Division Bravo if the

wheels of my Jeep had not somehow turned left at the dirt and gravel road toward the abandoned mine and the trail-head.

When Kerry saw my Jeep, he broke from his conversation with another man and came toward me. I got out and met him at the front bumper. "I'm going up to spike on top with the Indians," I said.

"What? You shouldn't do that! We don't have containment on that slope! It's bad enough we have the Indians up there, but every firefighter knows better than to sleep ahead of the fire." His eyes were wide, the stubble on his face was dark, and he looked a little mad.

"I know. The governor's office requested a team member be up there with communication capability in case someone needed help or something happened. I'm the logical one to go hang with the Indians."

Kerry grabbed my arm, a tight grip on my biceps. "Look, babe, don't do this. Think of the hotshots that got burned over. Think of that guy whose body you found. What are you doing going up there?"

He was squeezing my arm hard, and it hurt. I looked down at his hand, and he loosened his grip. I was suddenly questioning whether I should go myself. I tried to exude confidence. "Look, the other side of that cuesta is all shale and very sparse vegetation. There's a winding road that makes a perfect firebreak. All a person would have to do would be to run a few yards and there'd be a safety zone."

"I'm going to call Roy," he said, and he turned around and headed back for his truck.

I hurried to catch up with him, but he kept walking—and this time I grabbed his arm. "Kerry, wait a second. Will you just stop a second and look at me?"

He stopped and turned to face me.

"I'll be okay. I'm taking my pack and shelter, I'm taking my radio and a sat phone, and I'll be with a whole bunch of Indians who are going to be up half the night doing a storytelling ceremony."

As I spoke, he reached in his pocket for his can of dip. He took a pinch of tobacco between his fingers and stuffed it inside his lip.

"And Mountain will be there. I trust his instincts. I'll monitor the radio. Here . . ." I took out my small pocket notebook and wrote down my sat phone number, tore off the page, and handed it to him. "I've got to go into Pagosa Springs first. Then I'll head up on top of Chimney Rock for the night. Call me."

He reached for the slip of paper and squeezed my hand as he took it.

"Kerry, you need to get some sleep tonight."

He tucked the slip of paper in his pocket and reached over and smooched my cheek. I felt the bulge in his lip, reached my hand up and touched his jaw, drew my fingers down to his chin. His green-flecked brown eyes looked tired. "I might be able to sleep a little," he said. "The choppers don't fly at night."

◀ 27 ▶

The Land Deal

•

Thursday, 1945 Hours

At the shelter at Pagosa Elementary School, I asked the woman from the Red Cross if there were any Southern Utes staying there who'd been evacuated. She pointed to a man outside the school doors, propped against the building smoking. He looked lean and haggard and he had obviously not shaved or changed clothes in a while. "I don't know how many times I've told him there's no smoking on school grounds," she said, shaking her head as she walked away.

I went outside to talk with him. "I'm the liaison officer for the fire management team," I said. "Jamaica Wild." I extended my hand.

He looked down at it and thought for a moment, then reluctantly took it. His hand felt cold, his grip was limp, and I felt as if I'd just taken hold of a large clam. "Gary Nagual," he said. He threw his cigarette butt on the ground.

"It's dry here," I said, stepping on the butt with my boot. "You could start a fire doing that."

"When are we getting back in our houses?"

"When it's safe. Where do you live, Mr. Nagual?"

"Right next to me," a man's voice said. I turned to see Oscar Good, the rancher Mary Takes Horse had pointed out earlier that afternoon.

"Jamaica Wild," I said, "liaison officer for the—"

"I know who you are," he said, smiling, gripping my hand and shaking it. "Mary Takes Horse told me all about you."

"Oh, she did?"

At this, Nagual straightened. "I'm outta here," he said, and he strolled toward the parking lot.

"Don't worry about him," Oscar Good said with a wag of his hand. "He's not nice to anyone. He probably really needs a drink right about now."

I nodded my head. "I see."

"And if he had any cash, he'd be at the casino with the money burning a hole in his hand. Guy gets fifty thou every year without doing a lick of work, and he still manages to be broke nearly all the time."

I pressed my lips together, but didn't comment.

"You're the one who tried to go after Ned Spotted Cloud?"

"Yes, sir, I am."

"They said at the press conference that he'd been murdered."

"That's what the FBI and the coroner determined."

Oscar Good put his hands in the back pockets of his jeans and tilted his head up to look at the sky. Smoke from the Chimney Rock Fire had blown into Pagosa Springs, and with the air cooling slightly as evening came on, it had settled on the town.

"Can't say that I'm sorry. And Gary Nagual probably isn't either."

"The guy who just left?"

"Yup. Ned owned the land right next to mine, between me and the quarry. Gary rents the little house on that piece. Or he squats there, more like—I don't think he's paid Ned any rent in a long time. So Ned got tired of hounding him for money, and about two months ago, the old coot came over and threw everything Gary owned in the Piedra River. Television set, dishes, clothes, personal papers, everything. Just took it out back and pitched it in the water. When Gary got home from the casino that night, I had to call the sheriff or he would have went right over and killed Ned right then. Sheriff talked him down. Gary's still wearing the same clothes, after two months. I don't think he has any others."

"Well, that explains . . ."

"And if you're wondering about me, I'll tell you straight out. I tried to do a land deal with the Utes about fifteen years back. I own a little half-acre piece of land on the other side of Devil's Creek, right on the edge of their youth camp. It's landlocked by their land and the creek, and I can't even get to it, but it sure would have been nice for them to expand that youth camp a little bit. I offered to trade my half acre plus some cash for Ned's place, which is the same size. The tribe was going to compensate Ned some, too. He would have got well above market price. At the time Ned's land wasn't even being used—that little house was sitting vacant.

"Grampa Ned was on the Southern Ute Tribal Council back then, and so was Mary Takes Horse—of course, she still is. And they had a rule that anything to do with tribal assets had to be a unanimous vote. Well, guess who blocked the deal?"

"Grampa Ned?"

"You got it."

"That's too bad. But it doesn't seem like . . ."

"A reason to want to kill somebody?"

I nodded.

"Well, that's not all. Things got pretty heated between me and Ned, and we exchanged some angry words over the whole thing. And then . . ." Oscar Good bit his bottom lip and lowered his head.

I was quiet, waiting.

Good swallowed audibly, and then went on. "And then one day my two dogs suddenly developed seizures, all at the same time, and before I could get the vet out there, they both died. They twisted up and contorted in pain, and for an hour, they shook and yelped and foamed at the mouth, and then they finally gave out. We found a pan of antifreeze over on the other side of the fence, on Ned's land." He lowered his head again.

"That's terrible."

"I don't know if you can understand this, Miss Wild, a lot of people can't. But I don't have any family. My wife had died in childbirth a few years before that, and the baby died with her. Those dogs were my family. They were there for me when I hurt so bad I didn't want to get up some days. I guess I put all the heart I had left into those dogs. They were all I had."

I thought of Mountain, how dear he was to me, how he had filled my lonely life with joy, and I felt a tug in my chest. "I do understand, Mr. Good. I'm so sorry."

"I watched those dogs suffer something terrible. It was a horrible way to die, and there was nothing I could do. I still feel it to this day. Well, I would have killed Ned right then and there if I could have found him, but the weasel went somewhere and didn't come up for air for a couple months. Mary Takes Horse got him kicked off the tribal council after that. I've had a death wish for Ned Spotted Cloud ever since, and that's a fact. Everyone knows it. But I won't hesitate to add that I didn't act on it. Don't expect

me to cry at his funeral, though. I hope the sonofabitch suffered at least half what my dogs did. At least half."

At that, Oscar Good tipped his hat to me and walked
away.

A Feast of Sorts

Thursday, 2030 Hours

As I drove around to the east side of the mountain ridge topped by the two stone pinnacles known as Chimney Rock and Companion Rock, the shadow of the highland created early dark. It would not be sundown for almost another half hour, and yet, with the smoke in the atmosphere, it seemed much later.

Bearfat was standing in the parking lot in front of the visitors' center when I pulled up. A different young girl stood beside him. "Jamaica Wild!" he called, and waved, smiling. "I knew you'd be coming."

I got out of my Jeep. "I'm here at your request, I understand."

"It took some doing. I was afraid if I left the area, they wouldn't let me back in. But I told the guy guarding the gate out by the highway that I had to talk with the governor, and he let me make a quick run to Ignacio. There's no cell phone coverage here. I thought we ought to have someone who could get word out if we needed anything."

"Well, I'm here."

Bearfat flashed a wide, white smile at me. "It's going to be a good night."

I didn't understand his comment so I stood quietly. If there was one thing I'd learned from my dealings with the Tanoah, it was *When in doubt, don't talk.*

Bearfat was obviously testing me. He stood and looked down at me, smiling, hoping to make me uncomfortable. His young friend watched me suspiciously.

I bent down and picked up a tiny pebble from the parking lot. I acted as if I were enthralled with it, examining it carefully, turning it over and over between my fingers, setting it in my palm and raising it to eye level to look at it. I knew this game—the next one to talk was going to lose some power in the relationship. It wasn't going to be me.

Finally the girl with Bearfat spoke. "What about all that food?"

Bearfat was clearly chagrined. He broke off staring at me to glare at his companion.

"What food?" I said.

The girl simply pointed at the picnic table under the trees to one side of the visitors' center. Three large cardboard cartons sat on the tabletop.

"It's supper for the ones up on top," Bearfat said.

"How long has the food been sitting there?" I asked, walking toward the picnic table.

"About a half hour, I think. They're having a prayer ceremony at sundown. They will want to feast after that, but no one will eat until their prayers are spoken."

"Okay, then," I said, "should I take these boxes up with me?"

"No," he said. "We'll have the feast down here so everyone can attend. The prayer ceremony is only for the Puebloans."

"Oh."

"But you're invited," Bearfat said, smiling again.

"I am?"

"Yes, you and that wolf of yours. You better hurry. It's almost time for sunset."

As I drove away, I found myself shaking my head. *Bearfat!* I said to myself. *What kind of a game are you playing? And why do you insist on playing it with me?*

❀

I drove through the parking lot on the top and didn't see anyone around. I parked in my usual spot, got out, and walked past the comfort station, back across the pavement, and up the path leading past the Parking Lot site. To the west, the sky was dramatic: Peterson Ridge loomed in indigo relief on the horizon. The sun lingered on the rim of the ridge before saying good night, looking through the black and gray and magenta scarves of wind-blown smoke, illuminating these clouds of carbon from behind with a purple glow and red-feathered edges so that the whole atmosphere looked as if it had been washed with blood. Below, and to the southwest, an intense yellow incandescence marked the flame front, while smaller spot fires shone from within the dark relief of trees, like dozens of night-lit homes on the outskirts of a city.

I crossed the narrow causeway and heard a soft drumming sound. Then I heard a male voice cry out in falsetto voice: *Way-ah-hah-hah, Way-ah-hah-ah-yeh.* The drum grew louder, and more voices trilled: *Way-ah-hah-hah, hey-ah-eh-yay!* The smell of smoke from the fire was intense and heavy, but the voices were high and drawn, vibrating, penetrating the fog like a baby's cry, urgent and pure.

I climbed the rock steps to the Great House then walked along the wall, and as I rounded the corner of the structure, Mountain sprang toward me, his bridle in place, his lead trailing behind him. He squeaked and twirled as I patted and comforted him, and I found my hand softly pounding his back to the beat of the drum. I knelt and embraced my best friend, and he smiled and licked my ear. I took his leash and walked to the top edge of the ruin and looked down into the kiva.

The round stone-built room was filled with the native Puebloans, seated in circles emanating outward from a small, vacant hoop in the center. As the drumming and singing continued, two women took turns shaking pairs of prayer sticks embellished on the ends with feathers over the others at the ceremony. I watched as the pair went from person to person. They approached Momma Anna, who was sitting along the back wall. One woman reached high in the sky with her feathered sticks and shook them as though she were making rain, moving them downward until she shook past Momma Anna's shoulders and down her arms to her elbows and then into her lap. She stepped carefully to the side and the second woman held her prayer sticks low, then shook from the ground up, stooping to shake the feathered ends right over Momma Anna's crossed legs, then up her torso in front of her chest, in front of her face, over her head, and reaching upward to the sky. I started to sit down on the ground above the kiva rim, but a man stood and waved at me to come down the steps. Mountain balked and wouldn't come, so I took one step and stood for a while, then another, and then I sat down on one of the low steps. The wolf trembled and hesitated, but he carefully made his way down two steps and lay on the stone stair behind me. The song-prayer ended, and the man who had waved to me spoke in his native tongue. I didn't think it was Tiwa, because I had become familiar with the flat, nasal tones of that language through my work with the Tanoah. I thought perhaps this man might be Hopi, but I wasn't sure why. When he finished his prayer, the drum began to beat low and steady, *bom-bom-bom-bom, bom-bom-bom-bom,* and a woman in the center circle stood and offered a large abalone shell to the sky. I thought she was going to smudge by burning cedar, or perhaps even sage, but instead, she put two fingers into the shell and then put them on her tongue. Afterward, she made a circle with her fingers over her head and shook them at the sky and then circled them again over the ground.

As the drum beat on, *bom-bom-bom-bom, bom-bom-bom-bom,* the sky grew darker and it was hard for me to see what was going on in the round pit. It appeared that the abalone shell was being passed from person to person to repeat the offering, but I lost track of it somewhere in the second row. The sound of the drum was mesmerizing: *bom-bom-bom-bom, bom-bom-bom-bom.* I found myself swaying gently from side to side, rocking on my hips on the stone step. I closed my eyes and I could feel the drum as if it were my own heartbeat. I felt a bump on my elbow. I looked down to see that a woman was offering the abalone shell to me from her seat against the wall just below me. I reached down and took the shell from her, praying that I wouldn't make a mistake. I had only clearly seen the first woman's gestures, so I tried my best to remember exactly how she had performed the ritual. I put my fingers in the shell and found grains or meal of some kind in the bottom. I took a pinch and put it on my tongue. *Corn pollen.* Then I raised my pinched fingers and made a circle over my head, sprinkling some of the grains onto my hair. I reached to the heavens and offered some to Father Sky, then to the step below me, where I circled my fingers and offered pollen to Mother Earth. As I made this offering, the drum beat on: *bom-bom-bom-bom.* When I was finished, I looked to see what I should do with the shell, whether to try to pass it back to the woman who had just handed it to me or to move down another two steps and try to get it to the next person over against the wall.

But instead of the seated woman who had handed me
the abalone shell, Grampa Ned stood right next to me, his
large eyes looking directly into mine as I sat on the step. A
flap of skin hung away from his left temple and I could
smell the distinctive, acrid smell of burned hair and flesh.
He was smoldering, and his neck was black with oozing
clots. His chest, his back, and his shoulders dripped red-
black blood, and he wore a blanket of billowing layers of
tissue-thin ashes, which flaked off in bits and blew like tiny
cinders from a fire. He smiled at me, and instead of taking
the abalone shell I was holding just inches away, he held up
his own offering with his left hand. He held a bag made
from the tawny skin of an Indian woman's face, her long
black hair woven across the top for a handle. Ned Spotted
Cloud raised the bag and pushed it right in front of my
chest so I could see what was inside: dozens of human
hearts, some of them still beating, *bom-bom-bom-bom,* the
hearts he had stolen from the women he had known.

◄ 29 ►

Coyote and
the Desert's Blanket

Thursday, 2200 Hours

Later, after the ceremony and dinner and a storytelling, those gathered at the visitors' center milled around and talked. A few of the men smoked cigarettes.

I used my sat phone to call the ICP and check in. The Boss spoke in short, clipped sentences. Division Zulu, with its threatened power lines and potential for rampant spread in the national forest, was his chief concern. "We still don't have good containment on the eastern flank," he said, "so you keep your radio on and your sat phone with you. I don't give a damn what the governor says, if I say we need to evac those Indians, then that's what we're going to do. I'll call you."

Mary Takes Horse came up to me as I was hanging up. "How did you like the story I told the other time we were down here?"

"I loved it. With respect to men, I've known a few coyotes in my life, but I haven't met a bear yet." I thought of Kerry as I'd last seen him just a few hours before—his grizzled beard and driven look. "Or maybe those bears are hard to recognize."

She gave a pleased grin. "You should watch for that tenderness and devotion. That's the sign that you got a bear on your hands." Then her face grew serious. "Somebody said the fire burned across Oscar Good's ranch."

"Yes, but we have good structure protection. It got into the trees along the river and it shot up Devil's Creek, but they foamed his house and his barn, and they have crews working to protect all the houses along the river. I just got an update."

"At the press conference earlier, they said a member of our tribe was lost to an act of violence."

I nodded my head. "Yes, I know."

"Clara White Deer said you are the one who went looking for him."

I lowered my head. "Yes, ma'am, I did. But I didn't find him. Until later."

She was quiet.

I looked up at her.

She had her head tipped to the side, studying me, as she had earlier that day. "Do you know the story of the coyote who stole the desert's blanket?"

I wrinkled my brow. "No, ma'am, I don't."

"You listen for the next story. I'll ask Jimmy to tell that one. Have you met Jimmy?"

"No, I haven't."

She held up a hand for me to wait, then disappeared into the crowd. I took Mountain off into the bushes so he could relieve himself. Mary Takes Horse came back pulling a man in a cowboy hat by the arm. "This is Edgar 'Jimmy' Johns," she said. "He's an attorney for the tribe." Mountain was wagging his tail wildly and flicking his ears.

"Jamaica Wild. Pleased to meet you," I said. I stroked the wolf's head to try to calm him.

"Just call me Jimmy," the man said, as he reached into his pocket and pulled out a strip of jerky. He tossed it to Mountain, who raised up on his hind legs, paused for a second waiting for it, and snapped it out of the air like an outfielder catching a high fly ball. "I been giving him some of my homemade elk jerky. He really likes it." He reached down and patted the wolf on the back. Mountain made smacking sounds as he chewed.

"This is the girl who went looking for Grampa Ned. She wants to hear 'Coyote Takes the Desert's Blanket,'" Mary Takes Horse said.

Jimmy opened his mouth and nodded his head, as if he'd just had an *aha* moment. "Oh. Oh, right. Okay. I can do that one."

๑

Edgar "Jimmy" Johns stood before the crowd and waited patiently for them to quiet down. Mountain watched him eagerly, hoping for another wedge of dried meat. Jimmy held up a palm signaling for quiet. In the other hand, he held the same bear rattle that Mary Takes Horse had used at the previous storytelling ceremony. As she had done, he shook the rattle in an arc over his head, making a sustained sound like that of a rattlesnake warning of its presence. Then, Jimmy Johns held the totem high and made three sharp swipes downward, as if he were striking blows with a tomahawk. And then he began the story:

This was a while back, before people came to this place. There was this coyote who made friends with a young falcon. The falcon lived up high on the top of a canyon wall, and he would a lot of times go out for a mouse or a rabbit, flying way down from up there, way down to the bottom, and not get one. And when he did that a couple times, he would be too tired from the flight to make it back up to his nest. So the coyote would catch a little mouse or maybe a lizard and leave a little bit so the falcon wouldn't starve. And they became friends that way, after a while. So one day, the coyote was walking in the desert and he saw this little slot canyon over there on one side and he thought he just might go in that canyon and see what was in there.

Well, all of a sudden, that falcon swooped down from the top of the wall and he landed right in the coyote's path. "Don't go in there," he said.

"Why not?" said Coyote.

"The desert keeps her blankets in there," Falcon said, "and you must not touch them. She's very proud of them, and she only likes to show them when the light is just right."

But that old coyote, he did not listen and he went on in down that slot canyon. Pretty soon, he sees all these beautiful red and yellow and purple and blue blankets hanging all over the canyon walls. And the colors of these blankets are so beautiful that he cannot help himself, he just has to have one of them. "I just have to have that red and blue one over there," he says to himself. So he goes up to that blanket and takes it down from the cliff wall where it was hanging.

Right at that time, that falcon comes flying fast and he nearly crashes into Coyote. "Don't you take that blanket!" the falcon says.

Coyote just laughs. "I will look so good in this one. It must have been made for me."

But the falcon warns him again: "Don't you take that blanket! The desert will be angry!"

But old Coyote doesn't listen, he just has to have that blanket, and so he puts it around his shoulders and ties it under his chin, and off he goes, stepping high like a prairie chicken.

But he only gets a little way back down that slot canyon when there is a big rumbling sound and some of the red sandstone crashes down off of one cliff wall and almost hits the coyote in the head. The falcon, who is flying overhead, calls down, "See, I told you. You made the desert angry."

But that coyote didn't listen. He just started stepping real high again, showing off his new blanket, letting the breeze catch the corners of it and making the colors ripple in the sunlight.

Well, pretty soon the ground starts to shake and all sorts of stones come tumbling down off the sides of the canyon and one big slab falls right across the opening to that little slot canyon, trapping him in. And Coyote tries to push that big rock, and he shoves and he pushes, but it will not budge. "Help me, Falcon!" he calls.

Falcon floats above him in the sky. "You made the desert angry when you stole her blanket! You have to give it back."

Well, the coyote doesn't want to hear this, so he starts trying to climb up the cliff wall. He scrambles up a little way, and then the rock is too slick and too steep and he falls back to the bottom of the little canyon. "Help me, Falcon!" he calls again.

"You have to give back the desert's blanket," the falcon calls from the sky.

Finally it is getting pretty late and the coyote has missed his lunch and his dinner and he is getting hungry. The sky gets dark and it starts to get cold. Coyote's stomach is grumbling, and he wants to go to his den under the big cottonwood down by the river, where he has piled up some soft leaves and he has some old bones that might still have marrow inside. But he doesn't want to give back the blanket, especially because now it is pretty cold down there in that slot canyon. "I'll wait until morning," he says, "and then, when the sun starts to heat up the rocks, I'll give the blanket back. I just have to make it through the night without a meal."

But Falcon remembers how many times Coyote helped him out, and so Falcon goes and gets a mouse and he drops it in front of Coyote. So the old coyote has a little something in his stomach to get him through the night.

In the morning, the sun starts to warm the canyon walls, and the blankets begin to glow with color. Coyote unties the knot where he has fastened the blanket around his shoulders, and he holds it up. "I'll give the blanket back," he yells into the canyon, "if you'll move this rock so I can go home." His voice echoes in the canyon and pretty soon a rumbling sound starts, and the big stone slides back and the way is open.

But that old coyote just holds on to the blanket by its edges and out of the canyon he runs. And the rocks start crashing down from the canyon walls, and small stones rain down on him, but he just keeps on running. He's not going to let go of that blanket.

So now you might be walking sometime in the desert and find a pile of rocks in the canyon, or even maybe the rocks are still falling and they almost fall on you, because the desert is still mad about someone taking her blanket. And maybe sometime you see a coyote, but he is never sitting still, he is always loping along. The coyote is still running because he knows the desert is angry, but he never did give that blanket back.

◄ 30 ►

The Bear

Thursday, 2300 Hours

As I prepared to tuck in for the night, I took Mountain in the restroom with me and washed my face with the cold water. I heard noises in the shrubs outside, beneath the open window. Mountain went on high alert, the ridge along his back spiked with hair, his nose pointed upward, and his body quaking with adrenaline. I put a calming hand to the back of his neck and barely breathed, "Shhhhh . . ."

Moving carefully, I stepped lightly toward the door, and Mountain tiptoed right behind me, his head lowered now, ready to defend, attack, whatever was required. I pressed the flat of my palm right in front of his nose and whispered, "Stay!"

He tossed his head in defiance, moving his nose around my palm.

As quietly as I could, I slid the bathroom door open a few inches. Mountain scrambled on the concrete floor to try to get to the gap, so I quickly slid through and pulled the door shut behind me, leaving the wolf in the bathroom.

The noise in the bushes outside had stopped, and Mountain was now making all the sounds—scuffling back and forth on the concrete floor, leaping at the push-out window set high in the concrete block wall, yipping and barking.

I headed down the lamplit side of the building on tiptoe. When I turned the corner, the black darkness before me made it hard for me to see. I heard another sound of shrubs rustling right in front of me, and finally I gained my night vision. A small bear cub about the size of Mountain was looking up at me fearfully. I panicked immediately. *Where is the mother? If she catches me anywhere near her baby, she'll rip me to shreds!*

I started to back away when I heard a thumping sound. I looked toward it and saw a large black bear standing up, wrestling with a locked trash container, her coat shining like silk in the light from the side of the building. The Dumpster was metal and probably weighed hundreds of pounds, and yet the bear lifted it and rocked it and slammed it around. She held the two sides of it between massive arms, shaking it back and forth on the gravel pad. Finally, in frustration, she threw back her head and bawled, a low guttural *nnnnaaaaahhgggh!* Then she looked in my direction.

I knew I had been seen! I pivoted so quickly, I almost tripped over my boots, and I scrambled toward the door of the restroom. I could feel my heart beating so hard in my chest that it was like someone knocking at my ribs. A cacophony of shrubs tearing, limbs snapping, twigs breaking, and great feet pounding surged with me as I took the few long strides to the metal door, pressed it open just enough to jam myself in without letting Mountain out, and slammed it shut. Desperately, I fidgeted with the slide-bolt lock, all the while knowing it was so flimsy that the bear would have the door bent in, torn off its hinges, and smashed over my dead body before I could even get the bolt slid into the hole. I pressed my weight against the door, and a great *wwwwhhhockkkkk!* sounded as the door compressed, throwing me backward onto the floor. The door flew back and smashed into the block wall, and the bear stood on her hind legs peering in, her great mass more than filling the opening, so that she had to bend down to see inside.

When I went down, Mountain quickly moved between me and the animal, and he now stood with his lips pulled back and his teeth in a menacing grip, uttering a low, threatening growl.

The bear sniffed and hesitated. She did not look at me, but kept her eyes on Mountain. I could smell her raw, gamey musk, and I could feel her own fear, hunger, and desperation.

There was a moment of complete quiet. Mountain stood between my legs, his head thrust low and forward. I lay propped on my elbows looking up from the floor, afraid to move. The bear raised up slowly, her eyes above the doorway, then she turned slightly, dropped to all fours, and lumbered toward the back of the building where her baby waited.

Mountain started to lurch forward, but I quickly grabbed his hind leg. He turned and started to nip at me, but caught himself before his teeth touched my hand. "You stay," I said, holding his leg. He tugged the limb repeatedly, trying to wrest it from my grip, but I held firm, and we wrestled. He kicked at me and pulled powerfully at the leg I held, and he flailed his neck and head from one side to the other trying to break my hold. When he relaxed the leg for an instant, I grabbed hold of his hips, got to my knees, and threw my weight over him, my arms encircling his abdomen. I rode him over to the wall like that, pushed my feet under me, raised up enough to release one arm, and closed the now concave bathroom door, which no longer fit in the door frame, but rather swung from its hinges in the opening like a struck gong.

I turned to look at my best friend, my companion, my family. "You!" I said, and I threw myself back onto my knees and grabbed him around the neck. "You saved me."

Mountain wagged his tail wildly, looking over my shoulder on one side and then the other, still scouting for the bear.

◀ 31 ▶

The Dream Story

Thursday, 2330 Hours

I called in a bear report to the ICP and spoke with Ops Chief Charlie Dorn, who worked for the Department of Game and Fish in New Mexico. "You probably won't see her again up there, now that she knows there's a wolf around. She won't want a wolf near her cub."

"I didn't think so either, but I thought I ought to let someone know."

"Well, we'll notify the wildlife people in the morning, but there's nothing they can do in the dark anyway. They're not going to come set traps at midnight," Charlie said.

"I thought about warning everyone up here but they're all asleep. Do you think I should stay up and keep a look-out?"

"I wouldn't worry about it, Jamaica. You got a four-legged bear deterrent system right there with you. I don't think your mama bear will be back."

I already knew that bears avoided wolves from my experiences at home. My remote mountain cabin was near enough to a small spring that there were plenty of bears around in the summer. But none came within a hundred yards of my place, even with a Dumpster out back for an easy target. Mountain had marked his territory well, and the bears were forewarned. He and I often fell asleep on the ground outside my cabin, when I went out to talk to the stars. I felt perfectly safe then, and with Charlie's reassurance, I felt safe now, too. The bear had only charged to protect her cub. Now that she knew there was a wolf in the vicinity, she would move the cub out of harm's way.

I generally kept the backseat folded down in my Jeep so there would be plenty of space in the rear cargo area to transport Mountain. Tonight, I rolled down all the windows, left the hatch open, and unfurled my sleeping bag in the extended cargo area. It was too hot to get in the bag, so I stretched out on top of it, my feet hanging over the back bumper, my arm around the wolf, his back to me, his bridle on, and the leash looped over my wrist. The heat and the smoke made the air feel sticky and thick. I was so tired, and yet my mind was going in circles over the encounter with the bear, the vision of Grampa Ned, and the stories I'd heard.

After an hour or so of trying to sleep, I got up and pulled my boots back on, laced them up, and took Mountain for a walk in the dark. On the top level of the parking area, I noticed a round dome of faint light glowing above the Great House kiva. I made my way carefully across the narrow causeway to the ruin. The red glow of the fire blazing to the west made it fairly easy for me to see as I climbed the rock steps up to the ruin and the sloping path along the high wall. Once I reached the top, I approached slowly and looked down from above. I saw Momma Anna sitting in the kiva with a group of several women, a small lantern exuding soft, yellow light in the center of the circle. She looked up at me and Mountain standing on the rim and waved for us to come down. I tried to coax Mountain down the stone steps, but he trembled and balked, then finally leaped down them, nearly pulling me over. The women laughed, and my medicine teacher patted the ground next to her. I sat, and Mountain plopped on his side at my feet, still fretting over the unfamiliar and incomprehensible stairs. I leaned my back against the wall.

"We not see star," Momma Anna said. "Fire make sky look like gravy."

I smiled. "Yeah, it's pretty smoky."

"My people watch star here, time before time."

This startled me. "What?! Your people were here? At Chimney Rock?"

She clamped her lips tightly together, disapproving my question.

I couldn't help myself, I pressed on: "But I thought you told me your people came through the Eye of the Great Spirit, the Indigo Falls. Remember? You told me that story last year."

She made a little *tst-tst* noise with her mouth. "My people here, last world."

"Last world?"

She nodded her head.

I struggled to think of a way to get her to continue. I knew if I asked another question, I would face a wall of silence, perhaps for days. I was about to try making a statement to provoke more conversation when she went on of her own accord.

"Many my grandmother take care star." She made a long, sweeping gesture with her hand, taking in the arc of the sky as she moved, the motion as graceful as a dancer's.

At this, the other women began to watch Anna, some of them shifting their position so they could better see her.

Anna pointed the tips of her fingers straight overhead and began making an ever-widening circle—slowly, languidly, as if she were stirring the heavens with her hand. I found myself entranced by this, and as I watched, I began to feel sleepy.

"Many my auntie take care moon. Get up with moon like baby, watch moon like baby, only sleep when moon sleep." She opened both her arms wide and circled them outward as far as they could reach, and then scooped them together and brought them to her breast as if she were picking up a small child, gathering it to her in a fond embrace. I could not remember what she had said, but the dance of her arms through the air captivated me.

"These grandmother, these auntie, they learn count time. Star teach them. Moon teach them. They even count time backward. Back . . ." She drew one arm and then the other up from her torso, high above her shoulder, and then behind her as if she were doing a choreographed backstroke through the air. "Back, back, when only one woman come here through hole in sky. She bring a man with her to make seed. They make home by river down there, make her belly grow. They make children, and those children make more children. They call their relative Sky clan, all the one here. They take care of sky, that where they came." Momma Anna pressed her palms together as if in prayer and slowly pushed them high above her. Her face tilted upward.

I followed her example, looking up into the darkness. As I did so, I pressed the top of my head against the rock wall and thought how easy it would be to lean into the wall and fall asleep, just like that.

"Time move like star in sky." She opened her arms into a wide V, then drew her arms inward and crossed her palms over her chest. "Time move, and time move. Time always moving."

I felt as if I had warm milk flowing through my veins. My eyes burned and my eyelids longed to close. I couldn't help it, I opened my mouth into a wide yawn.

"Next time, the People say they must go into water, come up next world, Indigo Fall. So, they leave here, leave twin war god here . . ." She opened one arm outward, palm up, her eyes following her fingertips as she swept them slowly outward toward the two rock spires. "They watch over one true grandmother." She bowed her head.

⊛

When I woke up, the sun was starting to paint the tips of the Continental Divide pink. I raised up on my elbow and looked out the open back of the Jeep into the predawn light. Momma Anna was standing there with a towel over her shoulder and a bar of soap in one hand. She looked in at us, her head tilted to one side as if she were trying to figure something out. "You and that wolf," she said, shaking her head. "Sleep in same bed. *Tst-tst.*"

"I just had the strangest dream," I said, stretching. "You were in the kiva up at the Great House, and you were telling this story, and you were doing this incredible dance with your hands and arms, as if you were performing a ballet."

She smiled—a big, wide smile. "I like dance. I like grass dance, fancy dance . . ."

"No, this was something else. You were telling a story when you danced with your hands." I sat up and scooted to the edge of the Jeep's deck and started pulling on my boots.

"Dance always tell story."

Mountain rolled onto his back, happy to have more room, and he spread his back legs wide apart, feet in the air, his front paws curled up next to his chest, and his whole underside exposed in such a way that if it weren't so ridiculously comical looking, it might have seemed vulgar.

Momma Anna and I looked at him, and we both began to laugh. She brought one hand up and covered her mouth, but her eyes sparkled.

"That wolf has no shame," I said.

She turned and started to walk toward her makeshift camp under the big piñon. "We had bear here last night," she called over her shoulder. "Make bathroom door look like big bowl."

Hotshots and Shotguns

"We've had some bear trouble. I'm going to let the local Division of Wildlife representative talk about that in a minute. But before I do, let's have a little good news," Roy said. "One of the Three-Pueblos Hot Shots is getting out of the hospital either later today or in the morning, and he's going to come back here to Fire Camp."

The crowd erupted in applause. The woman standing next to me contorted her face to keep from crying and lowered her head. I saw her lips mouth the words *thank you*. Some of the hotshots hugged one another, shook hands, slapped one another on the back. There were few dry eyes in the crowd.

"Now, let's get back to the bear," Roy said. "The Blackfeet Hotshots Number Three are up on the top of Division Bravo. They've had to coyote up there, and last night a big black bear got into their food cache, tore into a mini blivet of water, and challenged the lookout. We think she might have gotten trapped with the fire between her and the river. I say *she* because they saw tracks—she's got a cub."

I was standing next to Charlie Dorn. I elbowed him and whispered, "You didn't tell Roy about my bear encounter?"

"You know how Roy is about you and trouble," he muttered under his breath. "He would have called out the National Guard."

The wildlife agent took over the briefing: "This she-bear may be reluctant to take her baby near the highway or down through the black where it's already burned. And they're starving. We're going to try to get up there and bait some traps so we can capture them and transport them to someplace safe. But in the meantime"—he held up a double-barrel pump—"we need to talk about these shotguns—a couple of these have already been issued to the crews in that area."

Some of the firefighters laughed and joked about bear hunting season being open, but the wildlife agent held up his hand to stop them.

"These shotguns will only be used to fire a beanbag round. That's a strong nylon pouch with about forty grams of lead shot inside. The beanbag is inserted into a standard twelve-gauge shotgun shell. When that shell is fired, the bag is expelled at around two hundred ninety feet per second. In flight, it spreads out and distributes the impact over about six centimeters of the target. It is meant to deliver a blow that will minimize long-term trauma with no penetration, but will briefly render the animal prone and immobile. Now, this beanbag round has a maximum range of around sixty-five feet, but it's inaccurate over about eighteen or nineteen feet. The idea here is to stun the bear and give you time to get away, not to harm the bear.

"This is just for your safety. We don't have enough of these shotguns for every crew, so you have to hand off to the next crew coming on when you go off shift. I want the

two lead resource advisors to each carry a rifle, though, if
you feel comfortable—I know some of you guys carry a
gun in the field to scare off varmints. Since you're out
ahead of the crews scouting for sites, you need the extra defense. But—all of you—please don't shoot her unless it's a
life-or-death matter. Remember, this she-bear is scared, too,
and she's trying to take care of her cub. That's a dangerous
scenario. If you can, keep alert and try to avoid crossing her
path. Radio back to the ICP and let us know if you see any
sign of bears, and we'll come in and take it from there."

⑤

After the briefing, Roy asked me to stay and speak with
him. "I want you to do a couple things for me," he said,
hurriedly.

"Sure, what's up?"

"Go into Pagosa Springs and get some flowers. Take
them to the victim's family."

"He just had the one daughter. No wife or anything."

"Well, take them to her, would you? Tell her they're
from the firefighters and the team."

"Okay."

"And get something for that hotshot, too, to give him
from all of us. One of the Information gals said to get him
a great big teddy bear, and we'd name it after the bear
that's been hanging around the fire line."

"What's the name of the bear on the fire line?"

"I don't know. You name her."

"Ursula."

"Okay. I'll tell Info her name's Ursula. Anyway, when
that injured hotshot gets here from Albuquerque, I want
you to take care of him. Take him around, let him talk to
the firefighters if he wants to. Show him that shrine they
made for the Three-Pebs over by the supply cache. Make
sure he has everything he needs. He'll be on crutches. But

he wanted to come back to Fire Camp, so you escort him, okay?"

"But isn't it Information's job to escort VIPs?"

He scowled at me but didn't speak.

"All right. You'll call me when you find out when he's going to be here?"

"Yes. I think Information has a big welcome party planned. They're getting a band and everything—some group of Forest Service folks who play bluegrass."

I cleared my throat. "Hey, Boss? The FBI has asked me to cooperate with them in the investigation."

"I thought you already did."

"They want me to talk to a couple people for them."

"Why you?"

"I think it's that thing about me and Indians."

He winked. "Ron Crane already called me about it."

"What? Why didn't you say so?"

"I wanted to see what you'd say."

"Nice. Real nice, Boss. So, what did you say?"

"I told Crane that I guessed a fire wasn't enough trouble for the likes of you. You had to get involved with a murder investigation, too."

I balled up my fist and punched him in the arm.

"Ow!" He grimaced, grabbing his biceps and rubbing.

"You deserved it," I said as I started to walk away.

He called after me, "You know I'm right."

◀ 33 ▶

Grampa Ned

Friday, 0900 Hours

I went to several stores in Pagosa Springs looking for a large teddy bear that looked like Ursula. One place had teddies in neon colors with plaid bows. Another had nothing but small stuffed animals. The gift shop in the public lands ranger station had a huge, lifelike bear, its fur the color of butter. The fur color wasn't right, but she was wearing a wildland firefighter outfit—a yellow shirt, green pants, little vinyl boots, and even a yellow helmet and Smokey Bear badge. I bought her.

When I set her in the passenger seat of my Jeep, she sat almost as tall as me. It was amusing at first to have a life-sized companion, but as we drove, the weight of her plastic helmet kept tipping her over onto me. I figured I'd have to strap her in when I had a minute.

۞

Nuni White Deer Garza answered the door of her own home. I had called before coming, and I was carrying an armload of flowers from a florist in Pagosa Springs. I handed them to her. "From the firefighters and the incident command team," I said.

She fought to keep her face arranged. "I'll be right back," she said. "I want to put these in some water."

She went to the back of the house, leaving me standing in the small entry area off the front room. I waited quietly. I could hear cupboard doors opening and closing.

On the wall to my right were several framed photos and mementos. One of them was a yellowed newspaper article featuring a large picture. I bent down to look more closely. The caption beneath the photo read: *The Queen and Her Court.* The discolored newsprint revealed the faces of several beautiful young women wrapped in fringed shawls. In the center, wearing a tiara and holding a bouquet of roses, was a young Nuni Garza. I checked the date on the paper's header, however, and realized that it was before Nuni could have been born. I started reading the article: *Clara White Deer was crowned queen of the Bear Dance ceremonies . . .*

Nuni came toward me with a pottery vase containing the blooms I'd just brought.

I straightened. "I'm so sorry for your loss," I said.

She dropped her chin to her chest and took a big breath. "I only just got to know my dad. That's the part that hurts the most. I just found him, and now he's gone." She set the container on the coffee table. "Sit down," she said, gesturing to the sofa.

I took a seat. "Your home is lovely."

She perched on a nearby chair, her back rigidly straight, hands clasped in her lap. "They won't let me in my dad's place. I was trying to help him clean up his place, clear everything out. My dad and I were trying to do that together, before . . . Anyway, the silly old fool, you saw how he saved everything. He knew it had gotten out of hand, and he asked me to help."

"You said you just found him?" I asked. "How did you find out that Grampa Ned was your father? Did your mother tell you?"

She snorted. "My mom? You've got to be kidding. My mother is the proudest woman I know. She never told a soul who fathered her child, not even me. When I was a teenager and started having questions, she just told me the wind blew really hard one day, and the next day, she was pregnant."

I gave a little smile. "It must have been hard for her."

"Well, it was hard for me, too. Anyway, to answer your question, Dad contacted me. Through his lawyer. He asked me to come back home to the rez, so we could get to know one another before . . ." She turned away and started tidying a stack of magazines on an end table.

"Before what?"

She raised her open palms in resignation. Her voice quivered. "I guess it doesn't matter now. He had lung cancer. They told him a couple months ago that he only had six months to live. He didn't want anyone to know. He was trying to do some things . . . to make amends."

"You mean like recognizing you as his daughter?"

She smiled a sad little smile. "Yes, that. And a few other things, too. He knew he hadn't led a good life. He wanted to make it up. Like the other day, the day he . . . died. I was there when he left the house that morning. I'd just made him breakfast. He told me he had to go someplace to return something, and then after that he was going to meet his attorney. But he never made it to the appointment. I don't know what he was doing inside the fire line."

"He was going to meet his attorney? Do you know who that was?"

"Yes. It's Edgar Johns. Everyone calls him Jimmy."

"I see," I said, remembering the storyteller from the night before. "Do you know what it was that your father was going to return?"

She shook her head.

"Do you know whom he had taken it from?"

"I don't know that either. He didn't tell me anything specifically. I just know he felt like whatever it was had cursed him."

"Cursed him?"

"Yes. When I first came back to the rez, he wanted me to help him clean up the house because he couldn't find it. He said it was something he took a long time ago, and he had to return it. That's why we were trying to clear out his clutter. Otherwise, I don't think he would have bothered, not with so little time left."

"But you didn't know what you were looking for?"

"No, not really. I think he took whatever it was from a woman, though."

"Really? Why do you say that?"

"When we were going through his things, he would often mumble, 'She's going to haunt me even after I die if I don't give it back, Nuni. We've got to find it.' "

I remembered what Clara White Deer had said about wanting something back from Grampa Ned. "Do you think the woman could have been your mother?"

Nuni looked me right in the eye. "Now, why would you say that? Does my mother seem like some kind of a witch or voodoo priest to you? How could she possibly haunt my dad? She never even spoke to him."

"How do you know that?"

"After my dad's attorney contacted me, I confronted my mother. She told me that Ned Spotted Cloud was as good as dead to her the day he left her pregnant and alone, and she'd never seen fit to resurrect him since."

"I see," I said, carefully masking my expression. "So you don't think it could have been something of your mother's he was concerned about returning?"

She shook her head. "No way. Neither of them ever

spoke about the other. Not even one word. Not to me, and not to anyone else. Whatever happened between them before I was born, it was over."

"Do you know anything about the Three-Pueblos Hot Shots?"

She drew her head back. "No, why?"

"Do you have any family at Taos Pueblo, or Tanoah, or Picuris? A first or second cousin, maybe? A great-aunt or -uncle?"

"We're Southern Ute," she said. "All Indians are not the same . . ."

"I know. But they marry sometimes into other tribes."

"We don't have anyone I know of at any of those places. It's pretty much just my mom and me. And now, my dad. And my husband, of course, but he's not from here."

"And do you have any children?"

A look of surprise took over her face. "No, why?"

"Never had any?"

Her tone grew stern. "I guess I don't understand where this is going."

"Never mind," I said, shaking my head. "It was a long shot anyway."

◄ 34 ►

The Attorney

Friday, 1100 Hours

I pulled up in front of Grampa Ned's house and saw the yellow crime scene tape across the porch entrance and the front door. Although the crime had occurred elsewhere, Agent Crane evidently believed that there might be evidence inside the home that would help him solve the mystery of who murdered Grampa Ned. I did, too.

I pulled down the road a few hundred yards and parked my Jeep under an old cottonwood. I walked back to the house and headed for the covered patio in the back that Alto Lefthand had built for Ned. Two strands of yellow tape crossed in an X over the sliding glass doors. I reached between the top and bottom strands of tape on the left side and tried the handle on the patio door. As Lefthand had indicated, it wasn't locked. I pushed it to the side and stepped gingerly through the opening between the upper and lower legs of the X, being careful not to catch the bottom one with my heavy boots.

"Hello?" I called, just in case.

There was no answer.

I stood in the kitchen and took in the massive piles of clutter. I thought for a moment. *If you were Ned Spotted Cloud, where would you hide some of your more important things?* I walked carefully through the hallway to the front entry. I looked to the dining room—piled with stacks of papers and cartons of receipts—to the living room, also choked with mounds of things. "Where's the bedroom?" I said aloud.

✿

I found several plastic containers stuffed under the bed. But the room was so massed with boxes, bags, and stacks of papers that I took one of the squat plastic tubs outside to go through it, since there was no place to set it down in the house. I sat at the little table on the covered back patio, sifting through papers, pictures, newspaper clippings, and small objects. "This is nuts, Jamaica," I muttered to myself. "You don't even know what it is that you're looking for." I pulled on the end of a bit of white cloth and found myself holding up a woman's bra.

"That looks like those cross-your-heart things women wore decades ago," I said, still talking to myself. "And it's white. Nobody wears white anymore." I dropped it on the table beside several piles of papers and photos I'd already gone through.

I continued to dig deeper into the box. Under some rodeo programs and a few utility bills, I discovered a packet of letters, tied with a string. The one on top was addressed to Ned Spotted Cloud, but no return address showed on the face of the envelope. The postmark read *Dolores, CO,* but the date was illegible.

Just then, I heard a car pull in the drive. I quickly jumped up and—again being careful of the tape—stepped through the open glass door and into the kitchen, dashed down the hallway and into the living room, where I could see out the big window. Edgar "Jimmy" Johns got out of a truck and slammed the door. He was wearing a cowboy hat and cowboy boots, and he had a toothpick in the corner of his mouth. Instead of coming to the front door, he made straight for the side of the house to go around to the back. I rushed back down the hall, through the kitchen, and out onto the covered patio. I started putting the things I'd set out on the table back into the plastic tub.

"I'll bet you haven't got a search warrant," he said.

I straightened. "I'm afraid not."

"See?" he said, pulling the toothpick from his mouth. "I could have won money if I actually would have placed that bet."

"I'm sorry," I said. "It's just that . . ."

"If you're trying to figure out who killed Grampa Ned, my money's on Gary Nagual, but you didn't hear me say that."

I stopped trying to cover my tracks and looked at the attorney's face. "The renter? Why do you think it's him?"

"He's under a lot of pressure for gambling debts. You know what Ned did to his things?"

"I heard. But Mr. Nagual just seems a little . . . out of it to me. I don't make him for a murderer."

Jimmy Johns pulled a chair out from the table, returned his toothpick to the corner of his mouth, and sat down. "You find anything good in that box?" he asked.

"I didn't get that far."

"Well, I'd prefer you didn't go any farther."

"Yes, sir, I'll just put these things back . . ."

He put a brown hand on top of mine to stop me. "Just leave it there. I'll take care of it. Where'd you get this from?"

"Under his bed."

He nodded his head several times. "Good thought, good thought."

I sat down in the chair next to him. "It seems like everybody who knew him had a reason to hate Grampa Ned."

"That's about right."

"So why do you represent him?"

He took the toothpick out of his mouth again, and waved it for emphasis. "I'm an attorney for the tribe. He's a member of the tribe."

"And do *you* have a reason to hate Grampa Ned?"

"Not that I know of."

"What can you tell me about him?"

"I already told you all about him."

"What?"

"Remember 'Coyote Takes the Desert's Blanket'?"

"Oh, the story. Yes. Oh, I see."

"Did you ever go to some of these places around here where the man of the house is a hunter and he's got a lot of trophies mounted on his wall—the stuffed heads of the animals, the racks of antlers, rugs made out of bear hides?"

"Yes, there are plenty of places like that all over the West."

"Well, Ned was like that about women."

"The desert's blanket?"

"Yeah. But it was more like the hunter. He liked to take a woman down, then take something for a trophy."

"You mean literally take something? Like something she owned?"

"Maybe that, too. But I was thinking more like a part of her."

Just then, a man's voice interrupted us. It startled me so much that I jumped up from my chair. "Is this a private party, or can anyone sit in?" Ron Crane holstered his automatic, having determined after watching us that Jimmy Johns and I posed no threat to the FBI.

I dropped my head. *Busted!* "Grampa Ned's attorney and I were just . . ."

"Breaking and entering?" Crane said. He waved two fingers at me. "I'll walk you to your car." Then he looked at the attorney. "Mr. Johns, I'll be right back."

At my Jeep, Crane said, "As long as you're meddling around in my case, could you go see Clara White Deer?"

"Meddling? You asked for my help."

"You call that help? I don't need you to break into Ned Spotted Cloud's house. I'm allowed to go in there if I want something. I'm the FBI."

"I didn't break in. The door was unlocked."

"You know, I think it would help me more if you worked *with* me. Last time I checked, I was the one in charge of this case."

"I'm sorry."

"So, what were you looking for in there?"

"I don't know."

"You don't know."

"No, I don't know. I'll know it when I see it."

"Sort of investigation by intuition? A little dash of trial and error?"

"Okay, Mr. FBI. You win. Clearly I'm no match for your superior powers of detection. So if you'll permit me, I have to get back to Fire Camp."

His face opened into a huge smile. He started to chuckle, then broke into a laugh. And kept laughing.

The sound of it was infectious. I tried to hold on to my indignation, to keep a straight face, but my lips wouldn't comply. I began to smirk, then a smile broke through, and finally I was laughing, too.

" 'Mr. FBI.' " He guffawed. "That was pretty good."

"You liked that?" I giggled.

He hooted and slapped his thigh. "Yeah, but the 'superior powers of detection' was the best."

"Oh, yeah?" I chuckled. "How about that 'investigation by intuition, with a little dash of trial and error'?"

We both roared with laughter, and Crane even gave a little shriek, which caused us to advance into further hysterics. I laughed so hard my eyes were wet, and I found myself holding my hand over my stomach, trying to catch my breath.

"So," Crane cackled, "who's your partner?" He pointed at Ursula the stuffed bear, who was slumped over halfway into my seat.

"Oh, that's Ursula," I sputtered. "I better buckle her seat belt or I'm liable to get arrested." I went around to the passenger side and belted the bear in.

Finally, the hilarity subsided, and Crane looked at me with a grin. "So will you go pay a visit to Clara White Deer?"

"I could do that. But I wouldn't know what to say."

"Get her to talk about Grampa Ned."

I shook my head. "I don't think that's going to happen."

"Just see what you can do, Miss Intuition." He smiled as he shoved the driver's-side door shut and went back up the road toward Ned Spotted Cloud's house and Edgar "Jimmy" Johns.

◄ 35 ►

The Long, Long Story

Friday, 1200 Hours

Information had asked me to drop some letters at the post office while I was in Ignacio. I drove through the short strip of downtown and saw Mary Takes Horse standing in the doorway of a small corner shop called Dancing Bear Trading Post. I turned onto the side street, found a place to park, and went to see the storyteller.

"You buying something or you wanting something for free?" Mary Takes Horse said when she saw me approach on foot.

"I'll buy you a glass of iced tea or a cup of coffee," I said, smiling.

"Not necessary," Mary said. "I got some coffee inside."

She handed me a steaming mug. The day was already blistering hot, and the coffee smelled burned, but I thanked her graciously.

"Your medicine teacher tells me you are a keeper of stories."

"I write a little, if that's what you mean."

"That's what I mean," she said, pulling a tall wooden stool out from under the cash register and sitting down behind the counter.

"I loved your story about the brothers," I said. "And the one Jimmy Johns told, too."

"Our culture is full of bear and coyote stories."

"Do you think Ned Spotted Cloud was a coyote, a trickster?" I asked.

She got off the stool and went to one of the nearby jewelry cases. "He stole a lot of blankets." She pointed to a silver bear paw inside the case. It was inlaid with green-veined turquoise. "You got a lot of bear medicine. I can see that about you. You should buy this."

I looked down into the case. "Why do you say I have a lot of bear medicine?"

"You remember I talked about that tenderness? You got that." She took the amulet out of the case and handed it to me. "But you're fierce, too, when you got something to protect."

"So how much is that?" I asked, studying the piece.

"Maybe if you get that fire put out, I'll make you a special deal," she said, smiling as she returned the silver piece to the case. "Pull up that chair over there."

Later, after we'd finished our coffee, I got up to leave. "You know, Clara White Deer told me that if she spoke harshly about Ned Spotted Cloud, you would do worse. But you seem very cautious when you speak about him."

She started wiping off the glass top of the jewelry case with a little rag. "He's dead. We can't give him a worse judgment than that."

"Well, thanks for the coffee." I made for the door.

"I watched that story unfold," she said, still rubbing the glass. "I watched it kind of like you watch on TV when the same show goes on for a whole week, night after night, and the people on that show start to grow older and maybe their kids grow up and get old, too."

"A miniseries?"

"Yes. Like that. This was a long story. A long, long story."

I held my hand on the door, waiting.

"It would take a lot of nights at the storyteller ceremonies to tell this one."

I hesitated. "Maybe they all start out as long stories, and we learn to choose the important things to tell."

"It all started when Clara White Deer was Bear Dance Queen . . ."

I turned and went back to my chair in front of the counter.

"She was a beautiful girl. So beautiful. She was beautiful even when she was a baby. By the time she was fourteen, she already had offers for marriage. But she was also smart, and she did real good in school. She wanted to be a teacher. She studied real hard, and her last year in high school, she got a scholarship to go to Fort Lewis A&M— that was a while after it moved from the old Indian school to Durango. And that summer, she worked in a little café here in Ignacio to make money for college.

"That café is not open anymore, but it was right next door, right there." She pointed at the wall. "Back then, Grampa Ned was in there all the time. He went in every day for his breakfast because he didn't have anyone to cook for him. Of course, we didn't call him Grampa Ned back then— he was still a young man. Oh, he was good-looking, too. He was the best-looking man I ever saw.

"I was a couple of years behind Clara in school, but she

was my best friend. I loved her like a sister. Her mother had taken sick when she was a little girl, and after a few years over there in Arizona, she died of the TB. Clara had to take care of her dad, and he drank. She couldn't wait to get out of here."

"You mean the reservation?"

"Yes. Lot of young people couldn't wait to leave, even back then. We were poor then, and there was nothing to stay here for—no jobs, no future. It's different now. We got the tribal growth fund and lots of economic opportunities for young people managing the tribe's interests. Anyway, back then, Clara couldn't wait to leave. She knew if she became a teacher, she'd always have a job and she could take care of herself.

"And that year, she got voted the Bear Dance Queen. She was the prettiest girl and real good, too. Everybody loved her."

"Did Ned Spotted Cloud love her?"

Mary Takes Horse threw her dust rag in a box behind the counter and rubbed her palms together rapidly, as if trying to remove something unpleasant. She stared at the floor, her lips pursed. Finally, she looked at me. "I don't think he ever loved anybody his whole life."

"What about Nuni?"

She spit air. "Another young woman, desperately needing to be loved. He just used her like he used everybody else."

"So Clara . . . she went away to school, pregnant?"

"When she came back to the reservation, she had two things: a baby and a teaching certificate. She never said one word about who the father was, and nobody ever asked."

"Still, people must have guessed."

"They could guess all they wanted, but she went away right when it happened, so they couldn't say for sure."

"Why do you think she fell for him?"

"Oh, he was handsome and he had more money than most of the men around here. And he didn't drink, that was one thing. He didn't drink, and he always had a good job."

"What did he do?"

"Oh, he always found something to do for the US government. Back then, those were the only jobs there were around here. He worked for them on the oil and gas reserves, as some sort of tribal representative or something. They got used to hiring him anytime they wanted something from our tribe—they'd call him up, and he'd go between and get the government whatever they wanted. They paid him pretty good.

"And he got himself on the tribal council and got involved with some land deals, too. He was on the council for a long time, but we finally had enough of him when the whole thing happened with Oscar Good. I found a way to get Ned out of there after that."

"And in the meantime, he fathered a lot of children? That's what Clara implied."

"Oh, we're pretty sure of that, yes. There was a lot of poverty for a long time and also we still have a problem with alcohol here. And a lot of young girls saw Ned's good looks and his fat wallet and they were ready to do anything to try to get in good with him. I watched this a long time, long time. Many girls, many women. I watched, and I never said nothing about it. I finally said something after Oscar Good's dogs died, something about that nasty old man and his character. But I only got him off the council. I didn't change anything for all the young girls before." She tidied a stack of papers next to the cash register, humming softly to herself.

I got up and tugged at my wildland pants to straighten them. "Thank you for telling me the story." I gave a respectful nod and started for the door.

"Could have been you, too," she said to my back.

"What?" I turned to look at her.

"All the girls wanted to be with Ned. He was handsome, and funny, and he just had a way with the women. Even as an old man, still."

I was trying to think of an answer when a crack of gunfire and the distinctive tinkle of shattering glass startled us both. Instinctively I dropped to a crouch. I glanced at Mary Takes Horse to be sure she was all right. Slowly, she lowered herself to a squat behind the display case, her wide eyes peering above the top glass at me. I held my hand up to pantomime using the phone. "Call 911," I whispered, and I checked the windows in the front of the shop for broken glass, but found none.

While Mary used the telephone to summon help, I pulled the door open several inches and strained to look down the street. After a few moments, I opened the door a little wider. Finally, I stood up and slowly slid through the door, edged to the corner of the brick building, and peeked around. I saw nothing out of the ordinary. I rapidly scanned the side street as far as I could see. And then I homed in on my Jeep.

The front passenger window bore a pattern in the shape of a spiderweb with a perfect round puncture in the center. And where Ursula the stuffed bear's helmeted head had been, a nebula of fluff, foam, and fake fur floated in front of the vacant headrest.

I drew back from the corner and took in a breath. The only sounds were the normal hum of traffic coming from down the street. I stood there for a moment, unsure what to do. I gingerly edged to the corner and looked around it again: the side street was empty, except for my Jeep—its window still shattered, Ursula's head blown apart. And no sign of who might have done it. I leaned against the building while I tried to think what to do next, but the bricks exuded so much heat that it reminded me of the burning man.

I pulled away and walked back the few steps to the door of the trading post. Mary Takes Horse stood inside, her mouth open, her face alert. She held the phone in one hand, ready to punch the keys with the other. She breathed a sigh of relief when she saw me. "Tribal police are on their way."

"I hope I have something stronger than bear medicine," I said, "because the bear just got blown away."

◂ 36 ▸

The Site

Back at the ICP, I asked to use one of the laptops in Plans while they took their lunch break. My request was granted, and I searched the Internet for information about archaeological sites in southern Colorado. Site 8AA.104 had been excavated more than twenty years ago. I didn't recognize the lead archaeologist's name, but the anthropologist listed was Elaine Oldham.

I learned that the little cave before which Crane and I had found the bear effigy had once been used as a granary, which was often the custom of the people once known as the Anasazi. The architecture of the site was certainly early Puebloan: before they constructed block wall structures, the Ancient Ones dug pits and made pit houses. Stone tools used to grind corn—called mano and metate—had been found there. The mano was the hand tool used to crack the kernels when rubbing them across the flat or scooped-out grinding stone, the metate. The presence of something the archaeologists called "flake" meant that blades and tools of flint had been made there. Evidently, none of the pots collected were remarkable enough to mention.

I found nothing noteworthy in the site details, but I printed what I found just in case. As I was waiting for the printer to warm up and feed out my page, Steve Morella and Elaine Oldham came in the room. Morella spoke. "Well, hey, stranger. Where is everybody?"

"Lunch, I think." I quickly logged off the Internet and closed the window of the browser.

"Must be. The parking lot was all but abandoned. What are you doing here? Didn't like the mystery meat they're serving in the chow tent today?" he asked.

"No, it's not that. Actually, I'm waiting for a call. I was just checking my e-mail." I walked to the printer, took the two sheets it spit out and rolled them into a tube, then stuck them in the side cargo pocket of my wildland pants. After the discovery of the bear effigy, I was pretty sure the site I'd been researching would be a sore subject with Elaine.

"So, there was nobody in the war room. Your IC's not here, I guess?" Steve asked. Elaine removed her hat and set it on a table, then wandered over to a row of fire photos pinned to a bulletin board and began studying them.

"No. Actually, he's the one I'm waiting to hear from. One of the Three-Pueblos Hot Shots is getting out of the hospital, and he's coming to Fire Camp."

"I know. There are flyers about it everywhere, even in the porta-johns. They're having a big party. How's he getting here?"

"I'm driving him."

"You're picking him up from somewhere, then?"

"Yes, as soon as I get the word, I'm going to Durango to get him."

"In your Jeep?"

"Yeah."

"I saw your Jeep in the parking lot outside. It looks like

someone used it for target practice. No one got hurt, I hope."

"No, it happened in Ignacio when I was in a shop there. The tribal police said that some kids on the reservation had been taking potshots at Forest Service vehicles."

"Does Mountain get to go with you to Durango?" Elaine asked, turning from the photos.

I hadn't thought about that, but I was pretty sure Momma Anna would enjoy a break. "That's a good idea. I think I'll go get him."

Just then, the fire management officer from the Columbine Ranger District, Frank McDaniel, leaned his head in the door. He smiled at us, white teeth showing beneath his perfect mustache. He spotted Elaine and said, "You owe me a firefighter time report for the other morning. I never got your hours."

She looked at him with a startled expression. "I do? Oh, okay. I'll get that to you. I guess I don't understand all these firefighter forms." She hurried out of the room.

I looked at Steve Morella. "So what are you and Elaine doing here in the middle of the day?"

He raised his eyebrows. "Trying to figure out where they want us to go next. I've done all I can in Division Zulu for now. We finally got the paperwork pushed through this morning so Elaine can drive her own rig on the fire. She needs to know where they want her this afternoon."

Just then, Elaine reappeared with a frown on her face. She scanned the room and then spied her hat on the table. Without saying a word to us, she snatched it up and left again.

"She seems a little out of her element," I said, smiling.

"She's been under a lot of strain. Elaine has a daughter with severe disabilities, you know."

I was only half-listening, thinking about the site information I'd just seen on the Internet. "Yeah, she mentioned that to me."

"Well, confidentially, she got word that the facility that cares for the girl is closing. I guess the only one that will take her now costs three times as much. It's got Elaine worried sick."

I nodded. "I can imagine . . ."

"Don't tell her I told you that," he hastened to add. "She's a very proud woman."

"Do you think—when she originally excavated—she could have missed the bear effigy we found?"

"Anyone could have missed it. The little recess was used as a small granary. No one would have expected to find an effigy in there, and as small as this one is, it would have been easy to miss. If they were limited on time or funding, or coming to the end of their contract, they might have had to make some hard choices about which areas of the site to finely sieve."

"But you think the effigy was from that site originally?"

"We won't know until we get to examine it, and perhaps not even then."

"I imagine the news of this bear is not sitting well with Elaine."

"Careerwise, it's probably like finding out you gave a winning lottery ticket to someone else," he said.

"And you're that someone else."

He widened his eyes and nodded. "Guilty as charged."

"Steve, could you help me find some information?"

"Certainly, I'll try."

I unrolled the report I'd downloaded off the Net and spread it out on the desktop.

He scanned both pages. "That brief form is from the Colorado Office of Archaeology and Historic Preservation's computerized database. It's not the main one that the contractors filled out originally. I can get you a copy of that. It'll have much more detail and a site map and personnel list. I have to request it, but I could probably get it for you pretty quick."

"How quick is pretty quick?"

"Maybe a day or two."

I rolled up the papers again and stuck them in my cargo pocket. "That's no good. I need it right away."

"Well, I could see if I could pull some strings."

"Would you?" I flashed him my best smile. "How long have you been working on the Pagosa Ranger District?" I asked.

"Seven years."

"Did you know Ned Spotted Cloud?"

"No, I didn't know him. Why?"

"I don't know. I'm just trying to figure out what he was doing at that site. Let me ask you one more question: do you know anything about a grandmother related to that site, or maybe to the bear effigy we found?"

He snorted. "A grandmother?"

"I know," I said, shaking my head. "It doesn't make any sense to me either."

◄ 37 ►

The Quick Way Down

When I got up to the parking lot near the top of Chimney Rock, there were no gatherings going on that I could see. I went to the area where I knew Momma Anna had made her camp and found her stretched out on her blanket under the tree. Mountain, who had been lying in the shade nearby, clambered up and greeted me with an attack of affection: circling, wagging, licking, and pressing himself into me.

"Heat make Indun tired," Momma Anna said. "Wolf, too. We take nap."

"Good idea," I said. I squatted down to look more closely at her. "Are you okay? Are you drinking plenty of water?"

She rubbed her hairline. "Just tired. That wolf wear me out."

I smiled and scratched Mountain vigorously behind the ears. "I know. How about I take him off your hands for a few hours?"

She leaned back again, reclining on her blanket. "Okay,"

she said, and she closed her eyes. "Your friend here," she muttered.

"My friend?"

"Mm." She didn't open her eyes.

"What friend?"

"I'm so-o-o tired."

I picked up Mountain's bridle and led him toward the restroom facility. The parking lot remained full of cars and RVs, yet there was no one in sight. I eyed the blown-in door of the ladies' room. A row of ice chests lined the other side of the building in the shade, and I opened one and scooped ice water across Mountain's neck and back. He shook the water out of his mane and then drank from the icy liquid in the cooler. Excited by the cold, he began to quiver and bound, straining against the leash, leaping in circles around me.

"Shhhhh, quiet!" I whispered to him. "Everyone's napping."

I loaded him in the back of my Jeep, and he settled instantly onto the blanketed rear deck, excited to be going with me.

"We're going for a ride!" I said.

I shifted the automatic transmission into drive and started down the steep, winding gravel road. Our speed picked up, our momentum increasing as we coasted rapidly down the narrow curves. The road was little more than one lane, and the edge was unprotected by guardrails or posts. I put my foot on the brake to slow the car, and I felt as if my boot had missed the brake entirely. There was no resistance, and my heavy lugs went all the way to the floor. The Jeep began going faster, and I stomped again for the brake, and this time I realized the pedal was there . . . but the brakes were not. A few quick, narrow curves demanded all my attention as I maneuvered sharp turns at a too-high speed. My disbelief kept me trapped in repetitive action as I continued to step on the useless brake pedal, all the while staring at the road wide-eyed, and muscling the wheel to navigate the sharp turns.

It was then that I saw the giant green sanitary truck lumbering up the road two or three curves below me, probably coming to pump the restroom holding tanks and porta-johns. My eyes quickly darted from one side of the road to the other, measuring. There was no way we were going to pass one another unless one of us stopped at one of the few wide spaces along the track.

By this time, Mountain had sensed my panic, and he moved up behind me, stumbling from side to side as he lost his footing, finally getting himself planted so that his head lowered enough to permit him to see out the front windshield. He panted heavily from the heat, and a huge strand of sticky drool dripped onto the side of my head and my ear.

"Mountain, get back!" I yelled as I maneuvered the steering wheel first one way and then the other as we careened ever faster. I worried that he'd become a huge projectile, perhaps sailing through the front window of the car, or snapping my neck as he slammed from the back into the front. "Get down, buddy! Lie down!"

Mountain licked his chops nervously and tried to lie down, but I had to jerk the wheel suddenly to manage a turn, and he rose to all fours again, straddling as wide a stance as he could manage.

The tires crunched along the gravel, spitting up a thousand tiny rocks into the undercarriage, against the oil pan, in the wheel wells, a deafening din of erratic drumming from under us. The treads were starting to slip and slide as we sped faster downward along the gravel, the Jeep skidding broadside into the curves as I cranked the steering wheel first one way and then the other in reaction to the switchbacks.

Mountain's jawbone banged hard into the top of my

head as he lost his balance, and I yelled "Damn!" above the Gatling-gun noise of the gravel against metal.

The sanitary truck chugged toward us, the driver gunning it hard to make it up the steep incline, and suddenly, perched high above the big green engine housing, I could see the driver's eyes, the alarm in his face. I had an insane stream of thoughts: *I should jump . . . but I'm on the side with the truck . . . it will hit me before I can . . . Mountain! . . . he won't know what to do! . . . he'll go over the cliff in the Jeep . . . a sanitary truck . . . why does it have to be a truck with a tankload of shit?*

All at once, the cliff edge began to pull at me. *I should drive right over and take my chances at flying . . . or maybe a tree will break our fall . . . gravity's bound to be kinder to us than what we're facing . . .*

The shit truck was almost upon us when I thought to grab the gearshift and pull it back from drive. A rapid transition from automatic to third, and I felt the engine squall—then low, and the car lurched and shook—there was rapid shuddering and a howling sound of metal shearing metal—and then I let go of the gearshift and reached my hand back and pulled up hard on the emergency brake. The Jeep staggered between stop and go and heaved and shimmied sideways toward the front of the sanitary truck—which seemed to be roaring as we came nearer, a high, sharp, sustained yowl of a sound. Mountain plunged forward like a heavy bag toward the front of the car, then— when the vehicle pitched sideways—he toppled onto his side and into the rear, up against the hatch door, then back into the spare tire. I tried to keep my eyes on him as I yawed first forward into the shoulder strap of my seat belt, then back against the headrest, then to the side across the center console, finally smashing back to the opposite side so that my head and neck went out the open window and my shoulder slammed hard into the door.

"Mountain!" I screamed as the car jolted and stopped. Through the web of shatter lines in the passenger-side window, and the prominent hole in the center of that motif, I could see the front grille of the sanitary truck, not six inches away from the Jeep, its pistons hammering, the blistering breath of its engine blasting at me, and I felt myself slipping away.

◀ 38 ▶

This Side of Hell

Friday, 1430 Hours

An instant later, I swam upward from a fiery, molten red world. "Mountain?" I sputtered with a hoarse, cracking voice.

I turned my head to the side and realized that it was still attached to my body. I felt the wolf's tongue lick my face. Mountain was doing his best to sit up in the cargo space behind the driver's seat, but he was too tall, and his ears splayed out against the head liner. He was trembling.

"Are you all right?" the truck driver called as he scrambled out of the cab.

I stared through the windshield. The Jeep was facing directly into the cliff wall on the inside edge of the road. "I'm good," I mumbled.

"Can you move . . . you know, your hands, your legs?" I turned slightly and saw a brown-skinned man peering in the window at me.

I wiggled my fingers, then lifted my palms to the steering wheel. I leaned forward and felt the shoulder harness scrape my neck. I reached down and unbuckled the seat belt, then tapped the toes of my boots on the floor of the car. "Everything . . ." My voice sounded as gravelly as the road. I cleared my throat. "Everything seems to be working so far."

"You want to try to get out of there?" He put his hand to the door handle.

"Is my wolf all right? Does he look like he's all right?" Mountain nosed the back of my head over the top of the headrest.

"He's really shaking. He looks like he's worried about you." The man opened the car door. "Let's see if you can get out," he said, reaching to try to help me.

"I'm okay, I can get out." I swung my legs to the side and climbed out of the Jeep. I pushed the back of the driver's seat forward and grabbed hold of Mountain's leash, still attached to his bridle. "Are you all right, baby wolf?" I asked.

He clambered cautiously out the driver's door and leaned into me, ears down. I dropped to a squat and began probing his body with my hands, groping his muscles, feeling for broken bones, cracked ribs, sore places. The wolf continued to quiver, his whole body vibrating rapidly, but he never flinched. I knew from experience that wolves could be very stoic; they could be in great pain and not let on. But I found nothing by palpating his exterior. Even if we had both somehow miraculously escaped major injury, we would be plenty sore in the morning, I was certain.

While I examined Mountain, the truck driver left briefly, then returned. "Listen," the man said, reaching into the Jeep and turning off the ignition, "it's a good thing you were able to stop. I thought I was going to T-bone you with the old poop-pumper." He attempted a smile. "I got the right front wheel of my truck into the cliff there, tore up the tire." He held out my keys and dropped them into my palm. "And I don't think you'll be able to drive that car anymore unless you get a new transmission."

"Yeah, I know. It was the only way I could stop. I had no brakes at all."

"Yeah?" He got to his knees and tried to peer under the car, then turned on his back and pushed himself under it beside the front wheel.

"Don't worry about . . ." I started to say, but I stopped and waited.

He wiggled out on his back, then rolled over and pushed himself up. He brushed the dirt off his hands. "Well, it was good thinking, what you did. That brake line right there has been cut. You wouldn't have been able to stop with it like that, just using the brake pedal. There's not a drop of brake fluid in that line."

"What?"

"You want me to show you?"

We both dropped to our knees, this time checking the rear brake on the driver's side. "See?" he said, pointing to a nearly severed line. "That's been cut. Looks like somebody took a hacksaw to it."

My first impulse was a surge of confusion and fear. But right behind it came a wave of seething rage. *Someone is trying to kill me! And Mountain!* "I need my sat phone out of my Jeep," I said. I clambered over the driver's seat. "Bunch of Ute kids taking potshots, my ass," I muttered as I reached onto the floor where my radio harness had landed.

"Beg pardon?" the truck driver said.

"Never mind." I straightened and strapped on the harness, pulled out the sat phone. "I have to make a call."

☉

My first call was to Roy. "Are you all right?" he asked.

"I'm okay. We—Mountain and I—just got tossed

around a little inside the car. I need to walk him and watch his gait, make sure he's all right."

"Do you need to have someone come? An ambulance? A vet?"

"No, I don't think so. I think we're both okay."

"You think someone tampered with the brakes?"

"The brake lines have been cut—front and back."

"Call the sheriff's office."

"I will. And the FBI."

"You get back to me on this."

"Can you get Ground Support to bring me a car? I have to go get Delgado Gonzales at the airport."

"Don't worry about Gonzales, his flight's been delayed a couple hours. Are you all right to drive?"

"I'm okay, Roy. We didn't crash. The truck stopped and I slid but I pulled up before hitting him. I'm going to be all right."

"Well, hell! This is—what?—three incidents on this fire now?"

"I know."

"Do you have any idea who got to your Jeep?"

"I'm going to talk with Ron Crane about that."

"Maybe you ought to at least report to the medical tent."

"I'm more concerned about Mountain. Let me walk him and watch him until he settles down. If I need to get him to a vet, I'll call you back. Otherwise, I'm going to pick up Gonzales in Durango."

"Well, that might be the safest place for you—away from Fire Camp. And I'll get someone else to come up to Chimney Rock for the night. But you be careful. Watch your back. You tell your FBI pal to report directly to me on this."

"There's just one more thing."

"What now?" the Boss snapped.

"I'm not sure if you understood that this happened on

the road to the top of Chimney Rock. Both vehicles are disabled. The way is completely blocked."

Roy was silent for a moment. Then he clicked right into gear. "Well, that's a major complication. I'll send my deputy safety officer over there. We've got winds picking up and shifting, and they've still got some reburning and spotting over on that east flank. I finally got an air tanker coming tomorrow, and we're going to bomb that slope with mud—but today or tonight, we could still have to evacuate the Native Americans."

"Well, until the tow trucks come . . ."

"Listen, if it comes down to it, we'll just have to walk them out."

My second call was to Ron Crane.

"You say what?" he asked, not believing what he'd heard.

"Someone cut my brake lines. I'm okay, but I had to grind up the transmission on my Jeep to bring it to a stop. I almost bought the farm."

"Any idea who it was?"

"I have a couple ideas. Could you find out something for me?"

"Probably. There's not much I can't access if I want to."

"You know where we found Ned Spotted Cloud's body? I want to know if he was working for the Forest Service or anyone else connected to that site when it was excavated twenty-three years ago. Or if the Forest Service needed permission from the Southern Ute Tribal Council to excavate—and if so, if Grampa Ned was on the tribal council then."

"I'm way ahead of you."

"And?"

"It's Southern Ute land. They had to get the approval of

the tribal council. Ned Spotted Cloud was a huge advocate for the deal. And a paid advisor."

"Advisor?"

"Yes. The Forest Service hired him—a way of swinging the deal. He got to stand around and look out for tribal interests, which pretty much meant collecting a paycheck for showing up every once in a while and watching them dig."

"And maybe picking up something if it interested him."

"Possibly so."

"Okay, thanks. There's one more thing: can you find out if Nuni Garza has had an abortion?"

"Ooh. You got me there. Unless they directly concern a crime victim, medical records are real hard to get without a court order. That can get complicated."

I was quiet, thinking.

"You still there?" Crane asked.

"Yeah, I'm here."

"This about motive?"

"I think so."

"Clara White Deer?"

"Yeah."

"I'll see what I can do."

"Thanks."

"Where are they taking your Jeep?" Crane asked. "I want to have a look at it."

"Probably someplace in Pagosa Springs. There's a public lands ranger station there. I'll get back to you with that information."

"And where were you with it today?"

"Besides Fire Camp? I was in Ignacio, you saw me."

"And you went straight from Ned's house to Fire Camp?"

"No. I stopped in to talk with Mary Takes Horse. And while I was in her shop, somebody fired a rifle through my passenger window and blew the head off Ursula."

"I heard."

"You already knew? Why'd you ask?"

"I wondered if you would tell me, or if you were going to stay a loose cannon."

"But the tribal police said that several Forest Service trucks—"

"Yeah. They called me about that deal. I don't think yours was a random potshot, though."

"Well, now I don't either."

"So, I'll go take a look at the vehicle when they get it to Pagosa. And you're looking at Clara White Deer then?"

"Maybe. I'll get back to you on that. I just need one more piece of the puzzle to be sure."

"Are you armed?"

"No, they don't allow weapons on a fire, unless they're issued."

"They issue weapons on fires?"

"Not very often. But every once in a while. We've got a few crews here that have shotguns with beanbag rounds because there's been a bear out on the fire lines."

"You need to be careful. Where are you going next?"

"To pick up one of the hotshots that got burned over. I'm meeting him at the Durango airport."

"You call me once you get your hotshot."

"I will."

卐

After I called the sheriff's office, I left the truck driver at the scene and told him I'd be back as soon as I got my wolf taken care of. Mountain and I hiked back up the road, and I let him off his leash so he could romp a little. He was clearly shaken by the event and stayed close by me, rather than scampering in the brush and sniffing at the vegetation. I watched his gait, but saw no signs of injury, and I was tremendously relieved.

When we got to the top, the winds had shifted straight

out of the west, and the smoke from the Chimney Rock Fire made the air thick and heavy. The color of the sky was brown, and tinges of orange formed a fiery circle where the light from the sun seared through the smoke particles.

I looked for Momma Anna and found my medicine teacher at the Great House. She was alone in the kiva, performing a ritual. I stood on the rim and put Mountain on a heel, and we waited and watched her.

Momma Anna held a pinch of something in the fingers of her right hand. She offered this from her heart, reaching outward to the east, dancing four steps in place, lifting her knees high. She turned to the south and made the same gesture of offering, dancing four more high steps. Then to the west, then to the north, and once again to the east—what the Tanoah called the five directions, with the east being both the beginning and the end. Then Momma Anna danced in place with her head lowered, facing the ground as she swirled her offering in a circle above the earth four times—this was for Mother Earth. Next, she raised her offering high above her head to Father Sky, turning her face upward, dancing her four steps in place, making four high circles with her hand. And finally, she circled her own heart—the Within—with her offering, dancing four steps, her eyes on her moving hand.

When she had finished the offering, she stood still and swirled the pinched fingers over her head, sprinkling the corn pollen and sage into the air. Then she rubbed her two hands together vigorously above her crown to disperse the last of the pollen, and clapped her hands together powerfully above her head.

She looked up at me as if she'd known all along that I was there. "You have question," she said.

This surprised me. Ordinarily, she saw questions as demanding and arrogant. I was not prepared for her to invite me to ask her for information. "Did you tell a story the other night about your ancestors being star watchers here at Chimney Rock?"

Momma Anna came up the steps of the kiva and walked straight to the fire tower. "They build great fire here, right here." She pointed at the fire tower. "Look south." She pointed back in the opposite direction.

Across the rim of the sunken kiva I looked down the backbone of the Chimney Rock cuesta and south through the valley carved by the Piedra River as it flowed to the San Juan River and beyond. The waterways looked like twisting steel blue ribbons. Despite the smoke in the atmosphere, there, in the notch between the mountain ranges, I could see Huerfano Mesa in northern New Mexico.

"Star people send message with fire. Here." She pointed again at the fire tower. "Use big rock send light, shiny black rock. Dark moon time."

"These were your ancestors?"

She didn't answer, but went on. "First woman come here through hole in sky, bring man for seed." She looked at me expectantly.

"Like the holes in the tops of the little pottery bears and seed pots that you make?"

"First one," she said, emphatically.

"I was going to ask you about your little pottery bears . . ." I looked at the old woman and stopped.

Her face was earnest and her eyes were shining. There was something here that she desperately wanted me to know, but I wasn't putting it all together yet. She walked right up to me, looked up into my face, and struck me hard on the cheek with the flat of her hand. "Wake up!" she snapped.

I clutched my cheek, shocked that this gentle, patient woman had struck me. "I am awake!"

She shook her head back and forth, hard and fast with frustration. *"Tcheee, tcheee, tcheee,"* she muttered, and she clutched her forehead with her hand. "We tell you story, but you . . ." She waved a hand as if to dismiss the thought.

"I what?"

"You . . . Just bring that boy."

"That boy?"

"Yes, that one coming now."

"The hotshot? The one who's coming tonight to Fire Camp?"

"You bring him me."

"I have something I have to do. I had a wreck . . ."

"You bring Talking Spider me. Here."

"Who's Talking Spider?"

"What you call? Delgado? You bring him."

"But the sheriff—"

"Leave wolf. He big part this story. You see soon enough."

Trophy Women

Friday, 1600 Hours

A man from Ground Support brought a rig for me to use and met me at the visitors' center. "They got a big mess on the highway over on the Pagosa Springs side," he said. "The smoke has been blowing out of the west and I guess the visibility is down to nothing. A semi jackknifed, another one turned over on the shoulder, and they had a twelve-car pileup. Nothing's moving on Highway 160, not even on either side of the roadblocks for the fire. After you take me back to Fire Camp, you'll have to go through Ignacio and back up through Bayfield to Durango to pick up that hotshot. His flight's been delayed, so you'll probably end up sitting at the airport waiting anyway."

I told him I had a couple of errands I could run to pass the time until Delgado Gonzales's plane arrived.

"Well, everyone in Fire Camp is excited about him coming. They're updating his flight status on the bulletin board every half hour. One more thing: here's some papers the IC asked to have dropped off at the Columbine Ranger District—their FMO is waiting on them. You have to go right by there when you swing through Bayfield, so I was thinking . . ."

I stopped by Division Bravo to see Kerry on the way to Ignacio. He hadn't shaved in three days, and his yellow shirt bore charcoal-colored stains. He was taking off his line pack at the back of a green Forest Service truck when I drove up. He didn't recognize the vehicle so he paid little attention to me until I got out and came up to him. "What's with the Ford?" His voice was hoarse from all the smoke he'd been breathing.

"I had a wreck in my Jeep. Someone cut my brake lines."

"What?! Are you all right? Was anyone hurt?"

"I'm fine. Mountain got tossed around in the back a bunch, but he seems all right."

He gritted his teeth. "Who did it?" His voice was barely a whisper.

"I'm not sure."

"You have no idea?"

"I didn't say that. I have a couple ideas. I'm on my way to find out which one of them it was."

He took hold of my arm. "You find me when you know. I want to be there. Don't try to confront this—whoever it is—by yourself. I'll back you. Just come get me."

I nodded my head. "I will." I looked at a line of twenty belly bags—gear bags used by helitack crews—each one paired with a flight helmet and a skein of rope, all stacked in uniform order on the side of the road. "What's up? You get a helicrew?"

"Yeah, finally got a rappel crew. The fire has worked its

way into a dozen different drainages on this side. There's no way to fight it but to drop crews in right on top of it. It's too dangerous to have firefighters on either side of the ravines."

"So, more chopper noise," I said, watching for his reaction. "You okay with that?"

He tipped his head back and rubbed his neck. "Of course," he said. "You know I used to rope down into action out of one of those birds."

"In Somalia?" I asked.

"In the army." His voice was soft.

I sensed an opening. "You're the perfect person to be running this division, then."

He looked at me. "I've got some experience."

I nodded. "I've got some experience, too."

Suddenly he reached out and pulled me to him, hugging me tight to his chest. I smelled the sweat and smoke in his clothes, felt the rough stubble of his unshaven cheek against my forehead. He reached up with one hand and cupped the back of my head, then pulled his own face back and looked at me. "You be safe, babe."

"You be safe, too," I said.

☙

When Clara White Deer wasn't at the school, I thought to look at the little café where we'd had lemonade two days before. She was there, in the same booth, writing in a notebook. I slid into the seat opposite her without waiting to be invited. She looked up. "Have a seat," she said.

"What did you want Grampa Ned to give back that he took from you?" I asked.

She chuckled. "You still stuck on that one? I pegged you for a smarter girl than that."

"Was it something of yours, or something he gave to you and then took back?"

She pressed her lips together in disapproval. "It was always mine. I never gave it to him. He stole it from me."

"And we're talking about an object here, right? Not Nuni."

She rolled her eyes. "Not Nuni. Of course not. People don't belong to anyone else. Nuni is not mine."

"Did you know about any of Ned's other affairs?"

She closed her notebook and pushed the pen into the coil binding. "I knew about all of them. Everyone knew about them."

"Did he take something from every woman he was involved with? A trophy?"

She shoved the notebook into her handbag, looking down into the seat beside her, where it sat. "He would have taken our very souls if he could have," she said.

"The thing he took from you—how did he know what would be a trophy for you in particular?"

"That's easy," she said. "He wanted to take my power. I'm guessing that was his pattern with all of them."

"And Nuni?"

"I love my daughter. But she has always been wounded by the abandonment she felt not having a father growing up. He figured out this weakness when it came time he needed someone, and he used it to lure her to him."

"Has he stolen something from Nuni?"

"He has stolen something from Life itself with Nuni."

I took a moment to think about this. "I know you said you don't have any grandbabies, but have you *ever* been a grandmother?"

She gave me a harsh look. "You know what? None of this is any of your business. I'm tired of you asking me all these questions about my private life, about my family. I don't have to answer them. I don't have to talk to you at all. Now leave me alone!" As she spoke these last words, she scrambled out of her seat in the booth, threw a five-dollar bill on the table, and walked away.

⑨

At the tribal offices, I asked to speak with Edgar "Jimmy" Johns. He showed me to a small office and offered me a seat in the chair beside his desk. "You know I can't tell you anything Ned told me in confidence," he said. "Professional ethics."

"I want to know about the Southern Ute Growth Fund."

"I can tell you some general things about that."

"Who gets an allowance from that?"

"Members of the tribe."

"And who qualifies as a member of the tribe?"

"Anyone one-quarter Southern Ute or more."

"And how do you determine if someone is one-quarter Southern Ute?"

"Well, in most cases, we already know that. Their people have provided their lineage. But we do occasionally have someone come looking for a share of the tribal growth fund that we don't know, and whose people we don't know—and then we have to ask them to prove their lineage. It all has to be well documented, which isn't always easy to do. You know, even well into the twentieth century, they didn't do birth certificates for Indians, even death certificates sometimes. So sometimes people have a hard time tracing their ancestors."

"Can you use DNA evidence?"

"We haven't had to do that yet. I suppose that could happen, but it hasn't happened yet."

"That's all I had, then, thank you," I said, and I got up from the chair to leave.

"There's a boy around who is just like his father," Jimmy Johns said.

"A boy?" I stopped and turned in the doorway.

Johns leaned back in his office chair. "Well, he is a man now. But he is just like his father."

"I guess I don't follow you. Why do you mention this, anyway?"

"I thought you were asking about lineage."

I nodded my head. "Yes. But how does this relate?"

"His mother is a Navajo."

"And?"

"And he found a way to get his share from the fund."

I was starting to realize how like the Tanoah the Utes were. Instead of handing me direct information, I was being given a riddle to solve. Because of my many experiences with Momma Anna, I also knew it was pointless to try to get information that wasn't being freely offered. "I had one more question." I didn't ask it, I made a statement—sometimes this worked. Not always. But it was worth a shot.

"Just one?" He grinned.

"What about grandchildren?"

"What about them?"

At least he didn't shut down! "I wondered if Grampa Ned ever admitted to having any grandchildren."

He rocked forward in his chair and stood up. "Not that I know of. Why?"

"I'm looking for a grandmother in this story somewhere."

He made a wide sweep with both his hands. "Well, just look around. They're all around you."

◄ 40 ►

Talking Shot

Friday, 1800 Hours

When I got to the Durango airport, there was still a wait for the incoming plane. I called Ron Crane on the phone. "Do you know anything about what Clara White Deer was doing the morning she reported Grampa Ned for going inside the fire lines?"

"I've already checked that out. She'd been to Pagosa Springs. She got gas there with a credit card and bought groceries about an hour before she reported seeing Ned."

"You say she bought groceries *before* she made the report?"

"Yes, I checked her credit card charges. Why?"

"She told me she was on her way to Pagosa Springs when she saw Ned."

"Well, that can't be. The incident report shows that she reported Ned's trespass at 1030 hours. And she was at the supermarket in Pagosa at 0930."

"No, I remember her saying she was *on the way* to

Pagosa when she saw him. It was the first time we met. We went to a café and had lemonade."

Crane was silent a moment. "You're sure?"

"I'm sure."

"Well, if that were true, why would she wait until after she'd driven all the way to Pagosa Springs, done her shopping, and gassed up her car to report Ned being in danger?"

"I can think of only one reason," I said.

"Okay, bye," Crane said, and clicked off the line.

Delgado Gonzales sported a white bandage on his foot, and he used crutches to keep from stepping on the injured appendage. Fortunately, he was in peak fitness, so the crutches did not seem to slow him down. In fact, his strong upper body flexed, his arm muscles bulged, and he looked as if he were enjoying using his strength in new ways.

The Durango airport was so small that I was able to drive right up in front of the building with the Ford I'd gotten from Ground Support. I tried to help Gonzales with his bag, but he insisted on slinging it on his back and crutching out to the car with it. He moved lightly, quickly, as if he'd been on crutches all his life.

"They've got a big party planned for you at Fire Camp," I said. "They even got a band. Everyone's so excited to see you."

"I wish my buddies from the crew could be here with me," he said. He wore a T-shirt with the same embroidered Three-Pueblos Hot Shots logo that I'd seen on the patches on the crew's Nomex shirts during Rescue Command.

"Well, we all wish the whole crew could be here, too, believe me. The whole camp has been worried about all of you. They've been sending you guys all their good thoughts and wishes, and plenty of prayers, too."

"Whatever they did, it's working, so tell them to keep it

up." He was quiet a moment, then said, "I wonder if you could take me someplace after the party."

"Well, I'll try. Where did you want to go?"

"There's an elder from my pueblo at Chimney Rock. I want to see her."

I sighed. "You're from Tanoah Pueblo?"

He turned and looked across the seat at me. "That's right."

"And you want to see Anna Santana, right?"

"You know her?" There was excitement in his voice.

"Boy, do I." I shook my head.

He grinned. "I see—she's teaching you." He reached across and shoved my shoulder.

I smiled back at him. "How'd you guess?"

"She told me she had a white slave!" He laughed at this. This was a common joke among the Tanoah when one of them befriended an Anglo.

I nodded my head, smiling. "Yup. I have to do all the white girl chores just for the chance to pick up a little Indun Way."

He laughed out loud, hearing me refer to another common expression among the elders of Tanoah. Momma Anna and her brothers and sisters often referred to their culture as "Indun Way."

"You know, you're all right," he said to me, and he reached into his bag for some chewing gum, took out a pack, and offered me a stick. I declined, but handed him a bottle of water from my own stash behind the seat.

After he'd unwrapped his gum and was smacking away on it, I tendered a question. Sometimes the younger Tanoah did not object to questions the same way the elders did. "Can you tell me why your brother Louie left your crew during the fire?"

Delgado Gonzales stopped chewing and grew quiet. Finally he said, "No, ma'am, I cannot."

We rode the rest of the way from Durango to Bayfield in silence.

⊛

At the Columbine Ranger District, I learned that the fire management officer—or FMO—was in the building next door to the main office. Both structures were former houses that had been rehabbed into offices and painted the familiar Forest Service green. In a small compound behind the two buildings was a fenced motor pool, and behind that was a corral with a horse grazing on the lawn. Seeing the animal, my heart suddenly ached for my former life as a range rider for the BLM. Alone in the remote backcountry, often on horseback, I patrolled literally thousands of acres of public land, riding the fence lines. It was a quiet, magic-filled life, a wild life, a lonely life. But it had also proven to be a dangerous one when I stumbled into a story that ended in several deaths, including my horse. My mind wanted to linger only on the idyllic days in scenic wilderness, alone with the forces of nature and the birds and the beasts. But the truth was another story.

I recognized Frank McDaniel's salt-and-pepper hair from behind. He was sitting at his desk, shoved up against a wall in a dark and crowded little front room, absorbed in some paperwork. He barely looked up when I came in. I stood over him for a moment, and then he recognized me. "Oh, sorry"—he stood up, a smile causing his mustache to curve upward—"I thought you were . . . never mind, I thought you were someone who works in this office. That's why I didn't pay any attention when you came in."

"They asked me to bring you these papers from the ICP," I said.

"Oh, right. Yes. Thanks. Saved me a trip over there. You know the highway's all bottled up."

"Yeah. Well, I just needed to drop these off. I have some-one waiting so I better go. It was nice to see you again."

"Hey, you're the liaison officer, right?"

"Yes."

"I've gotten at least a dozen calls for you."

"You have?" This puzzled me.

"Yes, I couldn't figure out why they kept asking to talk to Miss Wild. It happened so many times that I finally checked the incident action plan—they've got our numbers and names reversed. Your number is listed for me, and mine is listed for you."

"Oh," I said, remembering the calls I'd received with no one on the other end of the line. "This is the first I've heard of it."

"Well, unless you actually gave someone your number, they didn't have it. They called me instead. I didn't know what to do with that at first, but I finally figured it out, and started telling callers your correct number."

"Oh. Well, thanks very much." I started to leave, then turned. "By any chance, did anyone just hang up on you?"

"No. Why? You mean callers simply hung up on you when you answered?"

"Yeah. They did. Someone did. Several times."

"Well, I'm glad we got it figured out. They're supposed to correct it in the printout for tonight's briefing."

I walked out to the car where Delgado Gonzales was wait-ing, determined to draw him back into conversation. Appar-ently while I'd been inside talking to Frank McDaniel, he'd had the same idea. I'd barely put the key in the ignition when he said, "I'm sorry about earlier. I can't talk about it, though. But I did want to thank you for saving my brother. I pray that he makes it through this."

I turned and looked at him, and realized how afraid and desperate he must have been feeling throughout this ordeal. "I pray that he makes it, too. Momma Anna was just making offerings to the seven directions a little while ago. I'm sure she was praying for you and your brother, and for all the members of your crew."

He made a tight-lipped smile and gave a slight nod.

"It must have been hotter than hell in those fire shelters," I said as I put the car in gear and pulled out onto the road. "I start to roast in them when we're just doing a deployment for training, and that's only for a few minutes, without any live fire present."

"You can't even imagine," he said. "You can't breathe. You just want to bury your face in the earth and try to breathe the dirt, because it's cooler than the air. And the fire pushes such a wind ahead of it. You can't believe how fierce that wind is. It nearly took me up like a balloon, and I'm a pretty big guy."

"Of course, I wasn't as far inside the fire line as you were, but I got caught in the blowup myself. What I couldn't believe was the noise."

"Yeah, I don't think I'll ever forget that. That was the loudest sound I've ever heard in my life. It was like being inside a jet engine, maybe even louder."

This time it was my turn to smile and nod.

Delgado Gonzales talked nearly all the way back to Chimney Rock. I even managed to put a few questions to him and get a response. This might have served as our first real critical stress debriefing, for both of us.

"What were you thinking about, trapped in that fire shelter for so long?" I asked toward the end of our conversation.

"Well, we had a few breaks when a wave of fire would blow through and then we could hear ourselves talk for a few minutes before the next wave hit us. The first wave was terrible. Like I said, I could hardly breathe, and I nearly got blown over. I just knew we were all going to die. But after we made it through the first wave, I thought it was going to be all right. We counted off in crew order—just the way we always do when we line up at training—and we scooted ourselves and our shelters in closer together for more protection. But then, wave after wave hit. And when we counted off, each time we'd lose a guy or two who wouldn't respond when we called for him to count off. And I started to think, *This is it, this is the end.*" His voice broke and his lip quivered.

"That must have been terrible."

"The worst thing was knowing there were guys right there who probably needed medical attention, needed to be carried out, whatever. And I couldn't get out of my fire shelter."

I thought to ask if he was worried about his brother then, too, but I knew better than to say anything.

"When you train as hard as we do," Delgado said, clearing his throat and gathering composure, "when you work as hard as we do together, day in and day out . . . we start the season in early March with such rigorous training, you can't even imagine. We learn to carry more than our weight, we learn to take risks together, calculated risks, but risks just the same. We learn to face death when we walk into a fire, and we aren't afraid. We're family, we're that close, all of us. But in that shelter, I was afraid." He lowered his head and clamped his lips together.

I drove in silence, afraid to speak for fear I would say the wrong thing. Finally, after a minute, I said, "Are you married? Or do you have a sweetheart?"

It took him a few seconds to answer. He just kept slowly nodding his head up and down, his eyes unfocused. He had gone within. "My wife is pregnant with our first child. All my life I wanted to be a dad. We had a great dad. He taught us everything, and he loved us with all his heart. When my brother and I first joined the Three-Pebs, he was so proud of us. But he had a heart attack right before last Christmas and died. A few months later, when I learned my wife was pregnant, the first thing I thought of was how I was going to try to be as good a father as my dad was to us, so I could carry on his legacy in that way." He winced and closed his eyes, and once again lowered his head, unable to control his emotions.

Finally, he went on: "I think the worst thing about the time I spent in that fire shelter was knowing I was going to die, which meant I wasn't ever going to be a father to my own child. That was the worst thing of all."

◄ 41 ►

Celebration

Friday, 2000 Hours

The evening I brought Delgado Gonzales back, Fire Camp transformed from a battle outpost to a festival of revelry. The Blue Bandana Band played rousing bluegrass tunes, the camp kitchen had rustled up steaks for the evening meal and buckets of chocolate ice cream for dessert, and the evening briefing indicated that the news from the fire front was all good. Division Alpha, manned by the Southern Ute wildland crew, had contained the western flank with minimal damage to the riparian area along the Piedra. In Division Bravo, most of the coyote crews were reporting good black with little chance of reburn—only the recently deployed helicrew was still battling for containment, and they hoped to make headway when the wind died down after sunset. Durango was dispatching an air tanker the next day that would begin slurry-bombing the slopes on the eastern flank at dawn. Division Charlie had pumped water from Devil's Creek and the pond on the Laughing Dog

Ranch to an intricate system of hose lays that contained the fire in their sector without any structure loss on the ranch or in Camp Honor. Division Zulu had made progress, too: firefighters there were working successfully to keep the flames from the power lines. With any luck, the fire would be contained and in mop-up in twenty-four hours.

The best news of all was that ten more of the hotshots were to be released from the burn center in the morning, and all but one of the remaining eight had been upgraded in condition. One of the information officers made an announcement to this effect through the band's PA system, and a roar of applause and cheering rose up from the crowd like the smoke that had billowed all day from the Chimney Rock Fire.

My sat phone rang. Ron Crane began talking without any kind of greeting. "I've got Clara White Deer in custody. She won't talk, refuses to respond to questioning, she hasn't asked for a lawyer, didn't even want to make a phone call. She has motive and opportunity, and her story about that morning doesn't jive, but I can't hold her more than twenty-four hours without evidence. She's a real tough cookie. I did find out that she has been dating the owner of the service station in Ignacio. She might have enlisted his help or information in cutting your brake lines. We're trying to run him down to talk to him, but it's Friday night. His shop is closed and he's not at home. As for the gunshot through your windshield, I couldn't find the bullet anywhere in your car. If it went in through the window . . ."

"My driver's-side window was down. Maybe it went right through the car and out the other side."

"Parting your bear partner's hair along the way," he said. "I'll see if the Southern Ute Tribal Police can send someone to scope out the area where you were parked, look for casings or a slug."

I was quiet after that, thinking.

Crane went on. "Remember how I told you it's almost always the spouse?"

"Yeah, but . . ."

"Well, Clara White Deer is the closest thing we have to one in this case. She and Ned had a kid, and she's the only one Ned acknowledged. There must be some kind of bond there."

"What about your theory about the hotshot?"

"Yeah—oh, that reminds me: this is not for public dissemination, but the medical reports on that hotshot you found show that Louie Gonzales had severe bruising on the back of his head at the neckline, so possibly a closed head injury in addition to his burns. I think if Clara White Deer hit old Ned with the shovel, she probably took a whack at your hotshot, too."

☉

Later, I was standing to one side watching as Delgado held court seated in a folding chair with his crutches on the ground beside him—shaking hands, laughing, receiving good wishes from firefighters with moist eyes. He held his fists out in a wide V above his head, gesturing to show how he had held down the corners of his fire shelter against the savage winds of the firestorm that had ripped at the foil tent; then he stroked his throat as he spoke about inhaling the fiery hot gases and smoke. Each time he shared the war story of his entrapment, he told it with more and more gusto. As the story grew in detail and drama, something was healing in the storyteller, and Delgado began to look larger and stronger and more like a man with a purpose.

Someone tapped me on the shoulder, and I turned around to see Kerry grinning at me. His brown hair, which he kept short and neat, was dark with sweat and smoke, and spiked out from his head in places. He had a full-on beard in progress, and his skin was both red and brown from the sun. He had taken off his yellow shirt and was wearing a clean Forest Service T-shirt with his green Nomex pants and wildland boots, and I could see the muscles in his chest and shoulders through the soft cotton of his shirt.

"You have helmet head," I said, enjoying every minute detail of what I was seeing.

"I don't care," he said, his smile intensifying. He raised his eyebrows at me, then took my forearm and pulled me toward the grassy area where other firefighters were dancing to the music. Kerry pulled me toward him, encircled my waist with one arm while clutching my fingers in his other hand, and started to move as deftly as a trained dancer. He looked down at me, still smiling. "I've missed you, babe," he said.

"I've missed you, too," I said. "You seem more . . ."

"Shhhhh," he said, tightening his arm around my waist, "just listen to the music."

But I listened instead to his heart beating, my cheek against his chest, his chin resting on my head as we moved. I felt the strength in his arms guiding me, and I forgot about where to put my feet or which way to step and I let my senses run with the moment. I smelled him—his clean shirt exuding a hint of soap, his skin and his sweat and the smoke that had permeated his clothes and his hair, and that scent of *man* that he always carried—that fusion of hormones and DNA imprint that was uniquely Kerry. He twirled me around on the grass, and I looked out beyond his biceps and saw a fluidity to the images around us—the firefighters, the tents, the lake beyond, the band—everything swirling and nicely smudged at the edges like an Impressionist painting with a bluegrass soundtrack.

"We should go somewhere," he whispered, his voice soft and sensual.

I looked up at him and smiled. "Where?"

He glanced from one side to the other, still dancing. "Plans," he said. "They're all out here partying."

Inside the office that Plans had taken over, Kerry used a marker and a sheet of printer paper and made a sign that said DO NOT DISTURB and taped it to the outside of the door. He tipped the blinds upward at the windows so no one could see in, then turned off the lights and closed the door. He leaned with his back against it and looked at me. "Come here," he said.

I went to him, straddled his boots, and stepped into the circle of his arms. "Someone might come in."

"I'm right here," he said. "They won't get through me."

He tugged at my T-shirt and pulled it up over my head. I helped wriggle it off, then started pulling at his. The room was dim and dusky and the sound of the band outside and the firefighters talking noisily and laughing loudly was an intoxicating undercurrent. Our breathing was like another presence in the room—intense, passionate, rhythmic. I worked at Kerry's belt while he reached to unfasten my bra, his hands hot against my back, making short work of the fastener. He drew the bra around and down my arms and dropped it on the floor.

"You're excited," he said.

"How'd ya know?" I grinned.

"Look." He glanced at my nipples.

"You're excited, too," I said, unzipping his pants.

"How'd ya know?" he teased.

☸

Delgado Gonzales was not where I'd left him. The reveling, the laughter, and the band's volume had all escalated. The band had replaced their acoustic instruments with electric ones and had launched into a rockabilly version of

"Peggy Sue." It was almost impossible to hear my own voice when I shouted to a group near where the hotshot had been sitting. "Do you know where Delgado went?"

"Who?" one woman asked, straining to hear me.

"Delgado Gonzales, the hotshot with the crutches?"

"Oh, yeah," a man with her shouted. "He said to tell you he found a ride to Chimney Rock."

"Do you know who took him?"

"I think he left with that archaeologist."

"Steve Morella?" I asked, but he and the girl beside him turned and moved off to dance.

The music had a driving beat, and the others in the group didn't hear me. They nodded their heads and tapped their toes, their eyes on the musicians as my words vanished into the howl of guitars.

Kerry checked a couple sleeping bags out of the cache and we met up, as agreed, by the shores of Navajo Lake, about two hundred yards from where my ripped tent was staked. We spread the bags out on the ground, stripped down to T-shirts and skivvies, and lay down to watch the stars. Within minutes, Kerry began to snore softly. Right before I fell asleep, I thought about the moon forming a cradle to carry the dawn into the light.

๕

Kerry's radio sparked to life first. While he responded, I scrambled to pull on my pants, then stood up to search for my bra. Then my pack set sounded off.

The eastern flank had erupted again, this time at its northerly edge where the new heli-rappel team had been placed to close the gap. The fire had flashed in a narrow box canyon and quickly exploded up the slope. It was rapidly encroaching on Chimney Rock, and the Native Americans had to be evacuated immediately. A few hours after midnight, the winds had kicked up again unexpectedly.

Sunset had closed down all flight operations for the night, so the chopper couldn't get in to pick up the crew. There would be no help from the air until dawn.

My first thought, whether honorable or not, was for Mountain.

Kerry and I were dressed in seconds. Before he started to go, just ahead of me, he turned and looked at me for an instant. "Mountain!" I said. Then I hastened to add, "Momma Anna." He grabbed his radio harness and started running for his truck.

I tried to call Roy on my sat phone as I raced for the parking area, but I remembered that I had gone to sleep without plugging it in to recharge. I turned it off to preserve the battery and put my radio on scan. Traffic on the tactical channel was almost constant, so I dashed into the ICP and almost ran into Steve Morella in the lobby. "Oh, good," I said. "You're here. I have to go up to Chimney Rock and help evacuate the Indians. Will you let Roy or Charlie Dorn know I'm on the way there? And I don't know what you did with Gonzales after you took him to Chimney Rock, but you'll have to babysit him for a while longer. I have to go."

He gave me a puzzled look as I turned and hurried away.

◄ 42 ►

Chaos and Conflagration

Saturday, 0400 Hours

You couldn't have missed the entrance to Chimney Rock off of State Highway 151, no matter how hard you tried. Two sheriff's cruisers straddled either side of the road with their light bars whirling, a Colorado State Police car's LEDs danced in the entry drive, and a bevy of vans and SUVs queued up to load passengers.

Since I was driving a vehicle with no official identification, a sheriff's deputy challenged me as I pulled in. I reached into my radio harness and found my badge and flashed it at him. "I'm here to help evacuate the native Puebloans."

He leaned in the window. "We already started up top," he said. "Two of our deputies are helping bring the oldest ones down. The rest of the Indians are grabbing their stuff and getting ready to go. I'll radio ahead for my officers to hold traffic a few minutes and let you go on up, but after that, I'm shutting down all entries. We need to keep that road open for all those vehicles coming down. We need everyone out within the next half hour." He waved me past.

I drove the three miles up the steep and curving gravel road with my hands choking the steering wheel. I wanted to hurry, but the visceral memory of the accident just hours earlier suddenly overcame me—and I felt as though I were living a bad dream in which I knew what was about to happen and could neither prevent it nor stop my own momentum as I raced toward it. As I came around a bend, my headlights illuminated the scar on the cliff face where the sanitary truck had jammed its wheel into the rock just inches shy of the side of my Jeep. In my peripheral vision, I saw the wolf rolling past behind me, heard the thump as his body slammed into the side of the rear cargo compartment, felt the vertigo as my head and upper torso flopped forward and back and then side to side. My right ribs suddenly hurt and I felt my vehicle swerving off the road. I forced myself to breathe slowly, loosen my grip, and concentrate on the winding track in front of me. *You're all right,* I told myself, *you're all right.* But I was swimming through time, and now my thoughts raced ahead of me to Mountain and Momma Anna and the native Puebloans.

When I arrived at the parking lot on top, a sheriff's cruiser blocked the road. I pulled to the side, tucked into the soft gravel shoulder, and parked. I pulled the radio harness on over my head, put my arms through the loops, and snapped the strap that went around my back. I twisted my long hair into a rope and tucked it under my fire helmet, then strapped on my line pack and donned my gloves. I got Charlie Dorn on the radio and gave him my location. "Help the S.O. get everybody off that mountain!" he snapped. "And then you get down from there, too!"

A small group of Indians crossed the asphalt carrying

bundles wrapped in blankets. I ran to them. "Do you know where Anna Santana is?" I asked.

They eyed me with suspicion, their eyes squinting at me in my helmet and yellow shirt in the darkness.

"She is keeping my wolf," I thought to add, realizing they'd never seen me in full firefighter attire.

A round of nods erupted as they figured out who I was. One old man poked an arthritic finger toward the edge of the parking lot where I usually parked my Jeep. "Going out," he said.

"She's leaving? Do you know who she came with?"

They looked at me with blank faces.

"She doesn't drive. Did you see her leaving?"

They glanced at one another and shook their heads, then moved off toward a pickup in a nearby parking space.

The lot was full of people packing their things into their cars and hastily saying good-bye to one another. A deputy sheriff wearing a chartreuse neon vest and carrying a flashlight with an orange cone on the tip prepared to do traffic control. Another deputy was helping an Indian woman put her things in the trunk of her car. I checked in with him. "I think we got everybody. We're just trying to get them into their cars and keep them calm, and get them down the mountain in an orderly fashion," he said. "See what you can do to help."

I noticed Bearfat standing on the curb beside the comfort station and I spoke to him. "Has everybody gotten the news that they have to evacuate?"

He hesitated a moment, not recognizing me in the darkness in my helmet. "Oh, it's you, Jamaica Wild. Yes, I already told them. The sheriff talked to me about a half hour ago down at the visitors' center and I came up and told everyone. A deputy took two of the old Hopi men first. Everyone else is loading their stuff and getting ready to drive out. The officers told us to wait and they'd direct traffic so everybody didn't try to leave at once and end up in an accident. I think they're about ready to start."

"Is anyone resisting the evac?"

"Come with me," he said, and he walked a few yards toward the western cliff edge. Bearfat pointed down the slopes to the west just half a mile. A torrent of fiery orange tongues probed upward into the darkness while the burning belly beneath digested the forest and spat smoke so black that it was visible even in the night sky. "A bunch of them saw that and started leaving even before the sheriff got here."

"Are you taking a count or anything?" I asked as we started back to the parking lot.

"No. I didn't think . . ."

"Can you look around the perimeter and see if anyone is left?"

"Sure." He started to jog away.

"Wait!" I said. "Do you know where Anna Santana is?"

Bearfat gave me a sympathetic look as he shook his head.

As I hurried through the parking lot, I scanned for Mountain and Momma Anna. I helped a man put a large drum in the back of his car. Another man asked me to speak to his mother because she was afraid. I stood beside the car door and leaned down to look in the open window. "It's going to be fine, Grandmother," I said, addressing her in this way to show respect for an elder, as was the custom of Pueblo people. "There is plenty of time. We're going to get everyone down safely. You just stay in the car, and they'll let you know when it's time to go."

She reached a bony hand out the window and grasped the sleeve of my Nomex shirt, tugging my arm toward her. "I pray," she said.

"That's right," I said. "You pray."

"I pray for you," she said, and she squeezed my arm before releasing it.

As I moved on, I tried to be reassuring and helpful. I saw a clutch of women I'd seen with Momma Anna the first day of the ceremonies. "Is Anna Santana with you?" I asked, pulling off my helmet so they would recognize my long yellow hair.

They shook their heads no.

"Do you know who drove her here?"

One woman looked sideways at the others, then spoke: "Nephew bring."

"Her nephew?" I asked, my mind scanning the relatives of Anna's that I knew. "Is he here?"

The woman shook her head no.

"He didn't stay?"

She shook her head again.

"How was she going to get back home, do you know?"

"Nephew."

"The nephew was coming back?"

This time she nodded. "Come back after."

"He was going to come back to pick her up after the ceremonies here?"

She nodded again, this time more enthusiastically, as if encouraged that she was getting through. The other women nodded, too.

"So do you know where Anna is now? Where my wolf is?" I scanned the group hopefully.

They all shook their heads no.

"Well, thank you. You get ready to go, okay?" I said as I stuffed my hair back up in my helmet. "Go ahead and get in your cars, it will only be a few minutes now."

I dashed to the piñon tree where I'd seen Momma Anna's makeshift camp. It was dark in this little grove of trees, so I flipped on the LED headlamp on my helmet and took the Mini Mag out of my radio harness and shined it on the ground. The familiar multicolored Pendleton blanket still stretched across the dry earth with stones at the corners to hold it down. All her things lay in order beneath the tree. I knelt down and searched for Mountain's bridle and lead, but I didn't see them. It was then that I spied the drum that Momma Anna's father, Nazario, had made for her. I knew she would not have left without it—she was still here at Chimney Rock.

I ran back to the parking lot and began going from car to car, peering inside, asking for Momma Anna, for my wolf. I interrupted conversations without concern for how rude I must have seemed, and I seldom stayed to wait for an answer, having seen for myself before they even understood my question, if they did. My search yielded only a repeating chorus of surprised faces and heads shaking no.

By the time I'd reached the front of the parking lot, the viridescent-vested deputy was waving the first cars through to begin their caravan down the winding road to the bottom. As I came up to one side of him, he almost struck me with the cone-tipped flashlight, which he was waving like a conductor's baton, urging the traffic to move in a slow, steady rhythm. "Easy, there!" he said to me. "I didn't see you coming up."

"Officer, have you seen an old woman with a wolf?"

He stopped waving the flashlight and stared at me. "A what?"

"Has anyone come through with a big wolf?"

He frowned at me, the soft glow of the light through the cone making his face look like a jack-o'-lantern. "Is this a joke? I don't have time for jokes, miss."

"Never mind." I started to turn away. But I had to try

again. "There's an old Indian woman here with a wolf," I said. "If you see her, will you let me know? I'm on the evac channel with the sheriff's office."

By now, he was back to business, the traffic rolling slowly by to his direction. "If I see a wolf, I'll be sure to give you a holler," he said.

As the cars wheeled slowly past me, I saw smoke whorls dance in the yellow pools of light from the headlamps. I felt a gust of hot wind, and smelled the Chimney Rock Fire coming closer, its signature the scent of incinerating brush and heavy timber, the plants surrendering the last essence of their life into the clouds of hot gas as a wild and forlorn fragrance.

I ran to the comfort station and checked the restroom for Momma Anna. The concave metal door still dangled in the door frame, unable to fully open or close.

I took the trail down toward the stone basin, where I had first talked to the native Puebloans. The path looped past the Stone Basin site, around a pit house site, and past the Great Kiva. On the smooth flat of bedrock with the stone basin in its center, I paused to look through the junipers and down the hillside toward the fire. Along the jagged southwestern slopes of the mountain, the fire raged in a handful of narrow ravines that funneled the flames upward. From the shoulders of these flumes, curtains of smoke illuminated by red heat opened with the wind and closed again, and with another gust, I saw the leading edge of the blaze boiling out of a box canyon just a quarter mile below me. I turned to take to the trail again, shouting, "Mountain! Momma Anna!"

I jogged to the Great Kiva and shined my light around the edges. "Mountain!" I called. "Momma Anna?"

On the way back up the half-mile loop, I ran into Bearfat. "I think we got everybody," he said. "The last cars are rolling out now."

"My wolf!" I said. "Momma Anna. Did you find them?"

He paused a moment. "Well, I wasn't looking for them in particular . . ."

"Damn it, Bearfat! Did you see them?"

"Hey, calm down. I didn't see them, but that doesn't mean they didn't go down with some of the first ones. I told you a few people left even before the law got here."

"They're still here," I said, and I started to push past him. But I thought better, and turned. "But you're sure you got everyone else?"

"Pretty sure," he said.

"Thank you, Bearfat."

"No problem."

"You better go now, too."

"I will."

⊗

By the time I got back to the parking lot, there were only a few cars left in the line leading out and down the mountain. I skirted across the lower half of the lot, then up the few steps and across the upper section to the Parking Lot site. My radio crackled: "Chimney Rock evacuation is now complete. All personnel please leave the Chimney Rock mesa at once. Check in with Command when you reach the entrance gate."

I thumbed the mic. "Evac, this is Liaison Wild. I'm still looking for a missing party."

"Negative, we have everyone. Evacuate the mesa immediately. You are in danger."

"A-firm," I said. "I just have one more place to check and then I'll head right down."

"Negative. You will evacuate the mesa immediately. Request echo."

I closed my eyes and thought for a moment. "Echoing your command, I will evacuate the mesa immediately."

"A-firm."

I reached down and turned the radio off. "I didn't say I would obey," I muttered. "I just said I was echoing the command."

The upper Pueblo Trail of dirt, stone, and gravel escalated two hundred feet as it followed the narrow causeway to the Guard House site and upward from there, ascending a steplike rock outcropping to the Great House Pueblo at the top. As I started up the path, I heard a distant roar like the one that had first warned me on the morning I had gone looking for Grampa Ned. I turned and looked behind me. From this higher ground, a panoramic view of the western aspect of the mountain stretched below me. In the darkness, it looked like the black back of the slope had split open and erupted into five twisted rivers of yellow flame and a hundred tiny crimson craters—and the radiant halo around all these was a fiery incandescence that reddened even the smoke with a lurid atomic light. One seam flared. Trees began to candle. The pyre of dried brush and flashy juniper formed a fireball and shot celebratory sparks into the rubescent mantling that the inferno wore as it marched upward toward the rim of the Chimney Rock cuesta, now only a few hundred yards away. A torrent of hot wind blasted my face, caught the edge of my helmet, and threatened to lift it off, and the rope of hair escaped from beneath it and flew behind me like a sail.

I turned and ran up the narrow path in the dark. To either side of the slim stretch of trail, the edge dropped away sharply, but I feared the fire more. "Mountain?" I called. "Momma Anna? Anna Santana!" But the wind howled past me and shredded my words.

After the Guard House site, the way widened slightly,

but became rocky and entailed climbing up a stone stretch that made a natural stairway. I bounded up this and found myself out of breath at the high corner of the rock wall of the Great House Pueblo. The wall sheltered me from the wind, so I stopped to catch my breath. I started to call out again for Mountain and Momma Anna, but something caused me to resist. Instead, I made my way along the wall and up the inclined path to the next corner, pausing to listen for a moment. Then I headed up the remaining few yards to the top of the wall and the rim of the upper of the two kivas that were part of the Great House Pueblo. From this high point, I could see the entire sloping mesa of Chimney Rock below me. Trees had begun torching all along the western rim of the cuesta. A patch of brush near the stone outcropping I'd just climbed ignited, and I realized that the recessed stone circle of the kiva was probably my best safety zone. I switched on my headlamp and looked down into the darkness, and there I saw Momma Anna sitting next to Delgado Gonzales against the curving wall. They looked up at me in surprise as the glare of my headlamp washed over their faces.

I bounded down the steps. "Momma Anna, what are you doing here? Where is Mountain?"

She waved a hand, indicating I should come to her, but she did not speak.

"Where is Mountain?" I said again, louder.

She held a finger to her lips. Delgado pushed his hands against the wall and managed to stand upright on his one good leg. "Better come sit down, Jamaica," he said. "That fire is going to burn over us, and we'll be safer if we huddle down against this rock wall."

"But—"

Momma Anna interrupted me. "Sit down!"

Delgado added, "There's no vegetation in here, and

very little right around the Great House, so I think we'll be fine. You can take your pack off so you can sit more comfortably, but keep it nearby, just in case."

I took off my helmet, unhooked my pack and let it drop. I came and sat against the wall, next to Momma Anna.

"This boy Talking Spider from Tanoah Pueblo," she said.

"I know."

Momma Anna held her finger to her lips again. "We must talk quiet. You"—she pointed the same finger at me now—"listen."

The hotshot lowered himself to the ground, then scooted away from the wall to sit in front of the two of us, his injured leg extending straight out to one side. He leaned in so we could hear one another better.

"My brother was a wisdom keeper, a storyteller," Gonzales began. "Two are chosen from each generation—a male and a female—to carry certain parts of our culture. Some learn songs, some learn stories, and some learn wisdom."

"Knifewing have big honor," Momma Anna said.

Gonzales nodded. "Knifewing is my brother's medicine name."

Momma Anna continued: "He and next other young girl carry Star Woman wisdom," she said, and she placed a fist against her chest, indicating where they held this knowledge. "Star Woman first one. Come through hole in sky. Pull first man through for seed. She is here."

"She's here?" I said.

Again, Momma Anna placed her finger to her lips, indicating that I should keep my voice down. I looked around but couldn't understand the need for quiet. We were sheltered from the fierce winds preceding the fire, and even more, the atmosphere seemed to have suddenly become eerily silent.

"First woman, one true Grandmother, all clan. She is here."

The hotshot saw my confusion and intervened. "Every one of us at Tanoah Pueblo can trace our ancestry back to one woman. Our legends say she is buried here, at Chimney Rock. My brother Louie—Knifewing—was given the knowledge of the location of her grave site. We are lucky that archaeologists have never discovered it and disturbed it. It is sacred to us, and the wisdom is held closely by our tribe, shared with only two people from each generation. My brother was the lookout for our crew and when he was watching the fire through his field glasses, he saw someone digging at the grave of the Star Woman, our one true Grandmother. He left to go confront the man. That was before the fire blew up."

"You must clean drum," Momma Anna said, looking intently at me. She held her hand to her heart. "You have story, one day summon ancestors. Drum must be clear, make song."

I tried to muster patience with the old woman, but I could not. "What does that have to do with anything?" I shouted, and I stood up. "I'm sorry, but why did you come up here when you should have evacuated?" I looked at Gonzales for some support. I pointed at him. "You could have been burned again! You both could have. And where the hell is Mountain?"

Neither of them spoke, but they both looked beyond me at the rim of the kiva.

"I can answer that," a voice said from the darkness.

◀ 43 ▶

Grandmother Moon

"First, Jamaica, throw your radio and phone out in the center there," Elaine Oldham said. The sky was beginning to lighten slightly and she stood on the rim of the kiva in silhouette against a steel gray backdrop, her head tipped to one side, looking through the sight of a rifle she had jammed into one shoulder.

I stood up.

"Do it," she said in an icy voice.

"Where's Mountain?" I reached to my side to unsnap the strap.

"He's in the fire tower. Throw it. Into the center. Then put your hands on top of your head."

I did as she said. "Mountain's in the fire tower?"

"Lucky thing we had steaks for dinner tonight or I'd never have gotten him up there."

"But the fire!"

"He's safe enough. The base of that thing is solid rock."

"It's wood above the base. It's only about twenty feet to

the wood. The fire can easily ladder up those shrubs beside it to the deck. Let me go get him. I'll bring him back here, I promise."

"Let her go get the wolf," Delgado said, pulling himself up against the wall.

"Sit right back down, Gonzales!" Oldham yelled. "Don't any of you move, or I swear to God I'll shoot you all."

The hotshot lowered himself back to the ground.

"That's better."

"Elaine, you don't want to harm my wolf, you told me you loved him. You wanted to spend more time with him, remember? Let me go get him."

"It's too late. Besides, he's your baby, remember? Why should you get to save your baby when I can't save mine?"

I looked at her bewildered. "What does Mountain have to do with . . ."

"Be quiet! Just be quiet! I'll do the talking."

"Yes, let's talk, Elaine. Let's all calm down and we can talk about it." I started to move my hands from my head.

"Put them back—now! And don't you patronize me. I'm going to shoot the next time anyone moves."

I hesitated.

"You don't think I will? Believe me, I'll shoot you. And I'm a good shot, too. Out there in that godforsaken, stinking desert at Hovenweep I had to be able to hit a rattlesnake at a safe distance. I used to pass the time in the evenings shooting at tin cans. I'm not half bad, so don't test me."

Delgado whispered to me, "She's got a .270 rifle there. Do what she says." Then he called to Elaine, "At least let this old grandmother go, please."

Elaine thought a moment, shook her head. "Sorry, I can't. I'm going to have to kill all three of you. I can't risk having a witness again this time."

Suddenly, it was all clear. "You killed Grampa Ned, and Louie Gonzales was a witness."

"You seem surprised. I thought by now you would have figured it out," she said, her voice full of venom. "In fact, I thought you knew. You were the last one to talk to the hotshot. You kept asking me about the sites, about when I excavated them, about whether there was anything a pothunter would have wanted there. I knew you were trying to get me to incriminate myself. But I was right behind you the whole time."

"You slashed my tent. Went through my things."

"I had to. I tried to scare you off, but when I couldn't, I had to find out what you knew. I have a child to support, I can't go to jail. They'd just put her in some state-run institution and let her die. There's no one else to take care of her, especially now."

I was starting to figure it all out. "Grampa Ned was the father."

"He tried to deny it. Right from the beginning."

"He was an advisor on the site when you excavated it?"

"Don't judge me. Don't you dare judge me."

"No, I wasn't. I don't. I've heard he was very handsome . . ."

"You should have seen him back then." Her voice softened. "He was such a good-looking man, so charming. We spent all day, day after day, together one whole summer while I worked on that site. I fell in love with him. But when I told him about the baby, he denied it was his. He refused to see me, wouldn't answer my phone calls. I had to go away, someplace where it wouldn't be much noticed that I was pregnant, someplace remote where no one cared. There was a lot of stigma back then about single mothers, a lot of shame involved, not like today. I sacrificed my career going off to Hovenweep, to the middle of nowhere. I wrote to him, but he never answered my letters. And then, when my baby was born with Down syndrome, I had to put her in a facility. I never asked that bastard Ned Spotted Cloud for help until they told me the hospital was closing and I had to find her a new place for care. It's going to cost so much more. There's no way I can afford it." Her voice was rising in pitch as she spoke. "I needed his help. He wouldn't even have had to give me any of his own money. All I asked was for him to admit his paternity and she would have been eligible for an allowance from the tribal growth fund. But he refused. He refused and he called me a whore. He laughed at me and walked away."

"Elaine, hold on a minute," I said, "there are other ways to prove paternity. We can still—"

"I know that," she snapped, "but can you imagine what that would do to my career now, this late in life, when I'm practically disposable anyway? To have a paternity suit going, all that scandal? Maybe I could have done it, but it was just another expense, another cross to bear, all because of Ned Spotted Cloud. I didn't plan it. That morning when they called your team in to manage the fire, my boss asked me to go flag the sites on the eastern flank since I was familiar with them. I hiked up to that site and there was Ned. I stayed behind some trees and watched as he dug a hole and then placed something in it. I realize now there must have been a burial back in that little granary, under the floor—something I missed when we dug the site years ago. I was young back then and inexperienced. And I was distracted.

"Anyway, as I watched him, I just got more and more furious. He had obviously taken something from that site! Something from my site, and not even told me about it! Now we know what it was, it was that bear effigy."

At this, both Delgado and Momma Anna audibly gasped.

But Oldham seemed not to have noticed. "Do you know what that could have done for my career, to find something like that? It could have made all the difference! Anyway, I didn't know what it was then, when I saw Ned there digging. I was just worried about my daughter. I didn't know what I was going to do for the extra money. And he had treated me so rudely just a few months ago when I'd asked about the fund—I was still angry about that, so angry it kept me awake nights. For months, I had been lying there half the night envisioning him dying of some terrible disease and feeling the sweet taste of revenge. And here he was in front of me! So I waited behind the trees, and when he came down the path, I tripped him. He dropped his shovel when he fell, and I didn't even think about it, I just picked it up as he went down and hit him over the head with it."

"And Louie?" I asked. "The hotshot?"

"I had gone back up to the site and was looking for what Ned had buried when I heard that hotshot coming, so I just ran into the brush and hid again and watched. He looked all around, and he called out, 'Hello? Anyone here?' and then he went right to the spot where Ned had been digging! I couldn't believe it. He must have seen what I'd done. Otherwise how would he know to go right to that spot? So, while he was down on his hands and knees pushing the earth back into the hole, I came up behind him and hit him with the shovel, too. He had a helmet on, so I didn't know if I'd killed him, but I thought I felt the shovel blade connect with his head."

"Oh, my God!" Delgado cried out.

"It all happened so fast!" Elaine said. "I was horrified at what I had done, but I had to think what to do with the bodies. I could see from up there that the fire was coming that way, so I figured that would take care of everything—and that I'd better get out of there before it took care of me, too. I'd hiked in from right below the heel of the fire, so I just made my way back down. Then, when I got to Fire Camp later that day, you guys were in the middle of the transition and hadn't yet taken over, and I realized that nobody knew I'd been on the fire that morning. So I decided to act like I'd just arrived.

"But then, Jamaica, I heard that the hotshot made it out and spoke to you. And you started asking me all those questions. Then you went back to the scene again, and I heard the FBI had asked for your help so I knew that they suspected someone on the fire. I thought you already knew it was me and were just looking for enough evidence to have me arrested." She took a step back from the rim, the barrel of the rifle still pointed at me. "But you're not as smart as I thought you were. Too bad." As she had been speaking, I noticed the sky behind her had changed from charcoal to dark blue. Waves of black smoke passed over her head like fast-moving clouds. I could smell the fire, hear limbs crackling and popping somewhere near the wall of the Great House.

"Let me get Mountain," I said, trying to keep my voice calm. "Just let me go get Mountain. You can go with me. This elder and this injured man can't get anyplace fast—besides, the fire has them blocked in."

"No. You can't get him anyway, Jamaica. I locked him in the observation room on the top, and I made double sure he'd stay there—I locked the gate at the bottom, too."

"Give me the keys, Elaine. Let me go get Mountain."

"I threw the keys over the edge." She stepped back and all I could see over the rim of the kiva was her head and shoulders and the stock of the rifle pointing out from her shoulder. Wind began to blow above us, and Elaine's long white ponytail flew up and loose strands of hair blew into her face. She took her left hand away from the barrel of the rifle to brush the hair from her eyes.

I quickly turned my head and looked at Gonzales. He nodded. I sprang for the steps as I heard a rustling sound from the kiva wall behind me. Elaine Oldham struggled for an instant and then fired. The sound of the gunshot mixed with the wind and stretched into two distinct tones: first, a high, loud *ping*—and then a piercing crack which assaulted my ears just as I felt a knife blade slice open the side of my right calf. Something struck Elaine in the gut and she staggered backward, dropped the rifle, turned, and ran. I stumbled on the steps and reached a hand down to feel if my leg had been cut in two. It was then I realized I'd been shot.

I scrambled up the last two steps. Heat seared through the muscle of my calf like a stabbing hot poker. I stumbled and fell, saw the large rock Gonzales had thrown at Elaine. I grabbed the rifle and stood up. Gonzales had hobbled to the bottom of the steps. I threw him the gun. "You watch out for Momma Anna," I said.

I looked around for Elaine Oldham. A patch of dry brush had ignited at the base of the fire tower and flames were licking at the underside of the observation deck. I saw a shadow on the other side of the tower scrambling over the stone wall. I ran, limping, pain shooting up my side with every step on my right leg. I felt blood running down my leg into my boot, my sock getting wetter, and I knew I was bleeding a lot, that I needed to put pressure on the wound. I made it across the short stretch of trail to the wall in amazing time, given my injury. Hot gases from the burning brush just twenty yards from me burned my face. I peered over the wall to see Elaine Oldham hesitating at the edge of a large slab of rock at the rim of what was once the huge fire pit used for sending revelations and power to Chaco Canyon. Beyond her was nothing more than a long knife edge of shale that led up to the two spires, impossible to cross. Seeing that she could go no farther, Elaine Oldham stood on the edge of the stone and looked beyond. Just then, the barely visible new moon, a slender silver crescent no wider than a sliver, rose between Chimney Rock and

Companion Rock and hung in the sky, its faint glow illuminating the murderer of Ned Spotted Cloud in the promised magic of Lunar Standstill.

The wind died down, and an instant later, the birth of a new dawn began to burnish the tips of the mountains along the Continental Divide yellow-gold. While Elaine studied the thin blade of shale rim ahead of her, desperately looking for a way to get across it, I dragged my right leg over the wall, dropped silently down to the soft dirt, and then lunged across the rock slab and ambushed the woman with a powerful punch in the kidney. She gushed air, dropped, and writhed. Putting as much of my weight as I could on my left leg, I grabbed one of Elaine Oldham's hands and twisted it up behind her while she gasped from the pain of my attack.

"Get up," I told her, wrenching the arm up.

"I can't walk!" she said, sobbing. "My legs won't move."

"You'll walk," I said, yanking her arm again roughly, "or you'll fly. Right over the edge there. I'm through fooling around with you. I've got to get Mountain."

She struggled to her knees, then put one foot down and I tugged her upper arm to help her to her feet.

"Over the wall!" I yelled, pushing her. While she struggled her way over, I tore my bandana from my neck and twirled it into a long, slim rope of cloth. I forced my right leg up and onto the top of the wall and felt the fiber of my calf muscle rip and another flood of blood stream onto the leg. I pushed myself over, falling partly onto Elaine Oldham, who was on her knees on the other side of the wall, still gasping with pain and clutching at her kidney with one hand. I pushed myself up, grabbed one of her hands and then the other, and I tied them behind her with the bandana. It was then that I heard Mountain twenty feet above me in the glass-enclosed observation room of the fire

tower. He was hurling his body up and into the glass, yelping in fear and anxiety. The western edge of the observation deck was ablaze. The fire tower was burning.

Delgado Gonzales took charge of Elaine with the rifle.
"Get back in the kiva," I said. "Get down against the wall.
There's fire right up to the edge of the Great House."

I turned to the sturdy bars of the metal gate at the base
of the steps leading up to the deck of the fire tower. I pulled
and shook, but the lock would not give. Again, I hoisted my
right leg onto the stone wall on one side of the steps. I noticed the lower half of my brush pants was soaked with
blood on one side, but I didn't heed this. The winds had
died down and the sound of Mountain yelping and pounding against the glass above me was all I could think of. The
twenty-two–step stairway that led to the deck had a wide
wooden handrail but was open above that. I hung from the
rail by my hands while I found footing on the outside edges
of the steps, then maneuvered my way over the rail on my
stomach. The stairs forced me to put my weight on my right
foot, and after a few steps, I thought I would pass out from
pain and loss of blood. I put both hands on the handrail
well above where I stood and used them to help me hop a
few steps, but I didn't have enough strength to do many
like that. I was about to turn around and sit down and use
my triceps to lift my body weight a step at a time when I
heard the sound of breaking glass, and a spurt of red blood
shot out into the air and spattered my face. "Mountain!" I
screamed, and I half-crawled and half-scrambled the rest
of the way up.

Through the sliding glass doors I saw Mountain before
he saw me. He leaped into the air and yelped as he threw
himself again at the window he had just broken, but it was
too high for him to jump through with so short an approach. His right foreleg was matted and wet with red, and
bloody paw prints decorated the floor. I yanked at the han-

dle, but the door was locked. The wolf saw me and ran headlong into the glass, smashing against it with a powerful thump. "No!" I yelled. "Mountain, no! Stay. You stay. I'll get you out of there, buddy."

The sunrise had brought stillness to the air, and the smoke on the observation deck was heavy. Through the glass, I could see flames licking high against the windows on the other side of the deck, and I knew I only had minutes before it would spread to the roof. I looked around for anything I could use to break the lock or the glass of the sliding glass doors. There was nothing in sight. I pressed myself against the guardrail on the narrow deck and locked my hands onto the top. I kicked hard at the glass door with my one good leg, smacking forcefully into the glass with the thick sole of my boot. The solid pane of glass rattled but it did not break. Mountain hurled himself at the door again, jumping high and leaving a bloody streak from his paw down the glass. I was too weak to keep this up for long, so I took a moment to collect myself, took a deep breath, then carefully positioned myself to do it again with the maximum power I could muster. As I prepared myself to make another jab at the door, I heard a buzzing sound in the distance. "Please," I whispered to whatever benevolent spirit might hear me. I inhaled, raised myself up on my bent arms on the rail, coiled myself into a ball, and sent my left leg toward the glass like a cannonball. With a *thud,* the glass seemed to flex, and the aluminum frame sprung. I pushed myself away from the railing and tugged on the door handle with all my might. The door screeched and gave, and I managed to wedge it to the side a few inches. Mountain yelped and stuck his nose through the opening and tried to push his way through. The buzzing sound grew louder. "No, wait," I told the wolf, and I pressed myself against the door to force it back on its track. I gripped the open edge and I pushed and pulled, and I felt it snap back into the groove. I hauled on the handle and the glass slid to the side. I collapsed to my knees and embraced Mountain, sobbing. "I don't know how I'm going to get you out of here, buddy," I said, my arms around his neck. "The gate is locked at the bottom of the stairs, and I can't lift you over the handrail. Even if I did, there's a wall and no place on this side of it to go." Mountain whimpered and pawed at me, streaking blood across my shirt. As I started to get up, I realized that the buzzing sound had become a repetitive *throp-throp-throp*. It grew louder and louder and I felt Mountain trembling with fright at this strange noise. I stayed on my knees and took hold of his collar with one hand so he wouldn't bolt in fear, and I stroked his chest with the other. "Maybe that's help coming," I said in his ear.

When the percussive *throp* reached a deafening decibel and the fire tower began to shake with the vibrations, a man slid down a rappel line, pushed himself around the lip of the roof rim, and then placed his boots on the top of the guardrail. He jumped onto the deck and I saw that it was Kerry. But Mountain started to struggle and squirm, not recognizing him, terrified of the deafening noise and this stranger who jumped out of the sky. I held tight to his collar, but his strength was greater than mine, and Mountain wrestled himself free. He bounded past Kerry to one side of the deck and saw the flames there, then past us both again as we grabbed for him, escaping to the other corner, where he looked down at the stairs. I feared he would try to leap down them and further injure himself. "Mountain!" I screamed over the pounding *thwock* of the helicopter.

The wolf turned and looked at me, his eyes telegraphing his terror.

"Stay," I said, holding my palm up as a visual command.

Mountain's body quivered violently, but he obeyed.

Kerry eased past me, still wearing his rappel line, his palms up and open, moving slowly. I couldn't hear what he was saying over the thunder of the chopper's rotors, but I saw him talking to the wolf, then reaching out slowly and tenderly and taking hold of his collar. Kerry turned and shouted to me, "He's hurt."

"Can you get him out of here?" I yelled back. I put my palms on either side of the doorjamb and gripped the section of wall to help myself up.

Kerry pulled out his pack set and spoke to the helicrew. "We need to lift someone," he yelled into the radio. "He'll be dead weight, so you'll have to work him from up there."

Mountain was so frightened by the time they began to tighten the line attached to the harness around his middle that he simply went limp and surrendered. As they slowly raised him upward away from the deck of the tower, the life seemed gone from him, and I gasped at the thought. "I love you!" I cried out to him, and he turned his head. Encouraged, I called again, "I love you, Mountain. I'll be back. I'll be back." His ears flicked ever so slightly and I knew he had understood this last, which was something I said each time I had to leave him at home alone. I was certain that he had come to know what it meant—that even though we were about to be separated, we would soon be together again.

"You're hurt," Kerry yelled at me. "I didn't see that"—he pointed at my blood-soaked pant leg—"or you would have gone up first."

I started to answer, but we were both startled by the crack of a gunshot and a loud *ping* of metal, the sound so close and so loud that for an instant it cut through the deafening pulse of the rotating chopper blades. Kerry raced to the top of the steps and looked down. I hobbled behind him. Delgado Gonzales looked up the stairs as he swung the gate open. "I thought you might need some help up there," he shouted, a crutch under one arm and the rifle under the other.

"I'm going this way," I yelled, and I grabbed the handrail on each side and swung myself down a step. It was far easier going down than trying to lift myself up from above. I turned and looked up at Kerry.

"We should get you to a hospital," he shouted.

"You go with Mountain. Momma Anna is down below. And Grampa Ned's killer."

"You're in no shape—"

"I already got her," I hollered as I lifted myself up by my arms and gingerly lowered my left leg first onto the next step.

I turned again and saw Kerry clamping a line around his waist and then climbing up onto the deck rail and pushing off with his feet. As he did so, he reached his hand up and pressed away from the roof, then ascended upward, the orange flames behind him now devouring the opposite corner of the deck.

Gonzales was wearing my radio harness. "We've got to get down in the kiva right away," he said. "Here, hold this." He handed me the rifle. "Now, let me help you." Even though he had only one crutch to support himself, his strong arm lifted me by my right forearm, helping take the weight off my right foot as I hobbled toward the rim of the kiva.

Just as we started down the kiva steps, I saw the tanker coming, a cloud of red vapor forming at its tail. "Come on, get down!" the hotshot yelled at me as the SEAT thundered past, bombing the slope with slurry.

I sat on the bottom step and clutched at my calf. "She's all but over now," Delgado said. "Air support was what we needed all along." He bent down and ripped open the Velcro tab at the bottom of my Nomex pants. "Let's see what you got here," he said, rolling the blood-soaked fabric back.

I looked down at my leg, at a small, gelatinous orb of red-black blood in the side of the calf filling a well-defined hole. "It's stopped bleeding," I said. "It's clotted over."

Delgado squeezed the leg and pulled it toward him, and I shrieked at the pain. He examined the back side of my calf.

"Sorry," he said. "Looks like the bullet went in there and out the back, right through the muscle." He moved his head to one side to better see the back of the leg. "There's a larger wound back here where the bullet went out, and it's still bleeding quite a bit." Then he turned, and for the first time since I'd returned to the kiva, I noticed that Momma Anna was standing a few yards away. "Grandmother, can we use another piece of your blanket?" he asked.

Anna Santana tore two long strips of soft tan wool and Delgado used them to wrap my leg. He pulled them tightly enough to add some pressure, but not so much that they cut off the circulation to the rest of the limb.

"Where's Oldham?" I asked.

Delgado tipped his head toward the curving wall behind me. I turned in my seat on the steps and saw Elaine Oldham sitting with her back against the rock wall, her hands still tied behind her, and her outstretched legs straightened and bound at the ankles and knees, with strips of tan wool, to the hotshot's other crutch, which had been laid across the top of her legs to prevent her from bending them or getting up. Another strip of tan cloth had been tied around her mouth. "I didn't want her going anywhere while I went to see if I could help you. And she wouldn't shut up," Gonzales said. "I didn't want this good grandmother to have to listen to her."

As I was rolling my pant leg back down, I heard voices.

I stood up and looked over the rim of the kiva. Ron Crane and two firefighters rounded the corner and came up the path. Crane looked down at the scene inside. He pulled a pair of handcuffs off his belt. "Mind if I take Dr. Oldham off your hands?" he said.

"Not at all," I said, and I moved back to allow him room to come down the steps.

Seeing the blood on my pants, the other firefighters offered me help getting up the last two steps and onto the kiva rim. I heard the distinctive ring of my satellite phone. Gonzales, still wearing my radio harness, removed the phone from the holder and answered it. "Gonzales here." He handed it to me. "It's for you," he said.

◄ 44 ►

What's in a Blanket?

Sunday, 1400 Hours

The Southern Utes began by blessing the arbor, as they called the arena in the center of the Ignacio High School gymnasium. Roy, Kerry, Charlie Dorn, and I sat in an honored, front-row position on the bottom bleacher at the pow-wow honoring the firefighters and their victory over the Chimney Rock Fire. Mountain lay on the floor beneath my feet. Both the wolf and I sported bandages, and had orders to stay off our injured legs. An emcee asked us to stand for the Grand Entry, and Kerry helped me to my feet. The Utes had invited four drum groups to play for the occasion, and members of other area tribes had come in full regalia to dance.

Most of the native Puebloans had gone home after their evacuation from Chimney Rock, but a few remained an extra day to attend the powwow and celebrate the warrior spirit of the hotshots and the other firefighters. Anna Santana and her nephew had stayed to dance for Knifewing, who remained in the burn unit in Albuquerque in critical condition.

A day and a half had passed since I had found Momma Anna and Delgado Gonzales in the kiva of the Great House, but I had little recollection of most of it.

A monsoon rain had blown in on Saturday afternoon, just hours after Mountain and I were rushed into Pagosa Springs for medical care. The vet who had treated the wolf said that Mountain had come dangerously close to slicing through an artery in his front foreleg, but part of the sharp blade of glass had deflected off the dewclaw and the blood vessel was merely nicked. The pressure bandage Kerry and the helicrew had applied had stopped the bleeding, or the wolf might have bled to death. As it was, he garnered seven stitches, a gauze dressing on his shaved lower leg, an Ace wrap to protect the bandage so he couldn't lick the wound, and an L-shaped cast Velcroed around his limb and under his foot to deflect the weight when he stepped on that paw. I received seven stitches, too, a curious coincidence. The bullet had tunneled cleanly through the meat of my calf, and the punctured muscle had slowly drained blood while I'd pursued Elaine Oldham.

After our wounds were dressed, I had refused to be transported to the hospital in Durango for observation because it meant being separated from my wolf, and since the vet had no place for the two of us to stay together, I opted to go back to Fire Camp, against medical advice.

Roy was enraged when he learned this and sent us to the female staff cabin to rest. I remember only bits and pieces from the hours after that. I seem to recall that—as we were being driven to the cabin—I heard whoops and hollers, and I think I even turned back to see several of the camp's support crew dancing in the rain in front of the dining tent, reveling in soaked T-shirts and drenched hair. Or I might have dreamed it.

I do remember spreading my sleeping bag out on the floor so the wolf and I could curl up together, but after that, little more. The rain continued through the night, and I woke a few times to the sound of it on the roof. I slept with my chest and abdomen pressed into Mountain's warm back, my thighs pressed into his bottom, my arm around his middle.

While Mountain and I dozed, the focus of the incident management team had turned from quelling the fire to demobing the firefighters and dismantling camp. Ground Support hustled carloads of firefighters to the Durango airport, hotshot crews packed up their boxy buggies and bumped out to their next assignment, and the hard work of tearing down a tent city and organizing all the records fell upon the remaining support personnel. Most of the firefighters had gone home as well, but a core group from the Command and General Staff remained to transition the management of the fire to the local agency for mop-up.

Those who could get free to attend the powwow had come to celebrate. We all watched as the emcee, a woman from the Southern Ute tribe, read the names of the Three-Pueblos Hot Shots into a microphone. After the reading of the names, the host drum began to play. Eight men seated around a great hide-covered drum elevated on a stand began to pound with long cottonwood sticks padded at the end and covered with deerskin. The instrument had a deep, booming voice full of strength and pride, anger, joy, and sorrow. Its mottled, tan-and-white elk hide top carried scars from the fervor of the drummers. One man with loose, long, shining black hair started a low, rhythmic *bom-bom-bom-bom* on the drum. The others joined in: *bom-bom-bom-bom,* and every few beats, the leader would strike the drum hard, making a loud, booming accent. He raised his voice to an oscillating, high-pitched cry: *"Aye-yeh-ah-yeh, way-ah-hah-ha, way-ah-hah-ha."* The others joined in, repeating his cry in call-and-response style, their voices thin and high and sharp as knives, cutting through the pounding peal of the drum. I felt the sounds stirring me at my core, my spine tingling. I closed my eyes and listened to the song of the drum, and when I opened them, Momma Anna, Clara White Deer, and Nuni White Deer Garza stood before me.

"Come," Momma Anna said, holding out her hand. "You must dance."

"But my leg . . ."

"We will help," Clara White Deer said, reaching out and pulling one arm as Nuni reached for the other.

"Mountain . . . ," I started to protest, but Kerry had already reached down and grabbed the wolf's collar.

Clara White Deer had four shawls draped over her arm. She distributed them among us, and I wrapped myself in a beautiful red and blue shawl with long white fringe. Clara took my bent right arm by the elbow, and pressed up to show me that she would offer strength. Nuni took my left arm, and between the two of them, they nearly lifted me out into the arbor. Momma Anna stepped ahead of us, as light as a fairy on her feet, shuffling and bobbing in time to the drum. With the two strong women supporting me and the comfort of the shawl around me, I relaxed into the dance and felt myself shifting carefully from my good leg to a sort of well-timed limp on the other, moving with the rhythm of the song, bending my knees deeply with each step to create the rhythmic bounce that characterized the dance, padding in time with the three ladies. I stopped worrying about my leg and began to lose myself in the hypnotic rhythm. As I danced, I heard the drum and became mesmerized by its tone, felt it in my chest, so loud, so deep, its voice moving through my body . . . when suddenly it stopped.

We were standing before the head table where the

judges and emcee sat. Thinking the dance was over, I started to turn to go back to the bleachers, assuming my companions would turn with me and do the same. But Clara held tight to my arm. "Stay here," she said, as Nuni let go of me and went behind the head table. She returned with several young helpers, all carrying blankets and plastic laundry baskets filled with gifts.

The emcee announced that Nuni White Deer Garza wished to perform an Honoring Giveaway, and handed her the microphone. Nuni pulled her shawl tightly around her and spoke with a trembling voice. "I wish to honor my father for giving me the seed of life," she said. She picked up an eagle feather bound at the quill with a deerskin thong, and dangling small chunks of turquoise and short strands of trade beads. Her eyes glistened with tears as she laid the eagle feather on a folded Pendleton blanket held by one of the youths standing nearby. She picked up the blanket with its feather atop and carried it across the room to Bearfat, who was standing against the wall.

As she approached, his eyes widened, and he looked nervously from side to side.

"I have no known brothers or sisters," she said as she offered the folded blanket to him. "But I would like to call you brother and have you accept this gift," she said.

Bearfat stood stock-still, his hands at his sides, as if he were afraid to take the gift. He looked around the gymnasium. The crowd was silent, every eye on the transaction. Finally, Bearfat raised his open palms. "I accept this honor, my sister," he said, and he lowered his head as she placed the blanket in his hands. I saw him swallow hard, and he kept his head down even as Nuni returned to the head table.

"Next," she said, "I would like to honor my mother, who gave me my life." She reached under a piece of cloth in the basket held by her assistant and removed a gleaming glass tiara and held it up in her hands.

Clara gasped and let go of my arm. Her hand flew to her mouth, and I started to wobble, afraid to put much weight on my injured leg. Momma Anna saw my predicament and hurried to the side that Nuni had vacated and grabbed my arm.

By this time, Clara was weeping openly. "My Bear Dance Queen tiara," she said.

Nuni placed the crown on her mother's head, and I heard her say softly, "I found it in Dad's things."

Nuni was not finished. "I would now like to honor the brave warriors who captured my father's murderer," she said, and I felt my heart sink in my chest. If only she knew that this story was stained with the sadness of another daughter deprived of her father—a sister whom Nuni had never met, and a desperate mother with no honor and no hope for the future. Nuni's helpers came with three white plastic laundry baskets filled with presents, as she called the names of those she wished to honor:

"Delgado Gonzales." A few minutes of near silence ensued as the hotshot struggled to his feet and then crutched across the floor to accept the giveaway. A small boy brought a basket and set it in front of him.

"Anna Santana," Nuni said into the mic, and Momma Anna pressed her lips together into a half smile as the youngster set a basket in front of her.

"Jamaica Wild," she said, and a young girl handed me a folded blanket with beautiful horses in the pattern. Momma Anna took my elbow while I extended my arm and the girl draped the soft wool over it.

"And Mountain," Nuni announced, "the wolf." There was a ripple of laughter, but Mountain raised his head and flicked his ears when he heard his name. Kerry held tight to his collar as a small girl scuttled across the room with a laundry basket filled with rawhide bones, dog cookies, and squeaky toys.

Nuni handed the mic back to the emcee and the Southern Drum began to play.

☸

As we were leaving the gymnasium, I saw Bearfat outside talking to the young girl he'd been with on the first day I met him. She saw me coming and edged shyly away. Bearfat turned to me and beamed. "That's a good blanket you have there. Have you looked at it?"

"No, not yet," I said, unfolding it with his help. A string of horses adorned the blanket with a stylized row of tipis and moons along the edges.

"It's a Cheyenne Horse Legend blanket," Bearfat said. "Very special. Very good choice for you."

"It is?" I asked. "It's certainly beautiful. I love it."

"This blanket," Bearfat said, holding out one corner, "tells the story of a great warrior who had a beautiful shining brown horse. This horse was brave like the warrior, but one day the stallion was wounded in battle. The brave loved the horse so much that he stayed on the battlefield with the stallion, dressed his wounds with willow bark, and sang songs to draw the spirits to him. And in a few days, the horse was well enough and the two walked home. In return for his love and healing, the horse created a sacred tipi for the warrior, a place of love and magic."

"That's quite beautiful."

He scratched Mountain's ear and the wolf nuzzled his hand. "I think it is a perfect blanket for you, Miss Jamaica Wild."

"You got a blanket, too," I said. "What is the story of your blanket?"

"It is a family blanket. I have a sister," he said.

I thought about Bearfat, with his constant string of female companions, and I thought about the riddle that Jimmy Johns had given me to solve. And I thought that—if

I had solved the riddle correctly—Bearfat was about to learn that he had *two* sisters. "I was wondering if you would help someone," I said.

"You? Sure. Just name it."

"It's someone who needs to get her rightful share of the Southern Ute Growth Fund."

He screwed his face into a frown. "Who is it?"

"A young girl lies in a hospital with Down syndrome," I said. "She is the daughter of Ned Spotted Cloud, and her mother is now in the custody of the FBI."

Bearfat's eyebrows shot up.

"She needs family. The tribe. The support of the tribal growth fund for her care."

Bearfat swallowed again, as I'd seen him do inside the gymnasium when Nuni honored him as her brother. "I'll talk to J.J.," he said.

"J.J.?"

"Jimmy Johns, the tribal attorney. He knows all about how to do that. I know that together we can help this girl."

☸

I was in the war room, putting the last of my paperwork in the brown expanding file for the documentation unit, when Ron Crane came in the ICP. "Hey, I've been looking for you," he said.

"Agent Crane. What can I do for you?"

"I had two things, actually." He looked around. "Can I buy you a cup of coffee?"

"I think the mess tent is closed," I said. "But there might be some coffee down the hall in the little kitchenette."

He gestured for me to lead the way. "I have the I.D. on your ghost caller."

"Ghost caller?" I started to walk gingerly down the hall, favoring my injured leg.

"Hey, I can get it. Just tell me where to go."

"No, I'm okay. I needed to move a little anyway. And it's not far."

"You're a tough cookie," he said from behind me. "You know how you kept getting calls on your satellite phone and no one was there?"

"Oh, yeah. You traced that?"

"Yes. It was Elaine Oldham."

I paused a moment at the door of the kitchenette. "Oh, now I get it," I said, reaching for the coffeepot. "See, in the incident action plan, they had Frank McDaniel's number listed as mine, had them crossed."

"So she was trying to call McDaniel, her boss."

"Yeah. And she kept getting me. She was going to turn her hours for the morning of the murder in to him so he would submit them as a unit for payment from the fire, rather than fill out a crew time sheet here. That way, no one on the team would know she was even *on* the fire that morning."

He nodded. "That makes sense."

I handed him a cup of coffee.

He looked down at the cup. "When was this made?" he said, sniffing the black, oily liquid.

"I couldn't say," I said. "Sorry."

He set the cup on the counter. "Yeah, I did quite a bit of checking on Oldham. She was a pretty tough gal herself. Found out that when she was working out in Hovenweep she was all by herself nine months of the year out there. Only had folks working with her during the summer months when the students from the universities came to intern. A guy who does the road grading out there said she used to do all the repairs and maintenance on her own truck—had to. The nearest town was miles away and they didn't have roads straight through back then, like they do now. Even now, those roads aren't so good—they're dirt and gravel for the most part."

"Hey, watch what you say about those dirt and gravel roads. Those are practically highways in my neck of the woods. In northern New Mexico, they'll call a goat path a road."

He laughed. "Anyway, the guy told me she helped patch a split radiator hose one time when he was stranded, said she knew all about engines. I figure she's the one who cut your brake lines. Had to be."

I felt anger rising in my chest, and I dropped my head. Part of me wanted to hate Elaine Oldham for what she had done, nearly killing me. And Mountain. But another part of me pitied her deeply, even felt compassion. And I remembered what Momma Anna had said to me when she called me unclean, and I knew that I wanted my drum to sound as clear and proud and full of life and story as the drum I had danced to at the powwow. "You want me to make a fresh pot of coffee?" I asked.

Crane shook his head. "No, thanks, I can get some back in Durango."

"So that's the two things?" I asked as I started limping back to my files.

"No, that was the Elaine Oldham thing."

"Oh. And?"

"And there's the Jamaica Wild thing."

I stopped in the doorway of the war room and turned to look at Agent Ron Crane.

"I'd like to see you join us at the FBI," he said. "We could use someone like you. And I think you'd prefer the work—and the pay—to that little backwater job you have at Tanoah Pueblo. I'm going to recommend you to Quantico for training."

"Not so fast," Roy called as he came down the hall toward us. We both looked as he tipped his cowboy hat back on his head and strode toward the door. "I think I know Ja-

maica a little better than you do, Agent Crane, with all due
respect. She's an earth girl. She'd rather be with a mountain than a man," he went on. "She lives with a wolf in a
rustic cabin in the woods where there's no phones and no
TV. And the happiest I've ever seen her is when she's just
come in from a week of riding range, sleeping alone out
under the stars. You try to put her in an office and she'll
wilt and possibly die. I know you get to solve crimes and
catch bad guys, but you also spend a fair amount of time on
the phone, in the lab, and in those little carpet-covered cu-
bicles."

I smiled. Roy understood me better than I thought.

"But you're also right," the Boss said, "that she needs to
do something different."

Now I crinkled my brow.

"I think I got the answer, though, and I think it will suit
her better than going to work for the FBI. I'm going to recommend Jamaica for training as a BLM ranger. I'm tired
of looking out for her hide, so she's going to learn all the
skills she needs at federal law enforcement school and then
she can look out for mine. It'll keep her on the land, and
that's where she belongs. But I swear," he said, "this gal
can find trouble where they haven't even heard the word."

"Yeah?" Crane said.

"You're safer without her." Roy winked at me. "Hey,
Crane, would you like a cup of coffee?"

"I'm dying for one," the agent said.

Roy turned around and led the way down the hall "Let's
see if we can find some joe someplace else. That stuff in
there"—he said as they passed the kitchenette—"was made
around the end of last week."

"You must be glad the monsoons finally came," I heard
Crane say.

"Yeah, that's how it usually happens. We work to

contain the fires, but it's Mother Nature that always puts them out."

๑

Later, Kerry and I carefully loaded Mountain into the back of a rental SUV I'd been allocated for the drive home. The wolf was afraid of the new vehicle and wriggled and fought us, squeaking in fear as we lifted him in. I had to hold him and comfort him for several minutes afterward to settle him down. "Easy there, buddy," I said. "It's all right, we're going home." I sat on the rear deck of the vehicle and stroked the wolf as he lay across my spread-out sleeping bag in the cargo area, his cast extending straight out from his body. I stroked his chest and felt his racing heart slow. I rubbed his head and neck until his breathing leveled out. Mountain and I sat side by side in the back of the vehicle and watched as Kerry said good-bye to his crew, who drove away in the brush truck, headed back for Taos.

When I felt the wolf had calmed enough, I slipped down onto the pavement and turned and kissed his head. He gave me a pleading look. "It'll be all right," I told him.

Kerry closed the hatch and helped me around to the passenger side. "Thanks for driving us," I said.

"You couldn't have done it with your leg hurt like that. Besides, I drove up here in that brush truck with a bunch of stinky guys, and believe me, I'd rather drive home with a beautiful blonde any day." He pulled open the door.

I started to get in but there was something on the seat. "My blanket! I know I put that on top of my red bag on the floor of the backseat," I said, pulling out the Cheyenne Horse Legend blanket that Nuni had given me. Something was wrapped within it.

"What's in there?" Kerry asked.

I unfolded the soft wool layers and looked inside. Nestled within was the round drum Momma Anna's father had made for her.

"What a beautiful drum," Kerry said.

"Yes," I said, closing my eyes for a moment and clutching the drum and its blanket wrapper to my chest. Suddenly, I heard my own heartbeat in my ears: *bom-bom-bom-bom, bom-bom-bom-bom.* I opened my eyes again. "Yes, what a beautiful drum," I said.

**Bureau of Land Management agent
Jamaica Wild returns in**

Wild Sorrow

**from Mary Higgins Clark Award winner
Sandi Ault**

Tracking a wounded mountain lion, Jamaica comes across an old Indian School, where children were "Americanized" after being taken from their homes. As a snowstorm sweeps the canyon, Jamaica must take refuge in the abandoned school.

Exploring the building, Jamaica discovers the desecrated body of an elderly Anglo woman frozen on the floor. When the FBI takes over the murder investigation, Jamaica continues searching for the wounded she-lion and her cubs. As the dead of winter settles, arctic temperatures threaten the survival of the mountain lions—and Jamaica herself, as she is stalked by an unidentified killer...

The first in the series featuring Bureau of
Land Management agent Jamaica Wild

Winner of the Mary Higgins Clark Award

Wild Indigo

A WILD Mystery

by Sandi Ault

*The high desert of New Mexico becomes the
backdrop for this debut novel—one that
"crackles with life and novelty"*—of ancient
rituals, restless spirits, a desperate female
Fed, and a crime that could destroy an entire
culture...*

Bureau of Land Management agent Jamaica
Wild has witnessed the death of a Tanoah Pueblo
man—he was trampled by buffalo. After the tribal
government and local paper make allegations that
Jamaica caused the stampede, she is determined
to solve this mystery. But what is revealed is a
greater secret regarding the Tanoah Pueblo—one
that threatens its future and its past.

**The Washington Post*

M343T0908